ANNE McCLANE

THE TROUBLE ON
HIGHWAY ONE

BOOK TWO OF THE TRAITEUR TRILOGY

ISBN: 978-0-9977794-2-4
eBook ISBN: 978-0-9977794-3-1

First Edition

Library of Congress Control Number: 2018911422

Author photo by Matthew Foster
Cover and interior design by Shannon Bodie, BookWiseDesign.com
Source photos used in cover illustration:
 123rf.com, woman by Oleksii Zabusik
 Dreamstime.com, tree by Stephan Pietzko
 iStock.com, truck by Nameinfame, road and night sky by Jeremiah Gregory,
 highway sign by Aleksandar Nakic, jeans by Vladimir F. Loyd

Published by McClane Fiction, LLC
P.O. Box 24778
New Orleans, LA 70184

www.annemcclane.com

THE TROUBLE ON
HIGHWAY ONE

ANNE McCLANE

 McClane Fiction, LLC

1

South of Cut Off, Louisiana
One summer in the mid-twentieth century
Ga-dunk.

Birdie drove down Louisiana Highway One, the same stretch of highway she'd driven a thousand times before, it seemed. Galliano to Larose in the evening. Larose to Galliano in the morning.

Ga-dunk. She passed over a crosspiece for a bridge over Bayou Lafourche. *Ga-dunk,* over the other side of the bridge.

The night was complete darkness, no moon, the sky swathed in an inky haze. She'd left the Becnels late, waiting for Mr. Becnel to return home from a business trip.

She imagined the lights from her truck's headlights were the only lights for miles around.

You are a light for the world. Light your lamp where it shines for everyone.

The actual Bible verse was a little different, she knew. But that was how Momma used to say it to her. When she talked about her gift.

Birdie smiled wistfully. She still missed her mother. But she still felt her with her.

She missed Momma, but she didn't feel empty. Just like she'd never felt empty about Daddy. Her father—the source of her gift—had died when she was very young. Barely old enough to remember him. But he had passed on his traiteur ability to his little daughter, just learning to move in the world. It was Momma, and her brother, Ronnie, who had taught her the lengths, and the limits, of her ability. But Daddy always seemed present, especially in Momma's and Bubba's memories.

Now it was her mother who seemed present. Right now. She thought of Ronnie, and was glad she had just seen him recently. She thought of young Cecil, his precious son. A young man, now. Several years older than she was when Daddy passed the gift to her.

She reached for the radio dial. She'd reached the spot on the highway where she could pick up the radio station in New Orleans. And she was in luck, they were playing one of her favorites. "Amazing Grace."

She looked to her empty passenger seat and imagined Momma sitting right there. They would sing together.

Birdie hummed along, until the last passage. Then she sang aloud, her voice like salted honey. A warm, earthy, resonant note.

"When we've been there ten thousand years, bright shining as the sun, we've no less days to sing God's praise, than when we first begun."

Birdie didn't see the man standing in the road until it was too late. Too late for her.

She swerved to the right, the opposite side from the bayou.

In less than an instant, the steep embankment rose up, and her truck ended its collision course against a tree.

Her eyes opened, and her face felt wet. Something obscured her vision. She thought she'd gone into the bayou.

She drew the back of her hand across her forehead. Holding it out to the dim light of the dashboard, it was coated in a thick redness.

Help.

She would need to get help. It was too far to walk back to Galliano, and too far to walk forward home to Larose.

Home. Morris. He'd be angry about the truck. But he'd be more worried about her, she knew.

None of it would matter if she couldn't get out of the truck and flag down help from the road.

She turned toward her driver's side door, and focused her effort on the door handle. The front end of the truck was crumpled, and it kept her door from opening.

Looking through that window, a familiar figure appeared.

Help is coming to me, she thought.

As the figure grew larger in her view, she saw him. It was a man dressed all in white. Why did he look familiar?

That was the man in the road. What was he doing walking in the middle of the road? Can he help?

As the man came closer, her blood ran cold. He had a man's face, but there was something unnatural about it. Birdie thought of a picture book she had when she was a child. A picture book of Bible tales. One page showed the devil's face, when he appeared to Jesus during his forty days in the desert. He had bloodshot eyes, and a rapacious mouth.

That picture terrified her. And that's what the man's face looked like.

Now, he stood right outside the truck. Her limbs felt heavy. He held his palm up to the glass of her driver's side window. All she wanted was to turn away. But she couldn't.

She was transfixed.

She saw his palm pressed against the glass, but felt an invisible, icy pressure just above her heart.

Terror enveloped her. The pressure escalating to an inexorable conclusion.

In an instant, she was released. No more horror, no more pain above her heart. She could finally turn her gaze. She looked at the passenger seat, and Momma was there. The light of her smile made the devil disappear from Birdie's thoughts.

Birdie couldn't feel her own body anymore, but she could feel Momma take her by the hand. They left the truck through the passenger's side, and someone was waiting there for them. A warm, distant memory made concrete. It was Birdie's father.

The three of them made their way to the woods.

Like in a dream, Birdie could see her form in the truck, the blood on her face. The devil was nowhere to be seen.

Her heart ached a little for the Becnel children, and more so for Ronnie and young Cecil. Morris made her stop in her tracks. He couldn't live without her. She tried to turn around. To go back.

Birdie felt herself shrinking. She looked up, and her parents were on each side of her, towering above her. Gently, they each put an arm around her and carried her until she was whole again.

The woods never looked more peaceful. The cicadas sounded otherworldly, heavenly. The smell of eucalyptus enveloped them as they crossed the threshold.

2

Pismo Beach, California
Current day

Lacey Becnel inhaled the sea air. It felt good to stretch her legs, after nearly three hours in her Honda. She was sure Ambrose appreciated the break, too. He had been a trooper on the long, two-and-a-half-day drive along I-10 from New Orleans to Los Angeles. She might have been putting thoughts into his above-average St. Bernard brain, but he seemed to enjoy the gradual change in scenery as much as she did. From the saturated swamps of southern Louisiana, through the gently rolling Texas Hill Country, to the high plains and deserts of the Southwest, Lacey felt her horizon opening up. She couldn't remember a time when she felt more hopeful.

They had stayed at her brother Jimmy's house in Los Angeles the night prior, before making this final leg of the trip. According to the map on her phone, they were only twenty minutes away from their final destination in San Luis Obispo. It was only 1:00 p.m., and she didn't have anywhere to be until tomorrow. She could afford the quick detour off California

Highway One to take in the depths of the Pacific Ocean.

Lacey and Ambrose walked to the edge of the parking lot. Toward the pier, there was bustle—people eating lunch at open-air cafes, a few families out on the beach. She was surprised the beach wasn't more crowded, but then she remembered it was a Tuesday. A bicycle cop patrolled the area.

Fox would have had a field day with that.

She remembered a time in Pensacola, many years ago. He was relentless in his denigration of that city's bicycle patrol officers, all outside of their earshot, of course.

Lacey put Ambrose on leash and ventured out onto the path from the parking lot. She didn't plan to go all the way to water's edge, just a little exploration of the dunes.

"Do you miss Fox, Bro?" she asked the dog. He shook his head and sniffed the seagrass.

Guess that's my answer.

She caught herself, marveling at how easy it was to ask that question. It had given her great pains to even speak her deceased husband's name aloud, as recently as just one month ago. He had been gone nearly a year and a half now, but their life together felt more like decades ago.

She wondered how much of that perception was due to her transformation, and how much was due to the sheer volume of events that had transpired in the past month. And how much was due to Nathan. The man she had woken up next to, underneath an interstate overpass, naked as the day she was born, her singed clothes in a neatly folded pile nearby. The man she first used her transformative power upon. The power she didn't know she even had until she met him.

Ugh. Stop thinking about Nathan. Remember, hopeful. You're in a brand new state, about to start a brand new job.

She had been ready to stop thinking about Nathan. She had thought their meeting in the museum's sculpture garden put a nice punctuation to . . . whatever it was they had. Not a period, but surely an ellipsis. A definite sign that their relationship, such as it was, was on hiatus. He was a married man, don't forget. A married man with two children. A man in a very troubled marriage, but married just the same.

His surprise visit the night before she left New Orleans ruined all plans to put him out of her head.

Better yet. Quit thinking about lovers, and start thinking about your mutant powers. That's much more interesting.

Eli was supposed to be at her new job. While not the friendliest of people, he would be the only one there who knew her capabilities. He was such a mystery, she was curious to find out more about him. Where did he get *his* mutant powers? He seemed to have the ability to read her thoughts, which led her to believe he knew more about her healing ability than she did.

Her gaze focused on the interminable distance. The ocean was calm. For an ocean, she thought. When Lake Pontchartrain was calm, it looked like glass. Not the Pacific. A frothy white line marked the breaking surf. But very few white caps beyond that line. As if to prove her wrong, a wind whipped up the steep beach, blowing her wavy, tawny hair back behind her. It was longer than it had been in a decade, and she imagined she looked very dramatic. Like a superhero.

Thinking of Eli and white caps and superheroes, a new thought took shape. It had been trying to form on the whole drive out west, but kept getting drowned out by Nathan. The thought involved frequency. How many people were like her? She wished there was a support group, someone, anyone, who could tell her what to expect. *What to Expect When You Find*

Out You Have Mutant Powers. But maybe there was nothing out there, because there's no one else out there. Maybe her supernatural ability was exceedingly rare.

But her power couldn't be that rare. It even had a name, for whatever it was worth. A traiteur was an old Creole term for a healer. Her traiteur ability had been passed on to her by the mysterious Cecil. Cecil *had* given her a book. But it was all about quantum physics. Not quite the step-by-side guide she was looking for.

A pod of dolphins just off shore, headed south, captured Lacey's attention and brought her back to the present.

She considered taking a picture, but didn't know if it would turn out. And then she remembered she'd left her phone in the car.

"C'mon, Bro. If you're done, we should probably think about getting back on the road, anyway."

He huffed out a breath.

"I know, I know. I promise, we're almost there!"

They had wandered a little further than Lacey realized. And the grade back up to the parking lot was steeper than anything you'd find in southern Louisiana.

Another sea breeze buffeted her back. She turned around to get one final look at the ocean. The sea smelled different, different from the Gulf of Mexico, at least. Less decay, but more ozone.

Lacey turned around to continue her ascent. She heard him before she saw him, a male voice shouting, "Ma'am!"

Ambrose surprised her by barking in response.

"Ambrose!"

He rarely barked.

A bicycle cop was perched at the edge of the parking lot,

just ten yards away, towering over both of them. His height was enhanced by his impressive balancing act, straddling the saddle of the now stationary bike.

"Ma'am! You can't have your dog at this beach."

Lacey and Ambrose closed the gap. "We're getting ready to leave."

She vocalized each word, trying to sound like she was *not* struggling for breath.

"There's a dog beach just about a mile away. No dogs allowed here."

"I'm sorry, we didn't even mean to wander so far. We were just stretching our legs in the parking lot and got distracted.

"We've been in the car a while," she added.

He did not seem interested, nor did he seem like he would get out of the way anytime soon. Lacey wondered if he was planning to give her a ticket, and tried to get a read on him. He was very fit, the definition of his thigh muscles instantly visible in his uniform shorts. He might have been good-looking, but there was no telling what kind of eyes he had behind his blackout aviators. Lacey wondered where his weapon was.

He finally moved, letting Lacey and Ambrose pass. "Don't let me see you two out here again."

Who talks like that? Lacey thought.

She laughed to herself as she opened the door for Ambrose. It didn't matter if she had thought the cop was cute, Fox had completely ruined the whole idea for her.

3

San Luis Obispo, California

Twenty-four days.

Lacey fumbled with the laptop, set atop the desk, her tiny workspace in a cavernous warehouse studio, and tried not to think about how much time had passed.

Instead, she glared at the laptop, and wondered for the hundredth time about how much all the new equipment must have cost. Everything on the set of *Magical Choices*, from the cameras to the editing equipment to her laptop, was brand new and state-of-the art. At least, she was told it was state-of-the art, and she opted to believe it. None of it hit the production budget, so she didn't know how much the production company had spent on it.

She couldn't help herself. She'd been here twenty-four days now. And all but maybe four of those days spent here in this warehouse.

Right now, there was nothing left for her to do but wait, there wasn't even a scene shooting that she could watch. She Google searched "Restaurants San Luis Obispo," not confident she could trust the results. Her brother and his girlfriend were supposed to be driving up from L.A. this weekend, and she thought she'd take advantage of the rare evening off to share a nice meal with them.

Into her fourth week in California already, and she had eaten nothing but craft service leftovers and some frozen vegetables she'd stocked up on after one hurried trip to the grocery store.

She clicked on a result that looked like it was on the beach.

"Don't go there, it's awful," she heard a woman's voice behind her say.

Shit. Kandace.

The First Assistant Director on the project, Kandace Swade, had the habit of giving Lacey the stink-eye when she saw her on the internet. She had singled Lacey out for her particular brand of passive-aggressive "colleague-ship."

Lacey turned around to find Kandace standing behind her, her ill-fitting clothes on a disproportionate body. Pink cheeks that flushed every time she spoke. Kandace held a coffee mug with a wobbly straw hovering over the edge. Lacey knew the mug contained Diet Dr. Pepper.

Kandace was in "buddy" mode, an insincere smile plastered on her face and no hint of stink-eye. Lacey couldn't stop herself from noting the date and time.

Yep, that's the third instance of Friendly Kandy on a Friday.

Lacey's heart sank when she remembered each other instance preceded a request to come in to work on a production dark day.

"Sorry, Kandace," Lacey said as she closed her search results window. "I haven't had the chance to try any of the places to eat around here, I might try to tonight."

"Well, forget about that one," she said, setting down her mug and grabbing a seat from a nearby table.

Shit.

"Roger and I tried it, they told us it would take an hour to seat us, when we could see empty tables right behind the host stand. And there wasn't even a bar where we could wait."

"Huh," Lacey said. "That's good to know."

"Where did you wind up eating?" Lacey asked. After a very short time, Lacey had become self-conscious of using "y'all," because most of the people on the set had fun teasing her about it. But in this case, she really meant to say "you," because she was convinced Kandace's boyfriend Roger was fictitious.

Lacey knew all about making up people. She had spent so much time alone at her old job, as an executive assistant and bookkeeper in New Orleans, that she had created imaginary co-workers.

"Oh," Kandace answered. "We waited, and we ate there, and everything about it was terrible. The service, the food, everything." Kandace had one hand on her broad hip, and the other hand gesturing with tightly folded fingers. It appeared very practiced, like a politician telling "humanizing" stories.

Most of the stories Kandace told made her seem like a human with a pretty negative, or at least limited, point of view, Lacey observed. Even her description of Roger left much to be desired. Lacey once asked her what Roger was like—she had no pictures on her phone—and Kandace's response was, "Oh, you know, just an average guy. Nothing special." Lacey quit attempting to build bridges after that.

If you're gonna make shit up, go big. Go grand, Lacey thought. She was inspired.

"You know, a co-worker at my old job, Marva, she once walked right past the host—and past a line of about five people waiting—and sat right down at an empty table," Lacey said. She was surprised at how easy it was to invent a story about a make-believe co-worker, and even more surprised at how little guilt she felt over it.

That's how to make shit up.

It seemed to work. Kandace leaned in from her rolling chair. "Did they throw her out?" she asked.

"No! That's the best part of the story," Lacey said, trying to decide what the best part of the story might be. *Got it.*

"She sat there, quiet and patient as a dove, which she was not naturally, mind you, and the host, the people waiting, everyone just shrugged. A server came over right after that."

"Was she old?" Kandace asked. "She sounds old."

"Not as old as her name sounds."

"Well, I don't care how old or sweet she looked," Kandace said. "I wouldn't have just shrugged and let her take my seat, if I was one of those people waiting."

I'd imagine not.

Kandace stood abruptly, apparently done with story time. "Hey, I have news about Kevin," she said.

Here it comes.

"He's supposed to be here Monday," she said. "We have an iron-clad assurance from his people."

"What's your feeling about it?" Lacey asked.

"It'll happen. We're about to enter into breach of contract territory, and his people are smarter than that."

Lacey was surprised at the bullshit-free answer. Every now and then Kandace showed glimpses of the director she could be.

"Is everything ready?" Lacey asked. She knew the request to

come to the set, during what was supposed to be her time off, was coming.

"Yeah, you know, I think we're in good shape. The delays gave us the chance to get ahead of the curve. Can you get me a new Movie Marvel report?"

There were hundreds of reports in the production accounting software they used. Lacey had learned how to use it in just a few days, but she was still figuring out what Kandace meant when she asked for a "Movie Marvel" report. It could mean a budget, a schedule, a vendor list. Lacey had to guess according to context.

"Sure, I can get you a new schedule as soon as I plug in Kevin's revised date." Lacey hoped that was the right answer.

"Great. Email it to me as soon as you can." Kandace grabbed her mug of Diet Dr. Pepper and wobbly straw, and walked back to her office.

Lacey could barely contain herself. No request to come in tomorrow? Something didn't seem right.

Alone again, Lacey checked the time. 6:30 p.m. There was no telling when Jimmy and Monica would arrive. No huge rush to get that report to Kandace, but maybe she would earn some brownie points by dispensing with it quickly.

Ten minutes later, she emailed a revised schedule to Kandace, and reopened her search window. She wanted to go to somewhere on the beach, and maybe decide where to eat once they got there. She hadn't been to the beach since her abbreviated trip with Ambrose the day they arrived. She had been too busy since that time to attempt another excursion.

Her laptop pinged, a reply message from Kandace.

Thanks, looks good. Oh, am gonna need you on Sunday, after all, some last minute stuff.

Lacey's mood darkened. She waited before replying.

It could be worse, she told herself. At least she still had tomorrow off.

Sure, no problem, she replied. She made faces at the screen and a few obscene hand gestures.

Lacey opened the schedule she had just emailed, and checked the new estimated end date for the production. Her first thought surprised her. She thought of football. She realized she would still be in California at least halfway through football season.

Back home, everyone would be getting fired up for training camp, seeing how the new recruits looked, making plans for their fall Sundays. Usually, all the hype annoyed her. After Fox died, she intentionally drew back from fandom, relieved at the respite from days lost to tailgating and cheering the home team.

But she had a sudden renewed interest in the Saints. She'd have to be sure to get to a game once she got back. Fox's aunt, Tonti, had held season tickets for decades, probably as long as the team had been in New Orleans. She was sure Tonti would be glad to have Lacey's company at a game.

Lacey always had a bond with Tonti, and it had grown even stronger since Fox died. Tonti had only just recently shared her memories of Birdie, her childhood nanny. Lacey could tell she was digging deep to reveal how much she loved Birdie, who only worked for the Becnels for five years.

She had told Lacey "there's something in you that's like Birdie. That's all I know."

Thinking of Birdie, Lacey felt a pang. She was beginning to wonder if her "traiteur transformation" had been a fluke. She'd seen no sign of her healing ability manifest since before her failed effort with Nathan's father-in-law.

She hadn't been able to heal him. He'd been too far gone. And since then, her ability had gone silent. The thought that it might be gone forever, a "limited-time-only" phenomena, made her ache more than she expected.

And his father-in-law's death was a weight that sat right between her shoulders. The trial for the person responsible, Edmund Villere, was a cord that could pull her back to New Orleans before she was through with her work on *Magical Choices*. She'd had no word about the case for weeks, which had her counting her blessings and waiting for the other shoe to drop, all at the same time.

Suddenly, Lacey wasn't so eager to return to New Orleans and catch a Saints game.

She tried to focus on her present reality. *Quit thinking about the past. Or the unknown future. Focus on the now.*

Here, there were new people, and new things to learn, but so far, it hadn't been quite what she'd hoped for. Eli had been a no-show, along with the movie's star, Kevin Horner. They'd been delayed in Los Angeles, for reasons Lacey could never get a clear answer on, causing a flurry of rescheduling and up-ended timetables.

At the least, Lacey hoped Eli could help her figure out if the events of earlier this summer were just some chance accident. At best, she had hoped for intensive Jedi training under Eli; by this time, she was supposed to be able to at least sway the thoughts of some weak-minded fools.

She laughed at her own joke. *Yeah, if I was Eli.* She was supposed to be able to heal, and Eli had indicated, vaguely, that there were other things she might learn she could do. She had no reason to believe that she could read minds, like Eli apparently could. *Unfortunate that.* No, she'd come here for training on her own "gift"—a gift she knew little about, but that Eli seemed rather knowledgeable of. He was supposed to teach her the ropes, so to speak.

Instead, Eli was AWOL and she'd been left to her own devices as the production accountant on *Magical Choices* after only a week of training. Lynn, her short-term mentor, had told her, "You've got it figured out already, call me if you need anything," and promptly left to begin her maternity leave.

Lacey checked her phone again. She tried to break herself out of her bored-anxious emotional loop, which was only getting worse as the weeks wore on.

No word from Jimmy.

Her laptop pinged. Another message from Kandace.

Just found out the Moneyman will visit the set.

Lacey assumed that meant someone from the production company. Maybe the person responsible for all the "state-of-the-art" equipment.

Okay. Do you know when? she replied.

Not exactly. Some time in the next week and a half, best I can figure.

A message from Jimmy flashed on Lacey's phone. She wanted to end the digital conversation with Kandace quickly, before she read it.

Okay. How should we prepare for that visit?

Silence from Kandace. Exasperated, Lacey read Jimmy's message.

So sorry, Budge. Won't make it tonight, Monica stuck at work. But we'll be there early tomorrow. With a surprise you'll like.

Lacey knocked her head against her desk. Her anxious boredom threatened to overtake her.

Kandace replied. *Not sure yet. Let's discuss Sunday.*

Okay. I'm leaving shortly. I'll see you then.

Lacey didn't wait for a response before powering down her laptop.

4

Near Solvang, California

It was a long ride to Rideau Vineyard, and Lacey fought to keep her eyes open. In high summer, the rolling hills were baked to a yellow gold, and the drive lulled her into a dreamlike state. She hadn't slept well after another lonely meal of frozen vegetables and half a bottle of wine.

Her brother and Monica had arrived at Lacey's rental around eleven that morning, in an SUV with a hired driver. Jimmy announced his surprise (and the reason for the driver): they'd be drinking all day, on a tour of some of the Central Coast wineries.

His text was not mistaken . . . this was a surprise Lacey liked.

Jimmy sat in the front of the SUV with the driver—a friend of his, he said. Lacey sat in the back with Monica, who was lovely. Eyes the color of sepia that twinkled when she smiled, which was often. She wore her dark hair straight and long, framing her deep brown features. And she had a warmth to her that made Lacey feel an immediate affinity.

Back when Lacey and Jimmy were younger and both lived

at home, she remembered the girls Jimmy had dated always seemed aloof. They made Lacey feel like a snotty kid sister.

I suppose a lot of time has passed since then.

Lacey figured there must have been several women she'd never met, in the time her older brother had been in Los Angeles. Growing up, she and her brother had been close. Lacey had been at LSU when Jimmy moved out west with his best friend and bass guitarist, Dave Guidry. And once Lacey met Fox and got wrapped up in his life, she drifted out of regular contact with her brother.

But Jimmy had been there for her when she lost Fox, and then when she found out about all of Fox's infidelities. She was sorry that her misfortunes were the reason they'd become close again; but just the same, was very happy to have her brother back in her life. And she was also happy she had been there as his fortunes started to turn. His band, LeViticum,—she still didn't like the name—had just begun to break out.

They drove through a desolate, barren patch of land. A charred hillside piqued Lacey's concern.

"So, Chump," Lacey said to her brother, "where are you taking us again?"

"Don't worry, Budge. This looks like it was a controlled burn," he said, referring to the hillside.

"Where we're going—Rideau Vineyard—should be pretty green. It's a winery started by a woman from New Orleans."

"How do you spell Rideau?" Lacey asked. Jimmy spelled it out.

"I guess that fits," she said.

"There are some great wineries around where you're staying," Jimmy said. "This one's a bit of a hike from where you're at, but I thought you'd appreciate the connection."

The scenery changed to long, low farm fields, broken up again by rolling hills. Like the terrain couldn't make up its mind.

"For sure," Lacey said. "It'll be nice to see someone from home who made a go of it out here. And how do you know so much about wineries? And 'controlled burns,' too, since I'm asking?"

"Fifteen years in California. It's like a path to citizenship."

"Huh. Wouldn't have figured that for you . . . the winery part," Lacey said. She knew Jimmy as a beer-and-whiskey guy.

She smiled at Monica, who nodded knowingly.

"Just wait," Jimmy said. "After all your hob-knobbing on set with the movie stars and their sycophants, you'll be doing wine tours and bikram yoga and full body cleanses."

"How are those things even remotely related?" Lacey asked. "And I'm hardly hob-knobbing. I've spent the past month running reports and waiting around for the star to show up."

I'm not hob-knobbing now, at least.

Lacey thought back to her brief flirtation with Kevin Horner, whom she'd met while he was in New Orleans filming a different movie. The one little kiss they shared might've qualified as hob-knobbing. It made for a fun story, but one that she preferred to keep to herself. It wasn't worth the jokes her brother would make at her expense.

"Are we getting close?" Lacey asked.

"Yeah," Jimmy said. "Didn't you see the sign where we just turned?"

"Oh. No."

Patches of green lay beyond the low buildings they drove toward.

"I wonder how the water rations affect them here," Monica said.

"It's got to be a challenge," Jimmy replied. "I guess it ultimately raises the end prices."

"Yeah. It's a good thing I've had so little time, I guess," Lacey said. "Otherwise, I'd really miss a leisurely shower. The dude I'm renting from made me so paranoid about wasting water when I got the keys from him."

The patches of green bloomed into a tree-lined pathway opening onto a verdant expanse, set with wooden picnic tables. The driver pulled up to an adobe with a pitched roof, that looked like it would be just as home in a European vineyard as it was in California's Santa Ynez Valley. The lush flower garden that ringed the building bore no sign of deprivation.

The three passengers slowly unfolded themselves from the car. Lacey clasped her hands and stretched her arms above her head, yawned. She noted how petite Monica was. She went to Jimmy's side, and barely reached his shoulder. Lacey smiled. They looked good together.

The tasting room was elegant, but not stuffy. Wood paneling everywhere imbued the place with a warm and welcoming feeling. Lacey wondered if every winery tasting room was like this.

Guess I'll find out soon enough, since this is our first stop.

They listened to the spiel at the bar. Lacey and Monica started with the Syrah, Jimmy went for the Grenache.

Jimmy swirled the wine in his glass, and pulled out his phone. From another pocket, he pulled out a pair of eyeglasses.

Lacey guffawed. She'd seen her "bad-boy" brother's reading glasses before, but the amusement hadn't worn off yet.

"My little sister apparently finds the aging process amusing, Mon," Jimmy said. He rolled his lip and stuck out his tongue at Lacey.

She returned the look. "Whatever, Chump. It's not the aging process, it's the production you make of it."

"Production? Well, I never . . . " Jimmy put a hand on his hip.

Monica laughed. A pleasant, high, Tinkerbell kind of laugh. "I swear, y'all turn into twelve-year-olds around each other. I imagine it can get pretty annoying, but right now, it's funny."

Lacey smiled, hearing Monica use "y'all." Jimmy said she was from Baton Rouge.

Jimmy set down his wine glass, and tapped a reply to some message on his phone.

"Looks like Trevor is going to join us at the next stop," he said to no one in particular.

"Really? That's interesting," Monica said, one eyebrow raised.

"Trevor, your lead singer, Trevor?" Lacey asked. This was an intriguing turn. Jimmy was an "everyone's welcome" kind of guy, so she was never surprised when new people showed up anywhere Jimmy might be. It just so happened Trevor was a "new" person she was a little familiar with. And she wasn't opposed to becoming more familiar.

Jimmy looked down at Lacey over his glasses. "Yes, Budgie, Trevor, our lead singer, Trevor."

"You've met him before?" Monica asked Lacey.

"Yes, once, briefly," she answered. "LeViticum did a show in New Orleans back in June."

Lacey thought she saw Monica roll her eyes when she said the band's name. She smiled.

5

Edgard, Louisiana
One summer, several years after World War II

Ga-dunk.

Little Birdie awoke, happy, but unsure of where she was.

She wasn't worried about that yet, though. There was sunshine on her face, and soft grass at her back.

The feeling made her think of the time Ronnie took her camping. The air was cool and there were no bugs. Ronnie had said they didn't need a tent. He had rolled out his sleeping bag, his bedroll—he said they called it that in the Army—right onto the ground.

Ronnie had fashioned a bedroll for Birdie from an old sheet and a blanket from the hall closet. Momma had fussed at him, worrying over picking out burrs and trying to get the blanket clean. But Birdie knew Momma didn't really mind. Ever since he'd come home from Germany, Birdie knew Momma was just happy he was home—even though she was always saying, "Son, I don't know why you'd ever come back here."

Birdie didn't know what Momma meant by that. She was just happy her big brother was home, too.

He had written her letters, some from before she even knew how to read them. He had talked about taking her camping. And Ronnie made good on that promise not too long after he'd come home.

That first morning at Tickfaw, just as the sun was just starting to show in the pine trees, Ronnie had already been awake. He'd made a fire. He'd told Birdie she could have breakfast in bed. "That's the rules for camping," he'd said.

Birdie thought she might like to go camping every weekend after that, but they'd only gone the once so far.

Ga-dunk.

And that's what Birdie was thinking of, as she woke up to the smell of burning wood. And bacon. She was a little hungry now, come to think of it. She blinked twice and turned her head.

All thoughts of Ronnie and their time in Tickfaw vanished from her head.

Léon was lying beside her. Thick blood was everywhere—it was matted in Léon's fur and stained the grass all around him. His side rose and fell with slow breaths. A whimpering sound fell upon the air, but it wasn't Léon.

The sound escaped from Birdie, through pursed lips and teary eyes. She remembered where she was. She'd gone looking for Léon before dinnertime. He hadn't been home since breakfast. And he always came home around lunchtime, looking for table treats. She'd always sneak him some when Momma wasn't looking.

Birdie remembered finding him, lying in the field back behind the whites' cemetery. He must have fought with some kind of wild animal. Birdie had seen a coyote once, out on the batture, but that was a ways away from here.

She had thought he was dead. She'd put her hands on

his side, to see if she could feel him breathing. And then she couldn't remember what happened, or how she'd fallen asleep.

That made her scared. Very scared.

Even now, Birdie was reassured that her precious Léon, the dog with a lion's mane, was still alive, but she wasn't sure how long that would last. She pushed herself to a kneeling position and said a quick prayer. "Please, Jesus, please help Léon. And me, too, if it's not too much trouble." She reached her arms forward, intending to feel Léon's side again. A breeze ruffled her dress. But something wasn't right. There was more fluttering than there should be. She looked down at her dress, and saw tatters bounded by long, dark marks. Like it had been burned.

Birdie's fear grew.

How did this happen? And Momma was going to be so angry. She had just sewn her that dress, from a bolt of new material Mrs. Bergeron had given to her. "Okay, Jesus, I hope you can really help us both now."

Ga-dunk.

That sound must be from trucks out on the river road. It wasn't too far from the cemetery. She didn't want any strangers to see her and Léon out in the open, somewhere they shouldn't be.

Birdie pressed down the remains of her dress to cover herself. She reached out to Léon, who opened his eyes and blinked at her before she touched his side. She lay a gentle hand upon him, and he blew out a sigh. He tried to get up on his legs, paws struggling to get upright.

"Shhhhh," Birdie said. "Shhhh, it's okay, Léon. I think I can carry you." She wiped the back of her arm against her eyes, wiping away the tears. She had to be strong for Léon.

Little Birdie wanted to believe she could carry her beloved

dog, but he was just as big as she was. When she slid her forearms under his side, and strained to move him even an inch off the ground, she knew she'd have to come up with another plan.

"It's okay, Léon. I'm going to get help." Still trying to be strong, she couldn't keep her voice from cracking.

Her tattered garment fluttered. "Hopefully Momma won't see me, or she'll never let me back out again once she sees my dress."

Léon let out a low bark.

The sun was close to setting, and Birdie knew that's when the wild animals were the worst. She'd have to hurry for Léon. She stood and looked around, to make sure no coyotes were lurking. She took off as fast as her legs could carry her.

She didn't get far before big, strong arms caught her and held her close.

"Ronnie! What are you doing here?" Tears threatened again, but this time they were tears of relief.

"Why you so worried 'bout where I'm at? Momma's gonna start a bonfire, calling out everyone looking for you." He set Birdie down.

"Oh, Ronnie, Momma can't see me like this! And you have to help me get Léon!" Then a torrent of words tumbled out of Birdie until they turned into big, gulping sobs.

"I think there was a coyote and there's blood and you . . . and Léon . . . can't move . . . and . . . I thought he wasn't breathing!"

Ronnie laid a hand on her head and gently stroked her braids. He spoke slowly.

"Birdie. Where's Léon?" he asked.

Birdie grabbed her big brother's hand and pulled him back

toward where Léon lay. On arrival, they found him standing, ready to go, looking much better than he had just moments ago. Birdie ran to him and encircled her little arms around his head. She smiled and said quietly, "Thank you, Jesus."

Ronnie looked at his little sister, and then paced a circle around where Léon had been lying. He crouched down to get a closer look at the blood. He brushed his fingers over the grass.

"I swear, Ronnie, he was really hurt! I thought he was *dead*," Birdie said, her voice notching lower on the word. But she grew quiet as she watched her brother. He stood, folded his arms, and narrowed his eyes. He looked angry.

"Roberta, do you remember anything about Daddy?" Ronnie asked.

Now Birdie thought he was *really* angry. He never called her Roberta.

"Yes," she answered in a tiny voice.

"What do you remember?"

"I remember going out to the woods the day after Halloween, and Momma praying over his soul."

Ronnie walked over and laid a hand on her shoulder. Birdie winced.

"Sissy, what's wrong? Are you hurt?"

"You're mad at me," she answered.

He smiled. One of his big, light-up-the-sky smiles. "I'm not mad at you, Sissy." He kneeled down, his great form sinking into the scrubby grass. He was still a head above her, but no longer towering.

"I'm sad you don't remember anything about Daddy. He passed something on to you, and I wish he was still around to help you figure it out."

Birdie stared at him, confused.

"Guess it's up to me and Momma," he said under his breath.

Ronnie stood. "C'mon, let's get going before Momma calls down the rain."

"What am I gonna do about my dress?" Birdie asked, panic rising in her voice.

Ronnie looked her over again and chuckled. "Yeah, she ain't gonna be too happy about that. I'll talk to her while you go round the back and change."

Birdie was glad her big brother had found her. She was sure Jesus had heard her, and healed Léon, and then sent Ronnie her way. And she was happy that Ronnie would help her explain things to Momma.

She grabbed his hand as they walked toward home, Léon scampering ahead of them.

Ronnie looked down at Birdie. "Did you know that Daddy was what they call a traiteur, Sissy?"

6

San Luis Obispo, California
Current day

Lacey awoke, confused. She wrestled with a brief bout of deep-sleep-induced amnesia. Soft notes of something tangy reached her ears. It was much too languid for an alarm.

It was a harmonica. Someone was playing softly, a few notes at a time. Someone was trying to wake her. The thought of that someone made Lacey smile broadly.

She opened her eyes to peer at the back of a naked man, perched on the foot of the bed.

Trevor.

Trevor's head turned toward her and she shut her eyelids, a coy opossum. Seeing she was awake, he worked the tune-up notes into a full song, something quiet and soothing. Trevor's bungalow-style hotel room felt remote and secluded, but Lacey still wondered if neighbors could hear them. The music he made was low and melancholy, maybe not such a disruptive thing to wake up to, even if the neighbors could hear. She surrendered to the music—it was a melody she recognized, but couldn't immediately identify. She reflected on a snippet of last night's conversation.

Wine low in the bottle, the surf crashing, the stars twinkling, she'd admitted, "I'm a sucker for the harmonica." Trevor had looked at her, eyebrows raised.

"It's amazing how versatile it is," she said. "It shows up in rock, r&b, in country, even classical music."

Trevor's bright blue eyes had mimicked the stars overhead. She'd known she was talking too much and possibly slurring her words, but he didn't seem to mind.

"You'll be amazed how dexterous it makes the tongue," he'd said.

Lacey had spit out her wine then, immediately relieved it was a Chardonnay. The spots on the white linen tablecloth faded as quickly as they appeared. Trevor had been quite pleased with her reaction.

Back on the bed, the music faded. Lacey opened her eyes and checked the time on her watch. It was the only thing she was wearing.

She sat up in bed, tucking the sheets under her arms. She had a little time to play still.

"'Helped her out of jam I guess, but I used a little too much force,'" Lacey sang. She'd finally placed the tune, and she could swoon over his rendition of "Tangled Up in Blue."

Trevor faced her, sitting cross-legged. A tan line right below his waist revealed his true alabaster pallor.

"I only used the force required for the situation, darling," he said.

Lacey cringed inwardly at his choice of pet name. It was what Fox used to call her. Luckily, Trevor's Irish brogue and her dead husband's Cajun twinge sounded worlds apart.

"I'm surprised you don't burn," Lacey said, staring at his mid-section. "You're as pale as a newborn down there."

"My mother is Spanish," he said. "Note the lack of freckles?"

He rose up on to his knees and gestured his hands down the sides of his torso. He ignored his penis, which saluted at half-mast.

Lacey burst out laughing.

"Love, I'm the essence of 'what you see is what you get.'"

"Love. That's so cute." She gave him a quick peck on the cheek, hoping the positive reinforcement of the "Love" pet name would help it stick.

He moved to return the kiss on her lips, and Lacey leaned her head back into the pillow, bringing him with her. Trevor rose up on all fours, bracing himself like a bridge over her. Lacey stared at his biceps, and marveled at how quickly she'd gone from flirting to naked with Trevor Toomey.

"What are you looking at, darling?"

"Nothing," she said and smiled, and turned her head upward to look him in the eyes. "I liked your version of Dylan."

He sang the opening to her, returning the look, his husky, a cappella voice pinging a chord in her soul.

Lacey was amazed at how simple everything felt with Trevor. No initial awkwardness at his touch, no internal struggle over whether or not to sleep with him. As much as she didn't want to, she couldn't stop herself from thinking about Nathan. Everything with Nathan—even for as recent and fleeting as it was—had been like trying to resist a tidal wave. She wanted to resist but couldn't. With Trevor, it had been grabbing a hand and plunging in together with a running jump—giddy, joyful and undeniably fun.

They shared a knowing glance, and Lacey nodded. Trevor moved over to the other side of the bed. He grabbed a condom, laid back and slid it on, humming a song she couldn't make out.

Quit thinking. Lacey obeyed her own command and moved on top of Trevor, guiding him inside her. She began slowly, a light rocking atop him, savoring the feeling of him between her legs. Hands at her sides, eyes closed, she arched her back. She brought her head forward to sneak peeks at his lean, smooth body and lanky brown hair with hints of red. Suddenly, his blue eyes opened and focused on her breasts.

"Keep your eyes open, love, I want you to watch me," he said between stanzas of the song he kept humming.

She looked down at him and smiled. An early wave of pleasure made her shudder, and her rocking gave way to grinding. He stopped humming and let out a soulful moan in its place. She turned her head to the side.

She returned her gaze to him. He reached up and cupped her breasts, one at a time. His index finger brushed over her nipple, first her left, then her right. She gasped each time.

This feels too good to be real. The pressure was building up instead of her. His moans were rising in intensity, and she added her own to the chorus.

"You're phenomenal!" he said.

After they came together, and everything felt real again, Lacey almost laughed as she pulled off of him and collapsed back onto the bed. His exclamation in the throes of passion sounded funny to her. She decided to look past it and just take it as a compliment.

Trevor rolled off the bed and disposed of the condom. He jumped back onto the mattress and pulled her into a spooning position.

Lacey allowed herself a few moments to relax into his embrace, but she was beginning to feel like Cinderella a few minutes before midnight.

Just the previous afternoon, Trevor had met Lacey, Jimmy, and Monica at their last stop, a winery in San Luis Obispo. Lacey, tipsy and uninhibited from a full day of wine tasting, had been receptive to Trevor's flirtatious overtures.

She was disappointed when Jimmy and Monica had to cancel their plans for dinner to return back to L.A. Trevor, as it turns out, had booked a room in SLO, intending to stay overnight, and invited Lacey to join him for dinner. Though Lacey sensed all the markers of a set-up, she definitely enjoyed his company and could see no good reason to decline his offer.

Her eyes closed, back on his bed, she smiled. Lacey was surprised that she had slept so soundly in a stranger's bed. To awaken to that sound, and to one of her favorite Bob Dylan songs, it'd been surreal.

But now, the realization that it was already Sunday sat like a weight right between her eyes. That, and the lingering effects of the wine, contributed to the headache that gathered at her temples.

I could use some of that healing power now.

She still had enough time to get to the rental, shower, feed Ambrose, and make it to the studio by the time Kandace expected her. But she'd have to leave within the next few minutes.

"I can almost hear the hamster wheel in your head, love."

Lacey wasn't too stressed to appreciate that he'd gone back to her preferred nickname.

She rolled over and propped her head on her hand, supported by a crooked elbow.

"There's no hamster wheel," she said. "My mind is a blank. I'm so zen right now, I can barely stand it." It was a bold-faced lie.

He mirrored her side-propped pose.

"A likely story. Your twitchy foot kept me from falling back asleep." He popped up and grabbed both of her feet through the top sheet, like a pouncing kitten.

"Ah!" Lacey pulled her feet away. "I wasn't twitching my foot!" *Was I?*

"Zen is not the first word I'd use to describe you," Trevor said. "Lively, intrepid, maybe, but not zen."

She didn't want to leave. She hadn't had this much fun with a guy, with anyone, since Fox. Trevor had literally charmed the pants off her. Her stomach gurgled, and she thought of breakfast.

Ugh. No time for breakfast.

She rolled over and swung her feet to the floor. She sat for a moment with her back to Trevor. She felt the room spinning, and thought maybe she had arisen too fast. No, the room wasn't spinning, but it wasn't still, either. Whatever was happening, it had a sound, too. A rhythmic clanking from somewhere within the bungalow's bathroom. A little kernel of fear developed in her gut.

Now she felt herself moving back and forth, as if someone was standing at the edge of the bed and shaking it. She looked to see if Trevor was doing it.

Reclined on the bed, fingers clasped behind his head, he opened his hands and shrugged his shoulders.

"Earthquake," he said.

The movement stopped as quickly as it began. All became stationary again, but she kept waiting for the shaking to return. She was paralyzed, poised on the edge of the bed.

"What's wrong, love?"

"This doesn't freak you out at all?" She found her footing and stood, grabbing her clothes that lay in a rumpled pile near her feet.

"This one didn't last very long. I get more concerned when it goes on for a bit. And you hear crashing. Was this your first one?"

"Yep." She pulled on her jeans and fastened her bra, then turned around to face Trevor on the bed.

"Ha. And you were with me. You could say I made the earth move under your feet." He began to hum the rest of the song.

Lacey laughed. "Keep dreaming, love." She gave him a half-smile, but was too preoccupied with getting on her way and on with her day to engage his teasing any further.

Hurrying into the bathroom, she drew a line of toothpaste across her finger, and performed a quick, manual scrub of her teeth. She rinsed her mouth and finger, and righted the bottle of hotel shampoo that had keeled over in the quake.

She looked in the mirror, pausing to contemplate how she'd say her goodbye. She dabbed a smudge of stray mascara away. She resisted the almost instinctive urge to feel guilty and classify her departure as a "walk of shame." Because in truth, she didn't feel shameful at all.

I feel pretty good, and I don't look too bad, either. What am I turning into?

She answered her own question.

Someone different, that's for sure. Someone better than you were, I think.

Her departure was executed with tactical precision. A kiss that lingered just long enough, hoping to leave him wanting more. The look on his face as she said "bye" with a toodle-loo of her fingers told her she'd succeeded.

The cat who swallowed the canary. She was sure that's what her expression looked like, as she lingered in the lobby, waiting for the ride she'd hailed. She turned down the corners of her mouth, trying to appear more dignified.

Her Lyft driver played the 70s music station. She didn't ask Lacey if she wanted to listen to anything else. As they turned into the neighborhood of Lacey's rental, a harmonica solo heralded the opening of Supertramp's "Take the Long Way Home."

Lacey nodded her head. She was sure there was some deeper meaning there, but she didn't have the time or the capacity to contemplate it.

7

By Monday, Lacey finally felt settled. The whirlwind events of the weekend had shaken her up, in a good way. Saturday with her brother and his girlfriend reminded her of where she came from, and that, in essence, she was still the same person, just in a different venue. And her night with Trevor had been a brief, intensely satisfying respite. The evening made her feel like a new and improved version of her same old self. She longed to see Trevor again—but wondered if she would.

Sunday had just been her and Kandace. Lacey had arrived at the set at 9:50 a.m., bone-tired and a little frazzled, but still ten minutes earlier than she'd told Kandace she'd arrive. Kandace didn't arrive until 1:00 p.m. That only bothered Lacey a little bit, not as much as it might have just two days earlier. She began to feel that Kandace might no longer have her number. Maybe it was the palliative effects of her roll in the hay, or maybe it was because she and Trevor had their romantic dinner at the very place Kandace told her not to go.

She and Kandace briefly discussed what needed to be done for the moneyman's visit, and Lacey left the studio by 3:00 p.m.

For the two hours they spent together, even the wobbly straw and Diet Dr. Pepper were less irksome.

And Monday morning, she'd gone for a run, an earnest attempt to return to her three-times-a-week habit. That and a good night's sleep had done wonders to clear her head. Now, the set was a bustle of activity, but there was little for her to do. She had gotten ahead of all her work the day before. Kevin Horner was due to arrive midday, with preproduction meetings scheduled for that afternoon, and his first shoot tentatively scheduled for tomorrow. With no expenditures to track, she wandered to a favorite spot near the soundstage. It was a place, she discovered, where she could stand and observe undetected.

One of the crewmembers, a twenty-some-odd guy named Hans with long, dirty blond hair, was up in the scaffolding. She tried to remember his position—she would ask anyone she spoke to, trying to become passably fluent in the lingo—and she had asked this of Hans one late evening when they were each lingering around craft services. He's a Gaffer, she seemed to recall.

He fiddled with a light. Lacey tried to shrink back into her corner. She figured he could probably see her, but her presence didn't seem to faze him. The soundstage was otherwise empty, so there was really no better spot to stand around and do nothing and not get called on it.

The green screen area had been minimized, and faux furniture and faux half-walls installed for the interior shoots. Lacey thought of last week's scene with the Unicorn, the poor horse silent and impatient. She imagined the mare longing to shuffle her hooves and whinny, but she knew better. She was too well-trained and well-paid to give into it.

Lacey turned her head upward when she heard something from above, it sounded like Hans had cried out.

When he had Lacey's attention, he said, "Hey, hey, y'all," drawing out the word "yaalll."

"Do you mean me?" Lacey asked in a quiet voice. Apparently, her attempts to de-southernize her speech hadn't been successful.

"Yes, please," he said. "Can you go find some bandages? I'm on my way down."

Lacey caught herself before asking if he was hurt, and instead replied, "Yes, sure." She ran off to the supply room.

She was glad she had familiarized herself with the location of all the helpful things in the studio. First aid, private bath, the director's liquor stash.

She grabbed a roll of gauze, some sanitizer, and a handful of bandages from the first aid kit and ran back to the set. Hans was down from the scaffolding, standing off to the side, holding his hand. His dark t-shirt had a hand-print-shaped stain on it.

"Here, let me see that," Lacey said, setting down everything she had gathered. Hans had a nasty gash right through the center of his palm; a ragged, oozing wound.

She felt a shock as soon as she grabbed his hand, and felt a heat radiate from her arm. She knew instantly what was happening. Elation surged through her—her power had returned! With one hand still covering his, she reached behind her for the sanitizer with her free hand.

"What are you doing?" Hans asked, his eyes narrowed.

"Nothing, I'm cleaning your cut." Lacey kept her eyes down and her hands busy, trying to hide her handiwork. She wasn't ready to field any questions from Hans about her supernatural ability.

"What happened, how'd you do this?" Lacey asked, aiming to deflect his attention.

"Oh, nothing, my own stupidity." Now Hans was trying to deflect questions. Lacey guessed he'd rather not have the hassle of a workers comp claim. If she was successful, he wouldn't have to. She decided not to press the issue.

"It burns," he said.

"That's the sanitizer." It was a convenient cover for her power.

She felt her own heat subside, and held his palm open for him to see. A red line, an inch and a half long, dissected it. But it wasn't bleeding.

"What do you think?" she asked. "You might need stitches. You should go have it checked out." She knew he wouldn't, but felt obliged to say it anyway.

Hans curled his fingers, then flexed his hand. "I don't know, Y'aaall, I've had worse. If you bandage it up, I should be able to finish my work up there."

Lacey bristled. "My name's Lacey, you know. And I just want to be sure it doesn't get infected with all that dust and gunk."

Lank hair framed a smile on Hans' face. "I know your name, Y'aaall. And I'm not worried about infection, I think you burned up anything nasty with whatever you poured in there."

Lacey put some ointment and a gauze pad on the cut, and secured it with gauze tape crisscrossed over his palm in an "X."

"There you go, Jubilee," she said to Hans. Jubilee was the only X-Men she could remember that had something to do with lights. He didn't seem to catch the reference.

"You bored, Y'aaall?"

"No," Lacey said, getting defensive. "I was just taking a break, and I'm trying to get familiar with as much as I can while I'm here."

"Relax," Hans said, climbing back up the rigging. "I don't mind you hanging around. Actually, you're pretty good in a pinch. Stick around as long as you want."

"Thanks," she said. She checked the time. "But I should get back to work. Be careful!"

Lacey thought about what had just happened. It confirmed something she suspected. When she'd try to summon her healing power on her own, nothing would happen. She'd healed a cut on herself once before, but when she was without injury, nada. Crickets. She'd suspected there needed to be an injury, something to serve as a catalyst. Or, at least, she'd hoped that was the case. The cut on Hans's hand seemed to prove this theory. She made a mental note to ask Eli about it.

Kandace was sitting at Lacey's workstation when she returned. Lacey's joy over the return of her healing power was short-lived.

"There you are," Kandace said. "I need that report. Kevin Horner is only about twenty minutes away."

"Sure," Lacey said, sliding into her place as Kandace got up. Her coffee mug and wobbly straw was too close to Lacey's computer for her comfort.

"Which report?" Lacey asked.

Kandace huffed. "You *know* the one, Lacey. The one with all the budget numbers on the right."

There are a thousand reports you can get with the budget numbers on the right.

Lacey pulled a revised production schedule with overtime factored in, which seemed to be the one Kandace was looking for.

Kandace breathed down Lacey's neck as she peered over her shoulder at the screen. "Crap," Kandace said. "We're going to have to reschedule all the Liam scenes to meet this deadline."

Liam was the character Kevin Horner was supposed to play in *Magical Choices*. While he was young, to Lacey he seemed a little too old for a "coming-of-age story with elements of magic and light." Every bit of promotion for the movie boasted that tagline. Even the banner across the Movie Marvel report dashboard sported it. Lacey was sure she'd be fine if she never read those words strung together ever again.

The female lead's character was named Sinead, yet the story wasn't remotely Irish in any way. Lacey had only seen Mia Lindsey, the actress playing Sinead, once, when she'd watched the scene with the unicorn. Mia was quiet and seemed afraid of the horse when the camera wasn't rolling.

"Deadline?" Lacey asked.

"Yeah. Kevin Horner's a month late, but we still can't extend on the back end. We only have him for two and a half weeks."

"Oh, wow," Lacey said, trying to appear sympathetic.

"Yeah, tell me about it. Okay, thanks for this. I need to get it to Marco."

Kandace headed off to Marco's office and Lacey turned back to her computer.

A half an hour later, Kandace appeared again. And stayed.

Kevin Horner and Eli had been ushered into a meeting room with the director, Marco, and a line producer as soon as they arrived. Even though they had entered on the opposite side of the studio, Lacey couldn't help herself from staring in their direction. She wanted to see if Eli would acknowledge her. A slight turn of his head was all she got.

With Eli, that's enough. It means he at least knows I'm here.

Kandace appeared jittery, worse than Lacey had ever seen her. She wondered why Kandace wasn't in the meeting. She wished she was. Nearly two hours passed with the principals behind closed doors. Lacey was sure Kandace was going to wear a rut in the floor between her office and Lacey's desk. She imagined setting up a trip wire when Kandace wasn't looking. She was sure Hans could help with that.

Lacey wondered what Eli might be saying in the meeting. On the payroll, Eli Bardzani was listed as "Special Effects Supervisor," but she suspected his role might be something that transcended a job title. That seemed to be the case in the last production, the one he and Angele worked on together in New Orleans. Lacey hadn't been on that set, but she'd met much of the cast and crew during after-hours. Everyone seemed to defer to Eli, especially Kevin Horner.

Sometime around 4:30, Kandace shuffled back to Lacey's desk.

"I just got called in," she said. She grabbed a stack of reports from Lacey's workstation. "You sure everything's right in these?"

"I plugged in everything, exactly as you told me," Lacey said.

Kandace scurried toward the meeting room. "Be prepared for a late night," she said without turning around.

Whatever. And what does it matter if you screw up what you tell them, as long as I can back up the reports I've produced.

"Jesus," Lacey said out loud. *What the hell has happened to me?* She made an intention to be more charitable toward Kandace—the woman was annoying and passive-aggressive, but it didn't mean Lacey needed to be.

And the day started off so well.

Lacey sighed and kept herself busy with what work she could.

When the door to the conference room finally opened, Lacey thought of white smoke rising from St. Peter's Basilica. All seemed to be in good moods—Marco and Kevin Horner with their arms around each others' shoulders, Kandace on their heels, Eli and Tony, the line producer, in intense conversation but relaxed.

They were en route to the soundstage, and Lacey tried to shrink from view. To little avail.

Kevin Horner broke off from the director and headed toward Lacey. He was every bit the movie star in a white t-shirt and jeans, his blond hair a little longer than the last time she'd seen him. And he must have kept an insane workout schedule in the past month, because he was also significantly more ripped.

"Ha, ha—Nola Girl!" he said as he grabbed Lacey in a rocking embrace. "What are you doing here?"

Lacey caught Kandace's expression out of the corner of her eye. Shock and awe over the star's apparent affection for Lacey. It made the upcoming late night worth it.

"I'm working here!" Lacey answered. Her enthusiasm over seeing Kevin wasn't faked.

Kevin Horner let her go, and Eli appeared at his shoulder. Eli, by contrast, appeared exactly the same as Lacey remembered. Bald head, floating eye, and a barrel chest clothed in a multi-pocketed shirt. Lacey figured he owned the same shirt in multiple neutral colors. In a low and monotone voice, he said, "Hello, Lacey."

"Hello, Eli," she said, dropping her hands to her side and matching his intonation.

"You know him, too?" Kandace asked. Lacey wondered if she really couldn't stop herself from saying it out loud.

Eli turned to Kandace, hand to his temple. "Kevin and I met Lacey Becnel when we were in New Orleans for the last production. I'm glad she's here on this set, she has great capacity."

That shut everyone up. Even Marco, usually on some sphere high above everyone else, turned his head and took note.

It was short-lived. Marco went into director mode. Lacey imagined him with a bullhorn and flared pants.

"Kandy, get a skeleton crew for tonight. We're shooting scenes five and seventeen. Let's make a movie, people!"

With that, everyone scrambled.

At around one in the morning, Lacey found herself trying not to twiddle her thumbs. A thought occurred: maybe some part of Kandace does like Lacey, and finds her competent, and that's why she insists on making her part of these "skeleton crews" even though there's nothing for her to do. She tried to hold on to that thought as she sat far behind the line of cameras watching Kevin Horner recite inane dialogue with another actor.

Or maybe she doesn't like me at all and just wants me to suffer.

She tried not to think about Trevor. But it was so much more entertaining when she imagined him up on the soundstage with Kevin instead of that other actor.

Lacey had pieced together that these were the scenes with Liam and his best friend. The first, when he admits he has feelings for the mysterious Sinead, the second, when he and his best friend quarrel over the same mysterious Sinead.

Best friends fighting. Angele—her best friend from childhood and her connection into this whole, rather ridiculous world of show business. Who had recommended her for this job. Angele was one of the only people who knew about Lacey's supernatural ability, but she was hardly a staunch and loyal ally. She had been very vocal in her displeasure over Lacey's insignificant dalliance with Kevin Horner. But what bothered Lacey more was Angele's judgment of her healing power. Angele seemed to believe that Lacey should use her powers sparingly, if at all. That went against everything Lacey believed in. When she finally figured out how to use them, she intended to employ her powers as much as they were needed.

They had reached a truce, and things had been copacetic between them since Lacey had been in California. But if Lacey was honest with herself, she could admit that she was glad Angele was three hours away, working on a different production in Los Angeles.

She imagined a fight with Angele playing out on a soundstage.

Jesus. Maybe I'm *living out a coming-of-age story with elements of magic and light.*

She suddenly felt horribly clichéd.

"I like this story," a voice behind her said.

Lacey jumped in her seat and turned. Eli had a headset draped around his neck, and the perfunctory pockets on his shirt were near bursting with useful things.

"Eli," she stammered. "Don't you have stuff to do up there?"

"They just called a break," he said. "Were you paying attention?"

The corners of his mouth turned up, ever so slightly.

"Yes," she answered, defensive. "I was just thinking of Angele, though. My mind wandered just a bit."

"What were you thinking?" he asked.

Recalling the Professor X-like mind-reading abilities he'd displayed before, she thought, *I'm sure you already know.*

"Oh, nothing, I was thinking about what it would be like with her here on this set. I've never really seen her work, but now I have some idea of context."

Eli stared like he didn't understand her. His floating eye tracked right. Lacey resisted the urge to look in that direction.

After a near eternity, he said, "We will have the opportunity to work together in the coming days. Think of what you would like to learn. I've been in these situations before, I might be able to offer you some enlightenment."

Now it was Lacey's turn to stare like she didn't understand. *Is he talking about movie sets, or is he talking about the other thing?*

She decided to take a chance. "When?" she asked.

"When?" he repeated.

"Yes. When should I ask you the things I need to know?"

"When you're ready," he answered. His headset crackled, and he hooked the earpiece back in. He walked off without another word or glance.

"What if I'm ready now?" she said under her breath.

Is he implying I'm not ready?

Lacey returned to her desk, stewing over Eli's words, and wondering if she'd get any sleep at all in the hours ahead.

8

Lacey was curious when Kevin Horner's "guest" appeared at the studio the next day. Kevin signaled Marco, who called a break. He moved toward his guest, Allison, and gave her a tour of the set. Allison was a pale-skinned, leggy, strawberry blonde with a model-perfect face. She wore flats; with any sort of heel, she would have towered over Kevin.

Lacey, fighting fatigue after a sum total of three hours of sleep, found it hard to focus on anything she did. She watched Allison glide around the set, warmly engaging everyone she met, and assumed that she was like Kevin: an up-and-comer. She envied Allison's apparent ease.

Kandace tried to insinuate herself, placing herself in conspicuous locations, trying to insert herself in the round of introductions. Lacey did the opposite, retreating to a far abandoned corner of the set. The only disadvantage to that action was that she couldn't tell whether Kevin and Allison managed to skip Kandace.

Later, Lacey nearly collided with the couple on their way to lunch break.

"Nola girl!" he said. "I was looking for you earlier. Allison, this is Lacey, the one from New Orleans I was telling you about."

He was telling her about me? Why?

Lacey extended her hand. "It's a pleasure to meet you, Allison."

Allison grasped both hands around Lacey's. "Lacey! It's great to meet you, too! Kevin told me all about how you made him feel like a native New Orleanian."

Interesting. I wonder how I did that?

The three chatted for several moments, Allison saying how she'd been to Mardi Gras once a few years ago, when she was an undergrad, how much she loved it, and how she'd been wanting to go back for Jazz Fest.

Lacey had been positive Allison was an actress, but it wasn't until later that afternoon that Lacey found out Allison's vocation.

Allison had been sitting in a corner of the set, brows furrowed, reading glasses on, tablet in her lap. She called out to Lacey as she passed, possibly looking for a distraction. Lacey politely inquired about what she was reading, and when Allison rattled off something about "phase variations in vector controls"—her ears started buzzing and everything sounded hazy, but she took note. Allison was no actress, she was a graduate student in public health.

Lacey couldn't linger, and she didn't feel comfortable enough to ask just how on earth Allison had met Kevin Horner, but she was impressed. Allison seemed like she could fit in anywhere—a fashion week runway or a laboratory. She made Lacey think of Barbie.

Feeling more than just a little intimidated, Lacey was relieved when Eli appeared at her elbow. Lacey figured that must be a first.

"Lacey, I need your help with something," he said.

"Me?" Lacey asked.

Eli stared at her, his floating eye tracking right.

"Yeah, sure," she said. "It was nice talking with you, Allison."

Allison gave Lacey a megawatt smile. "No, Lacey, *stay*. Eli, you don't really need her, do you? I'm having fun with her."

Eli's face became all sharp and angry angles for a split second. And returned to its normal, placid demeanor just as quickly.

Lacey went lightheaded, and she couldn't make sense of the interaction between Allison and Eli. She grabbed the back of her neck, wanting to make sure her head was still attached.

"Don't you *want* to hang out, Lacey?"

Yes, I do, don't I? Lacey opened her mouth to tell Eli she was staying when his voice cut through her thoughts. *Lacey, you are needed. Now. Follow me.*

Lacey shook her head, disoriented, but Eli's voice was like a bucket of cold water over her scalp. She was at work. She worked for Eli. Everyone seemed to work for Eli.

She glanced at Allison as she left, detecting a slight notching down of her warmth and definitely a chill between Eli and Allison.

"Where are we going, Eli?" Lacey asked as she hustled to keep up with him. She wanted to ask him more—especially about Allison.

When he didn't answer, she figured it was not the time to barrage Eli with questions. But there was one she needed to ask.

"I'm asking because I need to check some figures and possibly re-run some reports. I don't have to do it right away, but if we're going to take a while . . . "

"This will not interfere with your other work," he said, interrupting her. He didn't slow down.

"Okay, then." Lacey decided to shut up.

Eli led her into an edit bay.

"Sit here," he said, pointing to a like-new loveseat set back from a row of huge flat screen monitors.

Lacey silently did as she was told.

Eli pulled a rolling chair up to the row of monitors and slid out a keyboard. He started tapping and images from various recently-shot scenes cascaded down the screen in dizzying array. Lacey felt motion-sick and turned her head to look at a blank wall.

"Pay attention," Eli said.

She stopped herself from saying, "I can't." She willed her gaze back to the screen. Mercifully, the images had slowed. Eli settled on the scene with the horse. The green screen was gone, replaced with a sylvan background, an enchanted meadow straight from a fairytale. A blank, negative, horn-shaped space sat atop the horse's head.

Eli clicked some buttons, and a cartoonish, spiraled horn filled the space. Punched some more buttons, and it disappeared. Again, and a more realistic horn appeared, but it looked pasted on the image.

"Are you watching?" Eli asked.

"Yes," Lacey said. Feeling feisty, she asked, "Do you want me to learn CGI?"

Eli ignored her question. "Do you know what the difference is between this . . . " The cartoon horn appeared again on the monitor directly before him, " . . . and this?"

The monitor adjacent blazed to life. The mare was there with the sylvan background, just like on the other screen, but on this one she had a perfect, spiraled bone emerging from her skull, coming to a perfect point in the upper left corner of the screen. She raised her forelegs in slow motion, and her mane bristled in an unseen breeze, the sun reflecting off the glistening horn.

"One is moving and the other is not?" she said. It seemed obvious.

"No," Eli said without turning around.

"Well, there's a lot different, Eli," she said, drawing out the "i" sound in his name. "What are you going for?"

"Think completion," he said.

Her brain started to hum. Suddenly, she knew he was trying to illustrate some aspect of her gift, but she couldn't see the connection yet. "The one on the right is finished, the work is finished. The one in front of you isn't. There's still work to be done."

"That's right," he said, finally spinning around in his chair. He looked at her with his one good eye.

"And to be more specific, there's a difference of about ten hours between the two."

"You did that work?" Lacey asked, imagining Eli planted in place for ten hours, taking no breaks. It wasn't hard to picture.

"No, not all of it," he answered. "But I want you to understand that you're seeing the result of the work, without witnessing the hours of effort it took to produce it."

"Yes," she said. "But isn't that how it's supposed to work? Isn't that why we're all here? No one wants to spend two hours watching someone do the monotonous behind-the-scenes work on a movie. They want to spend two hours watching the results of that work."

"You will need to maintain awareness of that time and effort," Eli said, his left eye still looking straight at her.

Lacey considered her next words. Simplest seemed best. "Why?" she asked.

"Because time and healing co-exist. They're symbiotic. The human body needs time to heal. If the injury or the illness is too severe, if it outweighs the amount of time available, time's up. So to speak."

Lacey processed his words. She thought of Mr. LaSalle—Nathan's father-in-law—and the gunshot wound in his stomach. "Is there something I can do about that?" she asked in a small voice.

"Yes," he said. "At least, to a certain degree. That's why you need to develop a deep appreciation for time. For how much you're able to bridge over, and how much is insurmountable, even for you."

"So I can control time?" Lacey asked. "Can I change the past or the future?"

Lacey lowered her voice as someone entered the far side of the bay.

Hopefully, they think I'm talking about a movie role.

Eli shook his head, exasperated. "No. I'm trying to help you with insight into *your particular gift*," he emphasized. "You don't have magical control over one of the fundamental elements of the universe."

Lacey's head hurt.

"Remember to be present," Eli said, standing. "The here and now is the only time we can affect. *Any* of us."

"Wait, Eli. I'm not sure I get this. Yet. Maybe I will, with *time*." She couldn't help smirking. Eli shook his head again.

"No, wait, please. I do have a real question, about something I might have recently figured out."

Eli tilted his head, waiting for her next words.

"So, my power needs a catalyst, right? There needs to be someone close by that needs healing, in order for my ability to rise, so to speak. Right?"

Eli rested his chin on his hand, looking like "The Thinker" statue. He nodded slightly. "You came to that conclusion on your own?"

Lacey became defensive. "Well, yes, it just makes sense, because I haven't been able to get *that feeling*, that heat, just thinking about it. And, there was Hans, the Gaffer . . . "

"He's a Grip," Eli corrected.

"Ugh! Okay, Hans, the Grip, had an injury on his hand, and . . . "

"You healed it."

Lacey crossed her arms across her chest, defiant. "Well, yes."

The side of Eli's face turned up, that expression Lacey interpreted as his version of a smile. "Then, your power must require a catalyst in order to manifest. In other words, you cannot 'conjure' it unbidden. Good work."

Lacey unfolded her arms and stopped herself from throwing them up in the air.

Eli walked toward the guy at the far end of the bay. "You're free to go," he said with his back to her. "And Lacey? Stay away from that woman. You have more important work to do."

Kevin Horner is a delight to watch, Lacey thought. *At least that makes the time go by faster.*

She had to wait for him to finish shooting a scene, she wasn't exactly sure why, but Kandace had been adamant about it. Lacey had tried to concentrate really hard when Kandace was talking to her and make her words speed up so she would finish and walk away in fast motion.

So she couldn't control time. But maybe what Eli was talking about was that she had to be sure not to *waste* time when someone needed healing. That her uncertainty could make the difference. She hadn't hesitated with anyone yet, or at least she didn't think she had. For as bad as she felt about Lawrence LaSalle dying, she didn't think hesitation had anything to do with it. She had run to his side as soon as she was able.

And maybe Eli didn't want her to *waste* time with Allison. But she still didn't know what his reaction was all about. Calling Allison "that woman." Eli was cryptic by nature, but showed a clear dislike for Allison that was exceedingly un-cryptic.

She wasn't ready to give up daydreaming about controlling time. Not just yet. It would be most convenient, if she could speed up everything around her in the studio, and slow things down back at the rental for Ambrose, she might not need to worry so much about him being alone. He had access to the yard, and had always been so self-sufficient, but Lacey worried that the cross-country drive and time on his own had taken a toll on him. He did seem to be enjoying the Central Coast's more temperate summer, though.

You're not being present, she heard a voice in her head.

Screw you, she answered in kind. *I can worry about my lovely, big-hearted, protective dog if I want.*

She tried to focus on the scene being shot. Kevin Horner delivered the wooden dialogue with just enough of a wink to charm the audience into thinking it might be better than it was. Lesser performers might let a twinge of resentment show, or worse yet, try to convince themselves that the role really wasn't as bad as it read in the script. Not Kevin Horner. He used his particular magic to transform this TV movie into something Lacey might actually want to watch. It made her look forward to seeing the movie he shot in New Orleans. It was slated to premiere on Lifetime next month.

"I don't care what the world thinks of Sinead," he said in character. "And I don't care what Sinead thinks of the world. I care about Sinead, and that's the heart of the matter."

"Cut!" Marco yelled.

The way Kevin said the name Sinead, she imagined a million viewers wishing he would say their name that way. But what was that line even supposed to mean?

Suddenly, Kevin Horner broke out into song, Don Henley's "The Heart of the Matter," a spot-on imitation of the voice and eighties-style inflections. He lampooned around the stage, putting his hand on Hans's shoulder as he tried to unrig something, moving on to someone else when Hans wouldn't play along.

He scanned the sparse audience assembled off the soundstage, and zeroed in on Lacey.

"Even if, even if, you don't love me anymore," he sang, pointing at her.

Lacey laughed and played along, mouthing a silent "Me?" and turned around, confirming there was no one behind her.

Turning her head forward again, she caught Allison standing off in a corridor directly to her right, arms folded. She detected a scowl on her face, but didn't want to linger to find out for sure.

Oops, Lacey thought. *I hope she knows Kevin and I are just friends. And really, barely that.*

Lacey imagined her reaction if she saw Trevor flirting with

someone in his audience. Her look would be similar, she was sure.

I'll have to make a conscious effort to not let that happen, Lacey thought. *That's a bad look.*

Eli's comment seemed less off-the-mark now. She thought about her earlier exchange with Allison, and something seemed really wrong about it. Lacey had thought she wasn't thinking clearly at the time, due to fatigue. But she was still fatigued, and now she could tell that something wasn't right about it. It was almost like Allison had cast a spell.

I definitely don't want to go up against a jealous witch. Literally.

Kevin Horner's song had run its course, and the set was finally breaking. Kevin jumped off stage and sauntered toward Allison. Lacey turned in the opposite direction, intending to find Kandace. She would get the plan for tomorrow and then race home.

Eli intercepted her before she reached Kandace.

"Bring your dog with you to work tomorrow," he said.

Lacey wasn't sure she heard him right. "Ambrose?" she asked.

Eli glared and waited a beat. "Do you have another dog?" he asked. Something like a smile appeared on his face.

"How did . . . " Lacey began to say, then stopped herself. Eli was doing his Professor X thing. A more practical concern needed attention. "I'd like to, but Kandace has told me I can't. Liability or something."

"I have already spoken to Kandace Swade about it. She is expecting to see your dog here tomorrow."

"Really? Does he get to be in the movie?" She was punchy and trying to be lighthearted, but she still entertained the thought. Lacey imagined the small audience the movie was likely to garner falling in love with Ambrose. Then she'd have to answer fan mail, choose his next roles—become his manager.

Eli sighed. "No, we don't need him for a scene. Will it be a problem for you to bring him tomorrow?"

"No, of course not. It will be nice to have him around."

"Good." Eli walked off. Lacey couldn't tell if he was speaking into his headset or shaking his head.

9

Edgard, Louisiana

One autumn in the mid-twentieth century

Birdie wasn't sure she liked being called Birdie anymore. Morris McIntyre had called her "bird legs" for as long as she could remember. Her legs were a little on the thin side, but she figured that was the way God had made her, so there was no point in wishing for something different.

Morris had turned from a scrawny kid to a pretty big youth just this past year. "Strapping," Momma called him. She wondered if he was as big as Ronnie. She couldn't believe it had been five years since she had seen Ronnie. So much had happened. Old age had finally gotten Léon. Ronnie had written Birdie a letter that made her feel better. He said that "Léon would have never made it as far as he did without her help." Only they knew the full story of what had happened that day. Though Birdie reckoned Momma knew a lot more than she let on.

Momma had gotten a new job, working at the grain factory on the river. She liked it better than her old work, and her pay was really good, but she still complained that "her back was surely gonna break soon." And Birdie was doing really well in school. Her guidance counselor, Mr. Coyner, was after her to start applying to colleges. Mr. Coyner was from up north.

She hadn't said anything to Momma about that. She hadn't said anything to anybody about that. But she wanted to tell Ronnie.

Birdie was expecting him any minute now. Momma wouldn't be home until five thirty, and she had told Birdie one hundred times that she needed to come home straight from school, tidy the living room, start dinner, and be ready when Ronnie came home. They expected him at four o'clock.

She had just finished browning the onions when the screen door opened. The scent of pork drippings and potent herbs wafted through the doorway.

"Little Bird, I didn't think it was possible, but that might just smell better than anything Momma's ever cooked."

Birdie wiped her hands on her apron and smiled wide at the sound of her brother's voice. And her eyes grew wider than her smile when she saw the little boy clasping her brother's hand.

Ronnie laughed. There were more wrinkles around his eyes and more gray around his temples than Birdie remembered. "Ha! I don't think I've ever seen that look on your face."

Birdie put her hands on her hips, not pleased about the surprise. She'd had no idea Ronnie had a child. "Well, this face is a lot different than it was five years ago." She gave her brother a quick glare, but was sure to give a smile and a wink to the child with bright eyes and a head full of coarse coils. He smiled back, but buried his face in Ronnie's leg.

Ronnie nudged the boy with his leg. "Cecil, say 'hi' to your Aunt Birdie."

Birdie didn't miss a beat. She held out her hand to Cecil and said, "Hello, Sir Cecil. It's a pleasure to meet you."

Cecil offered a tentative hand, and Birdie grasped it in both of hers. She gave him a 1,000-watt smile so similar to her brother's that Cecil had to recognize something of his daddy in it. He smiled back and lunged toward Birdie, arms wide. She scooped him up into her arms.

She shot another death stare at Ronnie while she held Cecil. The little child couldn't see her face.

"Daddy said you'd be mean," a small voice chirped as he hugged her closer.

A big, boisterous laugh came from Ronnie. "I said no such thing, Little Man. I did say your Aunt Birdie might be a little angry with me."

Birdie ignored her brother and hiked the toddler up on her hip to face him. With a wide smile and laughing eyes she said, "Your daddy thinks he's funny. Ha ha."

She tickled Cecil with her free hand and provoked a few well-timed giggles.

Looking at Ronnie, she said, "Little angry, maybe. But Momma?"

Ronnie looked sheepish.

Birdie wagged her head. "Of course. Momma knows. Why am I the last to find out everything?"

"It's a long story, Bird."

"I ain't going nowhere." She set Cecil down to return to the stove.

"Well, we'll be here for a few days," Ronnie said. He and Cecil sat at the kitchen table. "What's for dinner?"

"Pork chops."

"What time does Momma get home?"

"Five thirty."

"What does it take to get more than a one-word answer from Bird?" He bounced Cecil on his knee.

"Pork chops is two words," she said, and then couldn't suppress a laugh.

"Sounds like they're teaching you good in school," Ronnie said. "You know how to spell your food."

"They're teaching me *well*," she answered with a wink.

"You see that, Cecil? We need to send you to Bird's school."

A thought occurred to Birdie. *Is now the time to mention college?* She cocked her head at her brother, then decided to save her question for later.

✳

Momma spent most of dinner fussing over Cecil. Birdie tried to express her displeasure over being kept in the dark about being an aunt, but Momma either didn't hear her, or chose to ignore her. It was likely the latter, and Birdie knew better than to press her luck.

Cecil was put to bed, and Momma had followed shortly thereafter.

"She doesn't look good, Bird," Ronnie said. They sat across from each other in the den. Ronnie took up most of the new settee they had just bought. They'd had to go to New Orleans for it. Birdie couldn't believe how much Momma paid for it. She just said, "I ain't breaking my back for nothing," when Birdie tried to suggest a less expensive option.

Birdie began to worry. "Why? I know she's tired all the time, but I think that's just from her work."

"You heard her at dinner, same as me. They all say they're

working for a big, northern company, but the people running it are all the same as they've ever been. They're gonna find a way to keep you down, just like they always have."

"Don't you work for a big, northern company?"

"Yeah. Up north. Run by northerners. It's different."

"They don't try to keep you down, Bubba?"

"Oh, yeah, they still do. But there're a lot more ways for them to get caught doing it. And the trouble's worse for them if they get caught. Down here . . . "

Birdie remembered something Momma had told her. How the big boss at the factory was Mr. Savin. The Savins lived next door to the house where Momma used to clean. It was like she had switched jobs, but not employers.

Birdie began to worry more. "Do you think I could help Momma?"

"You already do. You take care of things here while she's at work. You do good in school."

Birdie thought of Mr. Coyner. Now might be a good opportunity to tell her brother about what he said. But leaving home for college was a weighty topic.

"No, I mean by going to work."

"That's gonna come soon enough, Bird."

She looked at her brother and thought again. "Ronnie, they're telling me at school that I should apply for college."

Ronnie looked thoughtful. "Who's telling you that?"

"The school counselor."

"What's his name?"

Birdie told him.

"He's not from around here, is he?"

"How'd you know that?" Birdie asked.

"Same thing I was just talking about, Bird. People from

around here are going to try to keep you down, same as they ever has. Momma's told me how good you're doing, how much you like school. That's good, and I hope it stays that way for a while. But keep your guard up."

Birdie cast her eyes downward. She was hoping her brother would encourage the thought of college. But he just seemed suspicious.

She looked up. "Ronnie, what's the real reason you came down here? It wasn't to surprise me with your son."

A sad smile crossed Ronnie's face. He stood up and rolled his shoulders. "Bird, things with Cecil's momma are not easy. Never have been. I knew you'd be crazy to meet him as soon as you knew about him, and I wanted to be sure I could get him down here before that. Does that make sense?"

Birdie tilted her head upward. "Not really."

She smiled and shook her head. "But it doesn't matter. You're forgiven."

He walked toward her and laid his large hand on her head. He turned back toward the settee.

"And the reason I'm down here is to check on you and Momma. Especially Momma. I should've never let five years go by."

"You don't need to worry about us." Birdie stood and put her hands on her hips.

Ronnie laughed and settled back down. "Oh, I know. But that doesn't mean I don't anyway."

10

Fatigue couldn't keep Lacey's mind from spinning. She couldn't sleep.

She wasn't comfortable in the rental. She wouldn't refer to it as home, not even in her head. It served a purpose, and the yard was somewhat lovely, but her home was on Florida Boulevard. She had no idea who her neighbors were here. She had seen a woman in her fifties tending a garden across the street, during the few times she had snuck away during a lunch break. And a lanky man in his twenties in the house next door. Only coming and going, never outside, even though his place had a porch with well-kept plants and a pristine bench. Lacey had figured his place must be a rental, too.

She almost missed her nosy neighbor Kravitz. Almost. She wondered if Tonti was keeping him entertained, since he had no one to spy on with her house lying empty. Tonti was supposed to be looking after Lacey's home while she was away. Lacey had meant to check in with her regularly, but that just hadn't happened as she intended.

She lay awake in the rental's bed, thinking of what she had to pack for Ambrose since she was bringing him to the set today. Travel water and food bowls, food, pooper-scooper. What did Eli mean about affecting the present? What was she going to learn today?

She tried to think of Trevor. Fun, care-free sex with Trevor. To no avail. Instead, complicated thoughts of Nathan kept rushing in where she least wanted them. It had been more than a month since she'd even heard from him. Why couldn't she let go?

She might have slept in ten-minute intervals.

What is wrong with me? I normally worry a lot, yes, but something really has me worked up about the day ahead.

On the drive into the studio, nothing felt right. Not Ambrose in the front seat of her car, not the whole idea of bringing him to work.

Ambrose was fine. His usual calm, massive self. Why couldn't she be more like him? Even though nothing felt right about bringing him, when she boiled it down, she was glad he would be by her side today. Maybe if he got hungry, he could eat Kandace.

The first half of the day was busy but uneventful. She had a high volume of visits from crew members, curious to meet Ambrose. But the distraction did nothing to abate her sense of unease. She kept waiting for the shoe to drop.

Sometime in the late afternoon, Eli appeared in front of her desk. She hadn't seen him nor heard from him all day. She was sure his appearance was the other shoe.

Ambrose had parked himself under the table that served as Lacey's desk most of the day. He moved from underneath it and sat by Lacey's side, looking at Eli expectantly.

Wordless, Eli stared at the dog, right eye floating. He held out his hand, palm up, fingers curled. Ambrose shook his head and walked toward Eli.

Lacey gasped. Ambrose was typically aloof with strangers. He was downright rude with Nathan. And yet, he had immediately taken to Eli.

You should learn to take a cue from him, Lacey.

Crap! Did I just think that, or was that Eli?

She glared at Eli, but he either didn't see it, or ignored it. He let Ambrose sniff his hand, then engaged in some generous petting. Still wordless. Lacey figured it would be the closest thing to affection she would ever see from Eli.

"Are you a dog person, Eli?" Lacey asked, feeling the need to fill the silence.

He looked at her, still patting the dog, but didn't answer immediately.

"I grew up with animals," he said

That would indicate he had a childhood, Lacey thought.

"Not in the way most people would think of it," he said.

Ah! He is in my thoughts! Stop thinking!

"I know dogs mostly as herders," he said, "not as pets."

Lacey wondered if Eli had grown up on a ranch. Then realized she had no idea where Eli was from. She was about to ask, when she saw Marco eyeing Ambrose from a distance. "What do you need him for?" she asked, motioning at Ambrose.

"Nothing," Eli answered.

What the hell?

"But yesterday, when you said to bring him . . . " she started. "Never mind."

Exhaustion got the better of her. She didn't even have the energy to be angry with Eli.

"Have you brought him outside?" Eli asked.

"Yes." She checked the time. "A few hours ago now."

"You should bring him outside again now," he said, looking down at Ambrose.

"He can hold his water longer than that," she said.

"You should bring him outside again now," he repeated.

"Okay . . . " Lacey looked behind her toward Kandace's office but she wasn't there. She counted her blessings. She hadn't seen her much today at all.

When she turned around, Eli was gone. She had wanted to ask what was so important about bringing Ambrose outside, but didn't know how to do it and not get an "Eli" answer. Now she didn't have to worry about it.

"Whatever," she said. She grabbed Ambrose's lead. "C'mon, Bro, 'the Professor' says you need to go outside. Hopefully Kandace won't get up my ass about it."

Hans passed within earshot as soon as she said it. He smiled at her and she shrugged her shoulders, looking sheepish.

I have got to remember my co-workers are no longer imaginary.

At the gatehouse, Horatio seemed nervous. He was a burly but sweet security guard, who would walk Lacey to her car when she left the set after dark, which was most nights. He was not much taller than Lacey, but almost twice as wide, and Lacey always felt safe with him.

He smiled at Lacey and Ambrose, but rubbed his palms against his legs. Sweat gathered around his collar.

"What's going on, Horatio?" Lacey asked.

"It's been pretty quiet today," he answered. He folded his arms.

"Yeah, for me, too," she said. "So why do I feel so spooked?"

He smiled at her and nodded silently. He blew out a

breath. He seemed unwilling to say anything about what was bothering him.

"You don't need to feel spooked," he said. "That's why we're here. To handle the spooky stuff."

"You're a good guy, Horatio," she said. "We're just going to visit our spot, we'll just be a few minutes."

He nodded and pressed a button, unlocking the door. A lone sycamore tree shaded a corner of the parking lot within view of the guardhouse. A small patch of grass surrounded it.

Walking across the parking lot, Lacey noticed orange cones blocking off the parking spaces nearest the entrance.

That's why Horatio's nervous, I bet. A VIP visitor. The moneyman?

If the moneyman was visiting today, why hadn't Kandace told her? Lacey's unease shifted into annoyance.

Ambrose was content to visit his outside spot, but even he seemed a bit confused by the timing of it. He ran around it, considered lifting his leg, but then seemed to think better of it.

All right, Eli, we're here, she thought. *What for?*

She closed her eyes for an instant, letting the afternoon sun warm her eyelids. She thought of the marked spot in the parking lot, Horatio's nervousness, and her own. The sun became a light bulb above her head.

"Oh," she said out loud. Ambrose looked up at her.

It was the moneyman who was making them all nervous. Well, her and Horatio, at least. Eli must have wanted her to make the connection herself.

What is it about this mysterious person that has me spooked? And Horatio, too? I wouldn't think anything spooks him.

Ambrose brushed up against her legs.

"You're no help, Bro."

*

By 5:00 p.m., she had convinced herself she was letting her own neuroses get the better of her. By most accounts, the day had gone well. Kevin Horner was rolling through his scenes; they were even preparing to shoot an additional one, ahead of schedule. Allison wasn't on set today, so maybe he was more focused without her around. Kandace had been more present in the afternoon, but Lacey had been able to read her moves, preparing her reports before she even asked for them.

They only had one hiccup between them. Lacey had asked, "So, are you expecting the moneyman today? I noticed some parking blocked off in the lot."

Kandace huffed. "I don't know, Lacey, he might come today. And we reserve parking for lots of people, anyway. Not just the VIPs. You shouldn't be so nosy."

Geesh! I didn't think my question warranted that response.

Lacey had let it go, still annoyed that Kandace only allowed one-way nosiness.

Eli had gone missing since midday, so Lacey had no opportunity to ask him more about it.

By eight o'clock in the evening, Lacey had Ambrose on his lead and was looking for Kandace. There was nothing left for her to do, and she was planning to go home. The door to Marco's office was closed, and Lacey stopped in front of it, listening for voices. If Kandace was in there, she would send her a text.

Standing before the door, Ambrose began to struggle, and growled low.

"Ambrose!" she said in a commanding whisper, giving the lead a tug. "Stop!"

And then Ambrose did something he had never done before. He disobeyed Lacey's command, broke from her grasp, rose on his hind legs to his full height and lunged at the door, checking his 160 pounds against it. Lacey stood, paralyzed with shock. She knew not to make any sudden movements. She tried to make eye contact with him. Then, as suddenly as he went for the door, he returned to all fours and lumbered past her to the end of the hallway.

She turned around, agape, and saw Eli at the end of the hall. He motioned her to the exit with a single nod of the head.

What the hell just happened? Lacey thought. She hurried to catch up to Eli and her dog, both of whom were nearly to the rear of the building already.

She caught up with them in a back corner of the studio. Eli had opened a utility closet, and stood in the doorway with Ambrose behind him.

"Eli, what the hell?" Lacey said, slightly out of breath. "What did you do to my dog?"

Ambrose gave a low bark.

"Okay, sorry, Bro," Lacey said. "I know you're your own dog, not *mine*."

Eli, silent, stared at her with his left eye.

"What is going on?" she asked. "What made him do that?"

"If you really want to know," he answered, "go back there now. They are about to exit the room. You were looking for Kandace, weren't you?"

"What about Ambrose?" she asked. "I'm not bringing him back there."

"We'll be outside when you're done."

"I don't want to leave him. Bringing him here was a bad idea all around."

"Leave him with me, Lacey. It will be okay."

Lacey was rooted to the floor in front of the utility closet. She wondered how long she could stay like that before she'd have to act.

Lacey, be present. Quit playing through scenarios. Leave Ambrose with me. All will be well.

Her eyes widened. *I hate it when you do that!*

"Get over it, and go," he said.

Lacey leaned past Eli, trying to make contact with Ambrose again. He looked up at her, wagging his tail.

"Fine," she said. She turned on her heel.

This is what I was waiting for with Eli? How is this helping me understand my gift any better?

She slowed her pace as she approached Marco's office, and took a few slow, deep breaths. Marco opened the door for Kandace, who came through followed by a man in a navy jacket and khaki slacks. He looked and smelled like high dollar. A subtle cologne, a musk with notes of bergamot, lingered. Lacey recognized the scent instantly—it was the same worn by her old boss. "A bespoke potion from a Paris parfumerie" was what Trip Carriere would say when asked about it.

"There she is now," Marco said, looking in Lacey's direction. Lacey turned her head to look behind her. No one was there.

"Yes, *you*," Marco said, playing magnanimous director. "We were just telling Mr. Savin, here . . . "

"Please, call me Gus," the man in the navy jacket interrupted. His accent was unmistakably New Orleanian.

"Yes, of course," Marco continued, "we were just saying how we had someone from New Orleans in our production crew."

Lacey stood and tried not to appear dumbfounded. She knew who he was, but had never met him in person. And had never seen his name associated with this production. Kandace wore a smug smile, obviously puffed up over being included in the meeting.

"You certainly picked the right time of year to be away," Gus Savin said. "The climate out here has been nothing less than breathtaking.

"Gus Savin," he said, holding out a well-manicured hand to Lacey. There was an antique ring on his pinky.

Lacey attempted a genuine smile. "Lacey Becnel."

"Lacey Becnel," he said, retrieving his hand and holding his chin. "Why do I know that name?"

Lacey tried to come up with some response that would have nothing to do with Trip and her old job, to no avail.

"You're Trip Carriere's associate! Or were, I guess I should say."

Lacey was surprised he didn't say "Trip Carriere's girl."

"Yes, I did work for Trip. I'm surprised you knew that," she said before she could stop herself. She figured Trip Carriere's associate would have been beneath his attention. "I've certainly spoken with several of your employees over the years."

"Her former employer is quite an antiques collector," he said, addressing Marco and Kandace. "And quite the character, too, I might add."

There's a euphemism if I ever heard one, Lacey thought.

Gus Savin looked over his shoulder. "Enrique, are you ready?"

Lacey noticed for the first time a young man in a seersucker suit, still in the meeting room. He was struggling with a ferret, trying to place him into a carrier.

"You should never have worn seersucker out here, and especially not when you have to wrassle with Percival," Gus Savin said.

Lacey tried to process what she was seeing and hearing.

The ferret might possibly explain Ambrose's reaction. But why on earth would one of the wealthiest old-money men in New Orleans be meeting with the director of a grade-C television movie, much less bring along his assistant and a ferret named Percival?

Gus Savin re-entered the office to supervise Enrique's efforts. Marco and Kandace acted like ferrets and moneymen were business-as-usual for them. Kandace stood, quiet, and Marco examined the door to his office.

"How long have you been here?" Marco asked.

Lacey turned, but wasn't sure if he was addressing her. "Excuse me?"

"Have you been in the hallway long?" he asked.

"Oh. I was here a few moments ago. I was trying to find Kandace. I just came back," she said.

Marco looked more closely at the door to his office. He ran his fingers along two fresh scratches in the door.

Oh, fuck, Lacey thought when she noticed what Marco was doing.

"Did you see anything?" he asked. "We heard a loud noise toward the end of our meeting, like someone banging against the door."

How to play this?

"Oh gosh, I'm sorry, that was probably me. I was carrying a box of files, wasn't watching where I going. I stumbled against the door. I'm so sorry."

Marco glared at her. "You shouldn't be lugging heavy things around," he said in a low voice. Lacey swallowed hard. "You, of all people, should know what a nightmare workers comp is," he said.

"That's on me, Marco," Kandace said, her voice bright.

"I'd asked Lacey to bring a set of reports to my office. I hadn't realized there'd be so many of them."

Lacey turned to Kandace, nonplussed.

Kandace actually smiled and touched Lacey on the elbow. "She's always trying to do too much."

"That's what I'd always heard from Trip Carriere," Gus Savin said, now back in the doorway. Enrique stood next to him, his suit lapels coated with ferret fur and a long lank of his black hair hanging in his face. He clutched the carrier containing a restless Percival.

"I can tell you're running a tight ship, here, Marco," he said, holding out his hand. Lacey could see the insignia on his pinky ring for the first time. An "S" set in a fountain.

"Thank you," Marco said. "I hire good people." He shot a laser-eyed glare at Kandace. "I'll see you to your car. I'll get you the details on that restaurant."

Something in the way he said "restaurant" made Lacey think he wasn't really referring to a restaurant. The way Marco and Savin spoke to each other gave her the creeps.

They disappeared down the corridor; beleaguered Enrique followed with the ferret. Lacey and Kandace stood alone. Lacey was ready for Kandace to do an about-face, but still wanted to recognize the charitable moment.

"Kandace, thank you," Lacey said.

"For what?" she said. She had a sly smile on her face Lacey had never seen before. "Marco is going to give me shit for my over-reliance on paper, but that's nothing new."

Lacey wasn't sure how to respond. She didn't want to look a gift horse in the mouth.

"Sorry for that," Lacey said. "I just wanted to see if you needed me for anything. I'm getting ready to head out."

"No, go ahead. Have a nice night."

"What time tomorrow?" Lacey asked.

"Eight thirty should be fine," she said as she headed toward her office.

"Okay," Lacey said to Kandace's back.

Lacey turned in a trance. On the way to retrieve her purse before meeting Eli and Ambrose, she pondered everything that had transpired over the last twelve hours. Nothing had happened as she expected. She wasn't sure what she had expected, but she was sure she had not anticipated anything as surreal as her encounter with Savin. Or Kandace covering for her.

11

On the way into work the next morning, this time without Ambrose, Lacey tried to remember everything she knew about Gus Savin.

She knew he was her old boss's adversary, an uptown socialite who had deprived Trip Carriere of his chance to be the youngest-ever King of Carnival (according to his telling). She also knew he was the premiere antiques dealer in New Orleans—and that he had a revolving door for employees. It was rare that she ever spoke to the same person twice, when his storefront would call Trip's office with rare book finds. Early on, years ago, there had been one man who called consistently—what was his name?—but he had left. Every recent dealing Lacey could recall, it was always someone different. Usually someone young.

But what did it matter, and why did she care? Because it was all so odd. Alternate universe weird. Eli had offered her very little—big shock there—when she retrieved Ambrose from him the night prior. He said something about animals sensing what humans can't, which was hardly revelatory to Lacey. And added that she didn't need to bring Ambrose to the set the next day.

He had turned on his heel and disappeared into the night. *Goodnight, Eli.*

Now, Lacey was dog-tired behind the wheel. She had dreamt of Nathan and the death of his father-in-law all night. It was dreadful, witnessing the life ebb out of Lawrence LaSalle over and over again. She had not had the dream since Trevor entered the picture. She blamed Gus Savin for the intrusion of old society New Orleans back into her subconscious.

Trevor is a lot easier to think about, she thought. *Think of Trevor instead.*

That didn't help much. She longed to see him again, and was wildly frustrated that she didn't know when it might happen. If she straight up asked to see him again, would that be too much expectation? She didn't want to talk to Jimmy about it. Being involved with his bandmate was fraught enough. Plus, the logistics were problematic. Trevor was staying three hours away, in Los Angeles, and she couldn't easily just pick up and leave her job to spend time with him if she felt like it.

She could tell Jimmy about Gus Savin, though. That would help. She would try to reach him today.

John Villere! That was the name of the person who would call for Gus Savin, way back when she first started working for Trip. How could she forget? He would always say his full name, "John Villere," when he called. And he always had an awkward joke, usually something about how he was no relation to the now long-gone New Orleans grocery store chain, Canal Villere.

Edmund Villere. The man who kidnapped her, killed Nathan's father-in-law, and was currently in jail, awaiting trial. How had she not drawn the connection until now?

Because there is no connection. Villere is a common name in southern Louisiana, she thought.

One was a very distant work acquaintance from years ago, to whom she only ever spoke over the phone. The other was a drug-addicted felon who would have killed her if he'd had the chance. Still, it seemed a weird coincidence.

She parked her car, waved at Horatio, and headed inside.

Lacey checked her calendar when she got to her desk. Kandace had scheduled a meeting at 9:00 a.m., which was in forty minutes, for just the two of them, in her office. She had booked an hour time slot for it.

Lacey panicked. This had to be it. Kandace would come down on her for the dog, for lurking outside the meeting room, for not being the good little toady she wanted her to be. Could she get fired? Could Kandace fire her? She didn't think she could. But Marco could. And Marco would give the task to Kandace.

Calm down, she told herself. *There's nothing to feel guilty about. And Kandace will smell the fear.*

She grabbed some hot tea from the empty break room. When she got back to her desk, she noticed the soundstage was eerily empty, too. It wasn't so unusual for the studio to be so empty this early, especially if the shoot was scheduled for the afternoon. But she would have preferred to have some distraction. She checked the schedule, and saw Kevin Horner was off today. But the other principals were scheduled for 1:00 p.m.

She smelled Diet Dr. Pepper. She turned around and saw Kandace with her mug and wobbly straw.

"Can you meet earlier than nine?" she asked.

Might as well get this over with.

"Sure," Lacey said. "Do I need to bring anything?"

"Just your brain," Kandace replied.

Lacey saw Kandace's laptop set up at the small conference table behind her desk, with two chairs side-by-side.

Doesn't look like a firing.

"It will go a long way with Marco," Kandace said, "if I show I'm really attempting to cut down on my paper use. He really is a rabid environmentalist. I had thought it was kind of an act."

Lacey suppressed a smile. She was certain everything with Marco was an act, but Kandace's olive branch felt very real. And she was relieved she was apparently going to keep her job.

"Is there something I can help you with?" Lacey asked.

"Yes, that's why I set this up. It's quiet this morning, and you seem like you're a good teacher. I was hoping you could walk me through some of the Movie Marvel reports."

Wow. Be nice, Lacey. Build a bridge.

"Sure, I'd be happy to," Lacey said.

They spent the better part of forty-five minutes scrolling through Kandace's screen. Lacey did a good job of silencing her internal dialogue and answering Kandace's questions respectfully. She couldn't tell if Kandace was really understanding what she was saying, but she asked questions like she was trying to.

When it was clear Kandace had reached her limit, she rolled her chair back from the small table.

"Are you up for spending more time on this, maybe in another couple of days?" she asked.

"Absolutely," Lacey said. "I'll even start writing down some shortcuts as I think of them, so we can make you a cheat sheet."

Kandace gave her the same sly smile she gave her last night. Had Lacey misjudged her from the beginning?

Kandace's phone flashed on the table. All Lacey saw was

the name Marco before Kandace jumped up from her chair, sourpuss face returned. She glared at Lacey and motioned her to the door with a nod of her head.

It was nice while it lasted, Lacey thought.

She wasted no time returning to her desk.

✳

Lacey entertained herself watching the afternoon shoot. The second male lead, Liam's best friend, seemed like he might actually be improving. Was Kevin Horner's influence upping the game of his fellow performers, after only a few days?

The guy practiced fencing in between takes.

Is there supposed to be a sword fight? She knew there was a new script just circulated, she hadn't thought the story could change so much to incorporate a whole new scene. She searched the server for the latest version of the script.

She stopped herself mid-way through. Meaningless script changes; endless delays; long, boring days; a colleague/boss she didn't enjoy working with. She didn't really care about any of it. The only reason she wanted to be in this place was for what she could learn from Eli.

How long can I do this?

She had worried that morning that Kandace might fire her. Would that be such a bad thing? The work was definitely an improvement over Carriere & Associates—she was rarely alone, for one, and she liked being part of a big project. But it was a project she didn't care about, and she still felt underutilized.

Underutilized.

What about her traiteur ability? With Eli a no-show for so long, how much time had she wasted? And she felt like their encounters this week hadn't advanced her understanding at all.

How did X-Men make a living? Was there money in the hero gig? Who pays them? If she could figure out how to harness whatever it is she has going for her, could she charge for it?

Absolutely not.

She knew, from what little she had read about the traiteur tradition, that traiteurs never asked for payment. And regardless of tradition, the idea wasn't even worth entertaining. *Sure, I'll fix up that gunshot wound, but it's gonna cost ya.*

No. There's no sense to that, and absolutely no honor.

She was going to have to figure out something to do to make a living wage, something that she didn't find horribly boring, that would at least keep her thoughts from straying all over the place. With Eli's apparent telepathic abilities, why was he working in movies in special effects? Would he even tell her if she asked?

An ideal job for her, she thought, would be something engaging, that kept her busy, and that might put her in the way of people needing healing.

She refrained from looking up, she was so sure a real light bulb popped above her head.

How had I not thought of this before?

A paramedic.

Maybe because I only just found out about my mutant power about, oh, sixty days ago.

She looked at the script she had opened on her screen. It was the most recent one, and she was perusing it for changes, but couldn't see a thing. She wanted to start researching paramedic training straight away.

Focus, she thought.

She tried to finish the task at hand. She found a scene near the end: Liam and his best friend have a sword fight with a centaur.

How on earth does that fit into the plot? And where did the centaur come from?

She closed the file and the folder she found it in. She made sure she didn't have any messages waiting from Kandace or anyone else, then started digging into what training she'd need to be a paramedic. In New Orleans.

A few hours later, she had begun a list of pros and cons. Was she too old? Could she trust her partner if she healed someone within sight of him or her? Perhaps most importantly, could she really heal people, and if so, what were her limits?

She minimized the window on her screen when she felt eyes behind her. There was no tell-tale scent of Diet Dr. Pepper, though.

She whipped around and saw Kandace, sans mug, statue-still with an ashen face.

Lacey recognized that look. It was the look reserved for only the worst news. Lacey felt a terrible pressure on her throat.

"Kandace. What is it?" she asked with a cracked voice.

"There's been an accident," she said, eyes staring forward.

Lacey rose, slowly. Kandace struggled with her words.

"Kevin Horner is dead," she said.

12

The last funeral she had attended was Fox's, eighteen months ago. Now, she was on her way to another funeral for another young man that had died too young.

The production had gone on immediate hiatus. The funeral was set for the upcoming Wednesday, in Los Angeles. Lacey and Ambrose drove down the coast highway to stay at Jimmy's house in Mar Vista for a few days. She wasn't sure what she would do after the funeral. Her brother told her she could stay at his house for as long as she wanted. LeViticum was set for several gigs throughout California and the Southwest, so he wouldn't be around a lot.

Which also meant Trevor wouldn't be around. But she wasn't thinking about him much, anyway. She was still in shock. Kevin Horner was so young, and so vital. It was so strange that he was gone. No, she wasn't close to him. But because her current employment, and her whole reason for being in California in the first place, was so interlaced with his part in that TV movie, her world at present was very much upturned. Herself and the dozens of other people affiliated with the production.

She had only seen Eli once since hearing the news. It was at the studio, before she had driven down to Los Angeles. From her time spent with Eli and Kevin in New Orleans, the two had appeared to be close. Lacey wondered how Eli was taking the loss.

Eli had appeared before her, at her desk, as she was securing the laptop. He bore no visible signs of emotion.

"Oh, Eli," she said, and walked out from her desk to offer an embrace.

Eli had accepted, stiffly, and disengaged quickly.

"You will go to the funeral?"

"Yes, of course," Lacey had answered. "It's not private? It won't be strange for me to be there?"

"No," he had said. "It will be a Hollywood funeral."

Lacey wasn't sure what he meant by that.

He had disappeared before she could ask him any of the one million questions going through her mind.

It had been a car accident. Kevin Horner was driving and Allison had been his passenger. She was injured pretty badly, but was expected to make it. This much she had gotten from Kandace.

She had gotten a little more from Angele. Angele was in Los Angeles, and they were supposed to go to the funeral together. The official word was that the toxicology screen on Kevin and the investigation was ongoing, so there wouldn't be any definitive answers for a while. But Angele knew from what she called "inside sources" that Kevin had not been partying prior to that drive. And that there was no other vehicle involved in the accident.

"There's something spooky about the whole thing," Angele had said in her trademark, cut-and-dried delivery. "Something doesn't add up."

Lacey couldn't stop herself from drawing the parallels to Fox. Young, and charismatic, and charming. And then gone.

Fox hadn't died in a car accident. No, the heart attack hit him as he entered the cold water of Lake Pontchartrain. But she'd always had an unnatural fear of car accidents. She'd been so certain there had been a wreck, during that twenty-minute lifetime between getting the call and seeing his lifeless body on the shore.

Lacey tried to steel herself for Kevin's funeral. She would know very few people, which would be a blessing, she thought. *This is not Fox's funeral*, she kept telling herself as she drove to meet up with Angele.

Angele was waiting for her outside the parking lot at the Grove, the outdoor shopping mall woven into Los Angeles's Farmers Market. She had told Lacey it would be easiest to meet there, no parking passes or security checks. Just a few months ago, Lacey might have been miffed that Angele wouldn't take the trouble to get her a pass onto Paramount Studio's lot, where she was currently working. But the circumstances of their meeting, and the fact that Lacey was over the whole movie business, made her appreciate the ease of the pick-up.

Angele was dressed in a black skirt, gray blouse, and heels. Lacey almost didn't recognize her.

She settled into the passenger's seat. "Well, this is all horrible."

"That's an understatement," Lacey answered.

They spent a few minutes discussing the latest details of the tragic story. Lacey had no updates on Allison's condition, and asked, "Is there any news about the girlfriend?"

"Yeah, I have news, all right," Angele said. "She's supposed to be there today."

"Holy crap. Like in traction, or what?"

"Probably in a wheel chair. I don't know who's gonna take her."

"Why not her friends or family?" Lacey asked. "Does she have somebody near by?"

"Not from what I hear," Angele answered cryptically. "I bet she'll hire a private nurse to bring her. I already hear she's planning on suing Kevin's estate to cover 'pain and suffering.'"

"Jesus, that's awful, if it's true," Lacey said. "Wouldn't his insurance be enough for all that?"

"Probably more than enough," Angele answered. "But I bet Kevin was sitting on a lot of liquidity. He'd been working a lot, and hadn't bought anything stupid."

"It's just so sad. And so weird. Her part in it, I mean," Lacey said.

"This wouldn't have happened under my watch," Angele said.

Lacey was certainly used to Angele's bold, even abrasive, proclamations. But this one seemed particularly over-the-top.

"Wow," Lacey said. "Do you really believe that? That you could have stopped the laws of physics somehow and prevented his car accident?"

"No, not that," Angele said, dismissive. "The girl, Allison. He shouldn't have gotten so serious with her, and he definitely shouldn't have brought her up to the set."

"Well, it all doesn't really matter now, does it?"

Angele ignored her last comment. "You look nice."

Lacey was past caring about Angele's abrasiveness. "Thanks. So do you."

"Did you bring that from home?" Angele asked.

Lacey smoothed the skirt of her conservative black shirt-dress with a free hand.

"Yeah," Lacey said. "I figured it was a good packing piece because it could work for a variety of occasions. Though I hadn't anticipated a funeral."

"You're probably going to see some heavy hitters there today," Angele said. "I think a lot of his co-stars from *Entanglement* may show up."

"Hmm. Okay. It's still really sad," Lacey said.

What a strange calculus this whole world operates on.

Lacey was certain she'd never understand it.

✳

Angele wasn't kidding. Lacey tried to keep her jaw from dropping open at the sight of all the celebrities. It was bizarre, seeing all those people she usually associated with the smell of popcorn, instead accompanied by the antiseptic-meets-floral standard odor of a funeral parlor.

And it wasn't just movie stars. Luminaries from music, the stage, nearly every corner of the arts milled about. Lacey focused on one musician. "Is he in the movie?" Lacey whispered to Angele.

"No. He wrote a song for the soundtrack," she hissed at her. "Can you at least try to act like you belong here?"

"I'll keep her in check," a low, monotone voice chimed in from behind them.

Eli was dressed in a dark suit, dark shirt, and a white tie. Strangely, it suited him. With his bald head, he looked like a formidable 1920s mobster.

"Lacey, can you come with me? Hello, Angele, it's nice to see you," he said all in one breath.

Angele motioned for Lacey to go ahead. "Hey, Eli," she said.

"I'm sorry to see you under these circumstances, but it's good to see you all the same."

He tipped his head silently toward her, and led Lacey lightly by the elbow.

"Are you doing okay, Eli?" Lacey asked as they walked to a less crowded area.

"I am well, thank you," he said. "And how are you? I wasn't sure how you'd react to funerals."

Lacey narrowed her eyes. *How I'd react? How much does he know about Fox's funeral?*

She stopped herself before answering.

"I'm fine, Eli. I'll be fine. But this is all just so sad, and weren't you close?"

"I was very fond of Kevin. Even felt a sort of a fraternal bond, you might say. This is, indeed, very difficult."

Eli's shoulders sloped, and his eyes misted over. Lacey was struck by how he became almost instantly vulnerable. She sensed a deeply-hidden tenderness.

"Do you understand what I mean by a Hollywood funeral, now?" he asked, recovering.

"Maybe," Lacey said. She refused the volley. "I am truly sorry and sad for you, and for Kevin's family."

"You can tell them that yourself," he said.

Lacey looked up and saw they were in a line, less than ten feet away from a couple linked together and receiving mourners. The woman was elegant, taller than the man, in a black prairie skirt and cropped black jacket. Her face was tear-stained. The man wore a turquoise bolo tie with a white shirt and a black suit. His eyes were moist, and he was an older version of Kevin Horner—in expression, stance, everything.

"Oh, Eli, no," Lacey whispered to him. "What would I say to them? I really barely knew Kevin."

"Tell them what you just told me," he said.

Lacey gauged the distance. Not long. "Did Kevin have any siblings?" she whispered.

"Yes. A younger sister. Look to that small couch," Eli said.

Lacey saw a girl who appeared no more than a teenager, sitting close to an older woman, maybe an aunt. Her eyes were dry, but she looked shattered, almost in shock.

Lacey suddenly saw herself in the girl. She couldn't imagine—never wanted to imagine—what it would be like to lose Jimmy. Losing a cheating husband was life-changing in every way. Losing a beloved brother would be a devastation.

Her heart ached. She whispered to Eli, "Their name is Horner?" She didn't even know if Kevin's name was real or a stage name.

Eli nodded.

The people in front of them moved on. They were face-to-face with the grieving parents.

"Mr. and Mrs. Horner," Eli began, his vulnerability resurfacing. Recognition lit up both their faces.

Mrs. Horner stopped his words with an embrace.

"Oh, Eli," Mrs. Horner said, "thank you for all you've done. And thank you for being such a good friend to Kevin."

Eli nodded. A tear slipped down his face. Lacey was stunned at the sight of it.

Mr. Horner grabbed Eli's hand in a firm shake.

"This is Lacey Becnel," Eli said. "Kevin and I met Lacey whilst filming in New Orleans."

"Look how lovely you are," Mrs. Horner said, embracing Lacey as well. Lacey felt something when they embraced, a pang in her solar plexus, and a radiating heat. Mrs. Horner held onto the embrace a second too long, and Lacey looked down at the floor when she disengaged, a little perplexed.

"How is Holly?" Eli asked.

Lacey looked up at the couple. Mrs. Horner gave her a sad smile, dissipating the awkwardness.

"She's having a very hard time with it," Mr. Horner said.

"Would you please go sit with her a spell?" Mrs. Horner asked.

The teenaged girl—Holly, Lacey assumed—was now alone on the couch, her face in her hands.

"Certainly," Eli said. "Is there anything else we can do for you? Anything you need right now?"

"Eli, you've already done so much," Mr. Horner said. "Thank you. I know the words are insufficient."

"No, they're not," Eli said. He grabbed Lacey's elbow.

"I'm . . . I'm so sorry," Lacey stuttered to the parents as Eli steered her toward the couch.

That was insufficient, Lacey thought.

Lacey and Eli stood over Holly on the grieving couch. Try as he might to be empathetic, Lacey thought he still might appear menacing to the young woman.

Holly looked up at Eli through parted hands. "Who *are* you?" she asked.

Lacey smiled. She'd wanted to ask Eli that question, in that same way, for months now.

"I've seen you with my parents at the hotel," Holly said, hands on her knees, revealing a face that was no longer tear-free.

"I'm sorry, we were never properly introduced," Eli said. "I'm Eli Bardzani. This is my friend, Lacey Becnel. May we sit?"

Holly looked at Lacey and pushed to one side of the couch,

silently telling her to sit next to her. Lacey smiled again and sat. She tried to think of something innocuous to say, that didn't include anything that would make Holly think about her dead brother. Nothing came.

"They're staying up in Los Feliz," Eli said. "Not too far from Griffith Observatory."

He gave Lacey an in. The planetarium, nestled on the southern slope of Mount Hollywood, was one of her favorite places in Los Angeles. The views were amazing.

"Oh, Griffith Observatory is awesome," Lacey said. "My brother has taken me there plenty of times."

Lacey winced right after she spoke. *Way to not mention brothers*, she thought. But it was impossible to think of Griffith Observatory without thinking of Jimmy.

"So did Kevin," Holly said. She perked up. "Well, he took me there once, at least."

Maybe that wasn't such a blunder, Lacey thought.

"You know, my brother moved out here a long time ago. On my very first visit, we went up there. Did you like it?" Lacey asked.

"Yeah. I mostly liked the view of the city from up there," she said.

"Was it during the day, or at night?" Lacey asked.

"Night," Holly said. "Well, we got there during the day, but stayed until the sun set."

"It's amazing to think of all those people down below, isn't it?" Lacey asked.

Holly nodded, then stared down at her lap again. Lacey glanced at Eli. He was expressionless.

Lacey moved her right hand from her lap, and placed it on Holly's knee. "I'm so sorry, Holly," she said.

This time was different from any other time. Lacey felt suddenly flush, but the heat didn't radiate. Her arm went numb, almost instantly. Holly began to cry, hushed sniffles emanating from her. Lacey wanted to move her arm, maybe place it around Holly's shoulders, but it wouldn't budge. She had a lead weight attached to her shoulder.

She finally managed to drop it to her side. Holly looked up.

"Thank you," she said.

Lacey wanted to ask "for what?" but the paralysis had moved to her throat. She gave Holly a weak smile.

Eli grabbed her good arm by the elbow. Things started to get back to normal. Lacey felt her voice return, and thought of something to say.

"Is there anything we can do for you, Holly? Anything I can get you? Some water, maybe?" Lacey asked.

Holly nodded. "Yes, thank you. Would you, please?"

Eli helped Lacey from the couch. "We'll be right back, Holly," Lacey said.

Lacey flexed her right hand. She'd regained control, but her arm was electric with pins-and-needles sensation. She kept flexing her fingers as Eli led her away.

"Eli, what . . . "

"Wait until we can't be overheard," he said in a low voice.

He led her outside. The harsh California sun was directly overhead. They walked toward a huge bougainvillea that offered no shade.

"Do you recall my words about time and your ability?" Eli asked.

"Yes, but I still don't really understand."

"Your ability will manifest in ways that are as different as people are different. But the constant is time."

"Still not understanding . . . "

Eli shifted his position. It helped block the sun from shining directly into Lacey's eyes.

"Try to think of it this way. For trauma-caused injuries—bone breaks, lacerations, gunshot wounds—your ability can "warp" time. Speed up the healing process."

"So I *can* control time! But only for injuries?"

"No," Eli said, "Your *presence*, and the ability that you have, 'tricks' time, as it were. You have no control over it." He stood, patient, motionless as a statue. Lacey thought of the Buddha.

She sighed, shifted, and found the sun back in her eyes. She returned to her original position.

"So what about other types of injuries?" she asked.

"It's different for those suffering emotional trauma, or chronic illness. Think about what just happened now."

Lacey bit her lip and cast her eyes downward. The sun was relentless.

"I felt something when Mrs. Horner embraced me. But not the 'my clothes are going to catch fire' heat. But then, with Holly, it was very different, and very distinct. The only heat was the kind that accompanies pins-and-needles."

"And how did they each seem afterward?"

Lacey thought about it. "Slightly better? A little less distraught? Or am I making that up?"

"No, I noticed an amelioration, too. You needn't be so distrustful of your gift, Lacey. It's quite remarkable."

This was a side of Eli she'd been hoping for.

"So, for things like that, I'm kind of like a respite? And, I'm just thinking this through, what did you mean by chronic illness?"

"It's an exponentially broad term. But it could mean things

like hearing loss, or migraines, or neuropathy. And, that's an appropriate way to think of it. Your ability provides a respite, but not a cure. Your presence can act like a balm."

Lacey considered. Being a balm sounded really nice. Not a bad ability to possess.

"So it's the same for emotional trauma, like losing a brother . . . ."

"Yes.

"You know, I've lost a brother," he added.

Eli stated it so matter-of-factly, with no change in his usual stoic demeanor, she wasn't sure she heard him correctly.

"Oh my God, Eli, that's terrible. I'm so sorry."

"It was a long time ago, and a story for another time. We should return inside now, and bring Holly the water we promised her."

Lacey was so stunned, all she could manage to say was, "Okay."

She followed him back inside the funeral home, wondering how much pain Eli kept below the surface. She'd been so focused on accessing his apparent knowledge of her ability. For the first time, she considered that maybe she could offer something to him, too.

13

Lacey and Angele sat across from each other, in the open-air concession outside the observatory at Griffith Park. An intermittent breeze blew the smog out to the ocean, in the stillness the scent of ozone lingered. They could even see the Los Angeles River glinting in the distance, snaking its way through the valley. The vestiges of a rare and welcome storm.

"When do you have to get back to the studio?" Lacey asked. "Or rather, the Grove parking lot?"

"Ha, ha. There's no rush. I wouldn't have agreed to let you drag me up here if there was."

"Gee, *dragged*," Lacey said. "I told you why I had a sudden yen to come up here again."

"Yeah, yeah. And that maybe you healed Kevin's little sister, too, but it was different and your clothes didn't catch on fire."

"Fine. We don't have to stay up here together if my presence is so onerous to you." She wondered why she never seemed to act like a balm to Angele.

"Oh, get over it," Angele said. "This is certainly preferable to the funeral. And I really want to hear the latest on your love life. How much time elapsed between your two different bedfellows?"

Lacey shook her head. While she knew the number exactly—thirty-one days—she wasn't ready to entertain Angele's judgment just yet.

"Not so fast. Last time we talked, you told me you were getting ready for a date. A guy who worked in Licensing, I think you said."

"Yes. And there's no story." Angele planted her hands firmly on the picnic table, like she was about to give a statement. "It was a non-starter, a dud, and there are no more current prospects. That's why I need your story, something vicarious."

The first tinges of deep blue showed on the eastern horizon, as the sun traveled in the opposite direction. Lacey sighed. "My two different bedfellows. Ha. This isn't the nineteenth century."

"Exactly! That's why I want details."

Lacey offered a very abbreviated version of her evening with Trevor. But then made the mistake of telling Angele that she'd been thinking of him, and hoping to see him again.

"Please! Don't tell me you're in love with him, after just one night."

"Who said anything about love?" Lacey was struggling to keep Angele from punching her buttons. "What's wrong with saying I want to see someone again, someone I had a really great time with?"

"Nothing. I'm just testing you. Because everything that went down with Dinner Jacket is still very recent, and that all moved very quickly."

"Do you remember his name is Nathan?"

"Yes. But Dinner Jacket is catchier. And less permanent."

"Right. Less permanent is right. There's nothing going on between me and Nathan," Lacey said. "There can't be anything going on with us."

Lacey was sure she hadn't told Angele what Nathan said to her. That he had said, "I love you." She was sure of it, because she hadn't told anyone. Nor had she told Angele—or anyone—about Nathan's visit the night before she left home. All of it added to the complication of Nathan, and she was not about to discuss that with Angele.

Lacey stood. "I'm tired of sitting."

"Me, too."

They strolled the promenade that spanned the length of the observatory. The crowd was light, and they found a spot on the low wall that hemmed the eastern end of the building.

The topic changed while they changed locations. Discussing the funeral, Angele asked what she thought of Allison's presence there.

"I barely saw her," Lacey said. "She had a horde of people around her the few times I got close."

"Yeah. It felt a bit orchestrated."

"Really? How can you orchestrate at a funeral? And from a wheelchair? Maybe people were just really concerned about her."

"Maybe orchestrate isn't the right word," Angele said. "It just seemed like everything, the crowd around her, was *engineered* to introduce some chaos."

"God, I sure hope not." But Lacey thought of her strange, spell-like experience with Allison, and admitted to herself that it was possible. She chose not to share it with Angele.

Lacey turned her back to the railing and stared off in the direction of the sinking sun.

"I need to think about getting back," Angele said. "Are you ready to go?"

"Yeah, I suppose," Lacey said. She brushed her hands along the lines of her dress.

They cut across the manicured lawn toward the parking lot. "I'm headed to New Orleans on Friday, so I have a bunch of things I need to finish up before I go," Angele said.

"Oh. I didn't know." Lacey stopped, surprised. She resumed walking when Angele didn't stop.

"I didn't tell you."

She raised her hands in exasperation, behind Angele's back.

"I saw that," Angele said.

"Saw what?" Lacey lengthened her stride to catch up to her. "You have another job there?"

"No," Angele said.

"Oh."

"Is everything okay?"

"Yeah," Angele said. "Dad has to get some kind of procedure done. Mom's going to need some company."

"Oh," Lacey repeated. "Procedure?"

Angele had told Lacey that her dad hadn't been feeling well, but had never elaborated. Despite Lacey's efforts to pry a few more details out of her.

"Yeah, something with his gall bladder, it's supposed to be fairly routine."

"Oh." Mr. Lee had trouble with gallstones, Lacey recalled.

"You want me to check in on Dinner Jacket while I'm in NOLA?" Angele asked.

It was Angele's classic parry, changing the subject away from her family. She decided not to push the subject.

"No," Lacey said. "But if you happen to find yourself in Lakeview, could you drive by the homestead?"

"I thought Aunt Tonti had you covered there," Angele said.

"She does, but I wouldn't mind another set of eyeballs. Plus, seeing you drive by will give Mr. Max something to yap about."

"I'll roll right up onto his grass," Angele said.

"Oh, Jesus. Please don't."

They shared a conspiratorial look and laughed. The tenor was reminiscent of the earliest days of their friendship. And for the first time in a very long time, Lacey didn't feel wistful for that long-ago era.

14

It was a whim.

Lacey tried to contain her excitement, because her impulses never seemed to turn out the way she wanted. But this time might be different.

She had parked her car after dropping off Angele. She knew her brother would be in town that evening, and hazarded the guess that Trevor would be, too. She had sent Trevor an innocuous text, *Hey, what's up,* and when he responded immediately, found herself stationary in her car, volleying texts that became increasingly explicit.

The thread concluded with his address. The pretense was she would meet him at his place in Hollywood, and they could walk to one of the spots on Sunset Boulevard for a bite to eat.

She needed something light. And not to eat. The day had been so heavy, on so many fronts, she was ready to not think about funerals, or dead loved ones, or really anything else for a little while.

Lacey called her brother before getting on the road to Trevor's place. She was hoping he was home, or at least close enough, that he could walk Ambrose.

"No," he answered. "I'm nowhere close. But I'll get someone to take care of it."

"Do you have a person for everything?"

"Pretty much. Anything else, Your Highness?"

"Ha. Thank you."

She was very grateful that Jimmy didn't need or want an explanation of her whereabouts.

Lacey drove around Trevor's block several times. She knew she would need to pay attention to how she parked. Car facing the correct way, wheels to the curb if her spot was downhill. That was, if she could find a spot. How had Jimmy, and Angele, made it in Los Angeles for so long? Things were much easier in New Orleans.

Finally finding a spot, she walked uphill to Trevor's place. A charming bungalow, with an airy yard full of rose bushes. It seemed like prime Hollywood real estate; she wondered how long Trevor had lived there.

The door was open, and Trevor leaned sideways against the doorframe. In jeans and an olive drab t-shirt that said "Degobah," his arms looked phenomenal. He gave her a lopsided grin. "Hello, love."

Entirely unexpectedly, her heart skipped a beat.

As she moved closer to kiss him hello, he circled his arms around her waist, pulling her to him. The kiss lingered longer than any friendly greeting had a right to. Lacey relaxed into it. His breath smelled minty.

Breaking free, Lacey took a side step, and pulled her hair behind her shoulders. "Hello, back."

They smiled at each other.

"C'mon in," he said, showing her inside with a sweep of the arm. "You look lovely, if you don't mind me saying. Basic black dress suits you."

Lacey considered saying something about the funeral, but then thought better of it. She hadn't sought out Trevor for a further rehashing of the day's events.

"Thank you," she said.

"Care for a drink?"

Lacey laughed. "More than you know. Yes, please."

She lingered in the living room while Trevor moved into the kitchen. There was a wooden bat enclosed in a glass case, hung horizontally over a mantle. It looked like a baseball bat, but the shaft was flat, not circular.

"This place is pretty well-stocked," he said, opening a cabinet. "What are you in the mood for?"

She moved to the kitchen doorway and tilted her head at him.

"This place?" she asked.

"Yes, it's a friend's house, love."

Ah, that explains how he can afford it.

"Oh. Got it. Is there any bourbon, by chance?"

He pulled out of bottle of Parker's Heritage. "This will do, I think. How do you take it?"

"Neat. Just a single, please."

Lacey entered the tidy kitchen and leaned against the granite countertop. The fading light from the kitchen window was warm against her back.

"You're glowing," he said with a wink. He handed her the drink and brought his empty glass to the refrigerator.

"You Yanks and your ice." He opened the freezer and popped one cube into the glass. "You've spoiled me."

He poured a more generous portion of bourbon for himself and returned to Lacey.

"Cheers," he said.

She clinked her glass against his. "Cheers."

"Care to sit?" He moved to the kitchen table.

"If you don't mind, I'd like to stand a while," Lacey said. "L.A. traffic, I feel like I've been in the car all day."

"Don't mind at all." He pulled a chair and positioned it so he was directly opposite Lacey. He stretched his legs out.

Lacey looked out toward the living room. "What's hanging above the mantle?"

Trevor looked at her quizzically. He craned his neck out toward the living room.

"Oh. It's a cricket bat. I suppose you wouldn't know that."

"I've heard of cricket," Lacey said. "It's like everyone else's version of baseball, right?"

Trevor laughed. She loved the sound of it. True, not forced.

"It's probably more like baseball is America's version of cricket."

"Is your friend a cricket player?" Lacey asked.

"Why're you so interested, love?" He pulled his chair closer.

"Just making conversation. Also, I'm a naturally curious person." Lacey set down her drink and flexed her arms behind her.

Damn, I'm preening, aren't I? This feels pretty good.

Trevor raised his eyebrows.

I think the preening is working.

"His father was a cricket player, if you must know. And he's traveling, so he won't be dropping in on us, in case you were curious about that. But since you like to make conversation, why don't you ask me what I did today?"

She took a step toward him. "I can do that. What did you do today, Trevor?"

"I tried surfing," he said. "I suck, but I'm hooked. I'm considering quitting the band and taking up surfing full-time."

She couldn't tell if he was joking or not. She didn't think her brother and the other members of LeViticum would like that very much.

He laughed again. "I'm not serious."

"Oh. Okay, that's good." After a pause, she added, "Because you can't quit the band before I've had the chance to see you perform live."

She had a brief flashback to a night in New Orleans, the one opportunity she had to see him on stage. Major events interrupted that chance—it had been the second time she'd come to Nathan's rescue. She tried not to think any more of it—especially not about the person at the center of those events.

"You've seen me," Trevor said. "I did a phenomenal rendition of 'Tangled Up in Blue.'"

"Yes, you did," she said, blushing. "But that was a private performance. I meant on stage, with LeViticum."

"You will soon enough."

"I hope so."

A part of Lacey wanted to plan. She knew in some late hour, she would look up their tour schedule, see when she might be able to catch one of their shows. That is, if she was even going to stay in California for any length of time.

I'm deviating from the whim. It's going swimmingly, don't stop now.

She shut down her straying thoughts.

"I *did* like the private performance, though." She looked

him in the eye, and it held to a long, knowing gaze, each from their separate posts in the kitchen.

Trevor stood and pushed his chair behind him. He walked toward her, the swelling in his jeans growing. He stopped in front of her, their faces an inch apart.

"You did, eh?" His voice was soft and lyrical, and he grazed his fingers along her cheek, gently tracing a line down to her shoulder.

"Yes," she said under her breath, and then brought her lips to his in a forceful stroke.

A sudden urgency fueled her movements as her hands grabbed his waist. She slowed enough to unfasten his jeans with precision. He took a slight step back to get his hands under her skirt, a caress over her hip before sliding her thong down. His fingers brushed against her center. She arched her head back, a voiceless moan escaping her as a long exhale.

She slid her hand in his briefs. "Oh, do you . . . " her voice was muffled. He pulled his face from hers, and she saw a twinkle in his eye as he reached into his back pocket. He produced a condom and sheathed himself while Lacey shimmied his briefs and jeans down to his knees.

He guided himself into her, while she gripped the countertop behind her. She thrilled at the sensation of being fully-dressed, standing, and feeling Trevor rock inside her. She marveled at his agility. She remembered what he had shouted in the throes of passion.

Their pleasures coalesced then receded in a sweet, simple rhythm. A graceful coming together.

"*You're* pretty phenomenal," she whispered as he pulled away.

✳

They kept to their pretense, and took a leisurely stroll up to Sunset Boulevard after composing themselves. Lacey reconsidered her prior frustration with the city. Even in late summer, the air was cool and mild. And the wealth of options for dining, entertainment, music—whatever the heart might seek—just a few minutes away, was certainly enviable. But she sensed that the time remaining on her successful whim was dwindling.

She endeavored to remain in the moment during their dinner. On the walk back, Trevor invited her back in, but she politely declined. He saw her to her car.

The heaviness of the day's events crashed in upon her as she drove back out to Jimmy's house. But she was grateful for the respite provided by her interlude with Trevor.

15

Galliano, Louisiana
One spring in the mid-twentieth century

Birdie wasn't sure why, but she thought of her old school counselor, Mr. Coyner. She hadn't seen him for more than seven years now. She'd just started this job, three months ago, and all signs pointed to positive. The Becnels paid her well, better than Mrs. Bergeron did. Truth was, that was all Mrs. Berge could afford. Birdie knew that, and didn't hold it against her. She'd learned a lot from her. A lot about traiteurs. She'd had to learn without asking too many questions, but Birdie excelled at that. She'd learned a lot through observation. Maybe that's why she was thinking of Mr. Coyner. That's why he always said she was "built for college." And maybe she was, but things just didn't turn out that way.

Funny thing about Mr. Becnel. Birdie's pay was double what Mrs. Bergeron paid. But while Birdie knew Mrs. Berge paid what she could afford—maybe more than what she could afford— Birdie suspected Mr. Becnel could afford a whole lot more.

So far, it was easy work. Mrs. Becnel stayed to herself, mostly. Birdie always checked on her, and would give her small, unobtrusive "treatments." Mrs. Becnel always had immediate relief, but never actively sought Birdie's care. She gave Birdie a wide berth. Birdie wasn't sure if it was out of deference or fear, but the end result was the same—she was able to do her job as best as she saw fit, with little to no interference.

Those kids were more than Mrs. Becnel had bargained for. And too many for her to handle. She wasn't built for it. Birdie figured she must be. Is that something? To be built for college, and built for rearing children, too? Maybe Birdie's make-up somehow captured both.

And she liked being with those children. They kept her too busy for her mind to wander.

Lord knows, it would be easy for her mind to wander down a dark path. Of sadness, regrets, and sorrow over those who've gone before her.

She pulled her truck along the side alley where Mr. Becnel told her to park. He'd insisted that Mrs. Becnel could provide transportation, but Birdie assured him that though the old Chevy didn't look like much, it was reliable, and it would all work out better this way.

Mrs. Becnel had sent a driver for her once, just once in the three months Birdie had been working for them. Her husband, Morris, had wanted to work on the truck, and Birdie knew some tinkering would be the best thing for him.

After her Momma died, she and Morris had moved down to Larose, and Morris had started working at his uncle's car shop. But business slowed around the same time Morris got the sickness in his legs. All Birdie could do was keep it from spreading. And then start working when Morris stopped getting a paycheck. That's when she found Mrs. Berge's 'help wanted' sign a few miles down Highway 1, in Galliano.

For the two years she worked for Mrs. Bergeron, Morris could still drive, and he would drop her off. But the sickness had weakened his muscles so much that it wasn't safe for him to drive that ten-mile distance anymore. When the Becnels approached her for a job, they not only offered more money, they also offered to provide Birdie's transportation.

But the one time she took them up on the offer was enough for her. Mrs. Becnel didn't come herself—she wasn't well enough that day—and besides, Birdie wasn't even sure if she could drive. The man who came for Birdie drove some busted up Ford older than Birdie's truck, and talked like those folks her Momma had always told her to stay away from. And on top of that, he was late. Birdie never found out who the man was.

She just made a gentle suggestion to Morris that maybe he could work on the truck on Sundays, her one day off, while she was at Mass. Morris wouldn't go, and Holy Angels was close enough that Birdie could walk.

Birdie pulled the truck into its spot at the Becnels and looked through the windshield. She felt a slight ping, like foreboding. She thought it was because she didn't see Foxy. The little boy would shadow Birdie as she looked after the twins, or served lunch to the older kids. He was just at the right age to be teased mercilessly by his next oldest brother, Lionel, who never answered to his proper name. So everyone just called him "Brother."

Foxy, always eager to escape Brother's enmity, wanted to help with his toddler twin siblings, even if he didn't know what to do. He was a sweet boy, gentler than his older brother. He wore his heart on his sleeve. And since Birdie's second day coming to the Becnels, he would wait at the galley door, the one closest to where Birdie parked.

She put her car key in her bag. The air was so still that spring morning, the sound of her shoes on the driveway, paved only with dredged shells, bleached white from the sun, resounded through the narrow alley way. The sky had a tinge to it that made Birdie uneasy.

So when she felt the sharp tap at her back, her scream was a little shriller, more fearful, than it might have otherwise been.

She turned around. "Foxy! How'd you do that?"

Little Fox's face crumbled, and a plaintive mew rose from his throat.

Birdie wasted no time. Her face broke out into a wide smile, and she scooped him up and placed him on her hip.

"Oh, child, don't be sad. You scared me, that's all. You must move like a cat!"

She moved the fingers of her free hand, mimicking a catwalk, and Foxy's face relaxed. Birdie kept at it until she produced a giggle.

"There, now." She carried Foxy through the galley door and set him down on the cedar planks. "Better?"

The little boy nodded. He gazed up at Birdie, and a shy smile brightened his cheeks.

"Good. Because we can't have you all crumpled up. That just won't do! Now, where's Sister?"

Even though Fox Becnel had three older sisters, and one younger, there was only one who answered to "Sister." Whereas Foxy and Birdie had a mutual admiration society, Evangeline was the one sibling Birdie counted on when she needed assistance wrangling the Becnel mob.

And she would need her help, since all the children were off school for the Easter break.

A young girl, tall for her age, poked her head around the

corner, but didn't enter the galley. Her unruly hair was in pin curls, and she wore a gingham jumper with bobby socks. Never one to be shy, Birdie wondered what had gotten into Evangeline.

"Hello, Sister. Your brother here gave me quite the scare when I drove up. Did he do the same to you?"

Apparently, Birdie breaking the ice was all Evangeline needed. She shook her head, took three strides into the galley, and faced Birdie, hands on hips.

"Birdie!" she said more loudly than she intended, and then lowered her voice. "Ms. Birdie, Camille is saying a big storm is going to hit, and she and Amelie got in a fight about it, and Mamere is in a very ill humor!"

"Is that so, Sister? Well, I'm afraid Camille might be right. We've got a storm sky this morning."

"Well, don't tell Amelie that. I think she thinks if she just pretends something bad won't happen, then it won't."

Birdie laughed. "None of that makes any sense, Sister. Can you keep an eye on things for a bit while I go check on Mrs. Becnel?"

Evangeline nodded, serious about her assigned duty.

Birdie realized her uneasiness hadn't gone away. It was a feeling of knowing something was going to happen, something momentous, but not knowing the particulars. Sometime after, she realized she was feeling what Momma had called the Sense.

It would turn out to be one of those watershed days. Those days where premonitions and powers and ominous signs all coalesce, and set things on a certain course from which there was no turning back.

While Birdie had no way to know that the job with the Becnels would be the last one she ever had, she would know from this day forward that there was where she was meant to be.

Mrs. Becnel had complained of a pain in her jaw, and a terrible ache in her temple on the same side. Birdie laid two fingers—with a very light touch—on her temple. Mrs. Becnel didn't like to be touched. When she checked on her later, before the storm hit, Mrs. Becnel was sleeping soundly. A point of fact, Mrs. Becnel claimed to have slept through the entire storm.

Birdie knew to count her blessings.

Camille's obstinacy was not among them. She was nowhere to be found, and the weather was about to take a terrible turn.

The radio in Birdie's truck had warned her about bad weather on her way there that morning. While she'd never seen a twister before, she'd read enough to figure that when the sky was dark, and the clouds were sharpening down into a point, that had to be a sign of a tornado.

The younger children were all indoors, anyway. By instinct, Birdie herded them all into the galley kitchen. It was narrower than any other room in the house; all the dishes were put away, so there was little to fly about. She had grabbed two blankets and laid them on the floor in a corner. She would make it a game for the younger children, but she would need the older children as accomplices.

She wasn't as sure about the bedroom where Mrs. Becnel slept, but let it suffice that it was at least on the ground floor.

Sister entertained the toddler twins, Foxy stood his ground against his older brother, and Amelie sulked on a corner of the blanket.

As if on cue, a terrible gust of wind rattled the window at the far end of the galley.

Birdie called Brother over to her, away from the ears of the younger children. Evangeline followed.

"Brother, please go round up Camille," Birdie asked.

He looked suspicious at first. But he must have weighed the opportunity—here was a rare chance to torment his older sister. He bounded out the room, and they all heard heavy footfalls on the stairs, two at a time.

The wind outside quieted, and Birdie breathed a heavy sigh of relief. Though the respite was short-lived.

It picked up worse than before, and Amelie quit sulking. She began to pace small semi-circles around the edge of the blanket. Birdie grabbed one of Amelie's hands in both of hers and forced her to a gentle stop. She pulled Amelie to the center of the circle formed by Evangeline, Fox, and the twins, Laville and Louisa.

"Who wants to hear the story of Armand the Alligator?" Birdie asked.

The toddler twins squealed and clapped, while Fox and Evangeline turned on quiet, bright smiles. Birdie looked to Amelie, a knowing glance of conspiracy and collaboration. Amelie relented.

Birdie had just gotten to the part where Armand locks the door to his alligator shack, heading out for his evening alligator stroll, when Brother appeared. Two telling things about his appearance: he was still, and he was pale.

Birdie asked Amelie to finish the story for her. The younger children sighed a collective "Awwww," but Birdie ignored it.

Off to the side, Brother told Birdie, "I can't find her."

"What do you mean?"

"I mean, I can't find her. She's not upstairs in the bedroom; she's not in the study. I even looked outside in the garden and she's not there."

Birdie looked out the window. She looked at the huddle of children on the blanket. And she knew what she had to do. Amelie had stepped up to shepherd her younger siblings.

"Children, I'm taking Brother to help secure the trellis. We'll be right back."

A flight of panic crossed Amelie's face, but she masked it well enough and continued Armand's story. Evangeline shot a glare at Birdie, but quickly turned her head away when Birdie answered with a wink.

Birdie knew there was nothing she could, or should, do to secure anything outside. The safest place for everyone was indoors. And she was worried about heading out there. But she also knew that she and Brother would have a better chance of finding Camille—two sets of eyes are better than one. And Brother was the most capable of taking care of himself.

They exited the house together, onto the side patio lined with brick. The trellis was thick with the branches of a climbing rose, pink buds peeking through dense foliage. The visible horizon was clear from that side of the house, but the light all around them was green.

"Come with me," Birdie said to Brother. "Stay close behind me."

Birdie led him to the back of the house. There, the sky was much more ominous, a mixture of green and gray. The funnel clouds much closer than just a few minutes before.

A copse of cypress, along the bayou and about thirty yards from the house, impeded the view of the horizon. And an inkling told Birdie that's where she'd find Camille.

Birdie broke out into a run toward the bayou. Brother struggled to keep up. Birdie found Camille, camera in hand, unaware of anything except the sight in its viewfinder.

"Camille!" Birdie yelled. "You're gonna get yourself killed!"

Camille didn't budge. Her lens was trained on the horizon, and she seemed unfazed by the fast-approaching danger.

Brother finally caught up and grabbed Camille's arm. "She's gonna get us all killed!"

Camille shoved her brother with her elbow, shaking him off. Five years older than him, she was still smaller by a few pounds and inches. He came back at her and took a firmer hold.

"Stop it! The both of you!"

A gale-force wind came at them, and it took effort to remain standing.

Camille finally removed the camera from her face. "Ms. Birdie, tell him to get his hands off me." She sounded much younger than fourteen.

The funnel cloud suddenly appeared to be less than a mile away. "You both need to run! Back to the house!" Birdie put her hand at Camille's back, right above the waistline of her pants, and shoved. Brother needed no such cue.

The siblings broke off in a sprint toward the house. Birdie ran just a few feet behind them. She saw Brother turn his head and she pointed a finger at him. "And don't look back!"

Without warning, a torrential downpour came down from the sky. Within seconds, the ground beneath their feet was saturated. Their footfalls sank deeper with every step, and there wasn't a square inch of anything dry between the three of them.

Brother reached the side door first and tumbled through it. Camille and Birdie followed close behind. All three of them were out of breath, sopping wet, and wired more tightly than a drum. Only Birdie knew how to handle it.

Brother had his hands on his knees, panting heavily. He straightened, and the look in his eyes was murderous. He stared at Camille.

Birdie grabbed him by the ear. He howled and turned his attention away from Camille.

"Brother! Go grab some linens," she said.

"Owwww. I don't know where the linens are."

"Of course you do. In the hall closet. Go grab enough to do the job."

Birdie hoped Mrs. Becnel would stay to her bed today. It would give her time to wash the linens later on, and no one would be the wiser.

With the threat of Brother's anger removed, Birdie laid a hand on Camille's shoulder. She was fretting over her camera, gently shaking the water from the lens. Birdie's hand was warm despite the wet chill she felt over her whole body.

"Child," Birdie said. Camille, sheepish, looked up into her eyes.

"You have an amazing perception of the world around you," Birdie said. Her voice had deepened an octave. "It is a gift. But you still have no sense of your place in the world. You cannot put yourself in danger like that."

Camille nodded her head and looked at her feet. Birdie turned Camille's face to hers again. "In the end, it wasn't just yourself in danger. You understand?"

Camille nodded again, and a tear rolled down her cheek. It blended with the rain that still stained her face.

"I'm sorry, Ms. Birdie. I'm so sorry. I didn't mean for you and Brother to have to come after me."

"I know you didn't, child."

Brother returned with a stack of linens. He shoved a third

of them at Camille, the look on his face still shooting daggers at her. But he was no longer ready to attack.

"Thank you, Brother." Birdie took half the remaining towels from him. "Now, you both get yourselves cleaned up."

16

San Luis Obispo, California
Current day

Lacey was running late. She remembered what Eli had said about time, and wondered if he'd be forgiving when she showed up ten minutes past their agreed-upon time.

She suspected not.

She checked her speedometer, and sped up five miles over the speed limit. The road was wide open.

Lacey and Ambrose had arrived back at the San Luis Obispo rental just seven hours prior. When Lacey had seen Kandace at the funeral, she gave every indication that the production would remain on hiatus, for at least another week. But Kandace called the next day and told Lacey to drop everything and head back up the coast. Something about a change of direction for the movie production and a possible new location. Eli was going to handle the location scouting, and would be in touch with where she needed to go.

She'd received a text from Eli, simply an address and a time. *Typical.*

She had managed just a few hours of sleep after she and

Ambrose settled back into the rental, before waking up and mapping out her route to the address. Her phone told her the address had a name: Sycamore Mineral Springs. And that she had grossly underestimated the time it would take it get there. She changed clothes, fed Ambrose, and flew out the door.

She had no idea what the place looked like, or why Eli wanted her there. Flustered, she turned at a sign that she thought read the name of the place, and found herself on a drive through a row of guesthouses. She pulled into a parking space and checked the time. 7:59 a.m. She was supposed to meet Eli at eight o'clock.

She tried calling him, he didn't answer. She began typing a text to him, frantic to get it sent with a time stamp of 8:00 a.m. or earlier. Her armpits were wet and she wished she didn't have a collared shirt on.

Why am I so worked up about this? Do I feel like I have to be perfect for Eli?

Lacey nearly jumped out of her seat when she heard a loud tapping on the window.

Eli stood in his standard fare of multi-pocketed shirt with cargo shorts. Lacey tried to open the door to her car, but he blocked it. She rolled down the window.

"I just tried to call you," Lacey said.

"I know," he said. "We need to go across the road, to the main campus."

"Okay," Lacey said. "I guess I probably shouldn't leave my car here, right?"

"No. Go back out to the road, and turn in the drive opposite this one."

"Okay." Lacey looked past Eli and didn't see his car. "Do you want to ride with me?"

"No. I will meet you there."

Eli walked off, in the opposite direction of where he told Lacey to go.

Lacey shook her head, took a deep breath, and pulled out of the parking spot.

✳

Lacey felt a surge of excitement as she read the sign on a small, white, domed building set against a hillside: *Healing Arts Institute.*

Eli had sent her this way after meeting her in the *correct* parking lot. He had told her she was to assist him in scouting this place as a location, but Lacey didn't know what that really meant. Looking around, significantly more relaxed than she'd been when she arrived, she was not opposed to finding out.

The whole resort was set against a hillside forest. The scent of eucalyptus was strong, along with something more pungent. Maybe that was the mineral springs?

She looked down the path in both directions. No sign of Eli.

She approached the door of the domed building and tugged on the handle. Locked.

That doesn't feel very welcoming, she thought.

"They're setting up for a wedding tonight," a voice behind her said. "That's the only reason it's locked."

Lacey whipped her head around to find a thin, elegant woman with a walking stick and dark sunglasses. She smiled at Lacey.

"Oh," Lacey said. "I was just curious as to what might be in there."

"All manner of things, depending on the day and occasion," the woman said. "Today, it's a wedding."

Lacey walked toward her. The woman held out her hand about two seconds too early. Lacey took a couple of quick steps to reach her.

"I'm Christine," the woman said.

Lacey introduced herself and shook the woman's hand.

"What a lovely name," Christine said, her focus still straight ahead. "What's your surname?"

"Becnel. Lacey Becnel." Christine released Lacey's hand.

"Is that French?"

"Yes. It was my husband . . . my late husband's name."

Lacey wondered why she felt so open with this woman.

"I can see why you kept it," Christine said. "French is so melodic."

Lacey nodded, not sure what else to say. This only made her feel more awkward, because she assumed Christine couldn't see her nod.

"I think your friends will be here shortly," Christine said. "And I will see that you get your tour of the institute, before your time here is up. You must be sure to take the waters while you're here. Farewell, Lacey."

Christine walked away, her walking stick leading the way.

Lacey watched her, mesmerized. Christine's long, diaphanous dress trailed behind her. Sunlight picked up silver strands in the lavender fabric.

"I see you met Christine. Good."

Lacey whipped her head around again. *Why am I so easy to sneak up on?*

Eli. With a guy she recognized, mostly from the edit bays at the studio. He carried some sort of tool with a laser pointer.

"You know her?" she asked Eli.

"Yes," he replied. He stared and said nothing further, right eye floating.

Lacey looked to the guy whose name she couldn't remember, but he was busy pointing the laser off at some trees behind the dome.

"Okay," Lacey said. "So what do you need me to do?"

"Meet people. Be an ambassador. If we wind up filming here, we'll need a face to interact with the employees and owners."

Lacey looked down at her feet, then at the red beam flitting about the trees. She felt her ire rise up, and didn't tamp it down.

"Isn't that a little sexist, Eli? Woman just needs to smile and make people feel comfortable?"

Eli stood, implacable as ever, though one corner of his mouth turned up, almost imperceptibly.

"No. It's not sexist. It's a meritocracy. You are the available resource best suited to that job. Do you really want me or Roland to try to cover that function?"

Lacey looked at Eli's urban safari attire and dour expression, and edit bay Roland's fascination with his instrument. She relented and laughed. "That's actually humorous, Eli. I didn't know you had it in you."

"I wasn't trying to be funny," he said.

"I know," Lacey said.

"Christine lost her eyesight when she was four years old," Eli said.

"Excuse me?" She still was not used to Eli's propensity to turn the conversation on a dime.

"The woman you just met, Christine," Eli said.

"Yes, I know who you're referring to, it's just . . . never mind," Lacey said.

"Measles," Eli said.

"Oh," Lacey said. She wondered how old Christine might be.

"She's not from here," Eli said.

"Okay," Lacey replied. She was afraid of what Eli would answer if she asked where Christine was from. "She seems to manage very well."

"Yes," Eli said. "She has developed other ways of seeing that are quite remarkable. You should spend some time with her. As part of your ambassador duty."

Lacey nodded slowly. "I see. I mean, okay."

"We'll be working here for at least a week. If you would like to stay up here, the cabins on the other side of the road allow pets. A number of them have been allotted for crew, one of them can be yours if you wish."

Lacey considered. It sounded ideal. She already felt more at ease in this place than she'd felt anywhere in town. "Really?"

"Yes. I won't need you back here until 5 p.m., so you could make the move now if you choose."

He tapped Roland on the shoulder and the two of them strode off up the path and into the woods.

"Wait," Lacey said, not loud enough to be heard. "How do I know which one I'm supposed to go to?" she asked the air.

She checked her watch. She had roughly seven hours to figure it out.

Lacey sighed and set off down the hill to her car.

17

The next morning, Lacey sat out on the back patio of her cabin, with a cup of coffee (the coffeemaker was new and the cupboard was stocked), Ambrose at her feet. She watched the sun slowly make its way over a distant, eastern ridge. This place was a definite upgrade from the rental.

She took stock of the week ahead. Plenty of time to figure out what "being an ambassador" was. If all it meant was exploring the beautiful grounds and meeting people, she could definitely handle it. Ambrose was welcome to explore with her, which was a bonus. She would have to go to the studio on Tuesday, but she could still plan to have her breakfast right there, in that very spot, for the rest of her stay. Not to mention she'd get to run the trails around here, a huge improvement from where she'd run around the rental, for sure.

It felt heavenly.

Lacey smiled and Ambrose stood, stretched, and settled back down, this time next to the vacant seat to Lacey's left.

As beautiful as the accommodations were, reminders of coupledom were everywhere. The two seats out on the patio.

Two sinks in the bathroom. A king-sized bed. She thought of Nathan then, and her eyes widened.

Not Fox, not memories of coupledom once shared. And not of Trevor, her current paramour.

But of Nathan. Of coupledom that had never been, and that could not be for the foreseeable future. Most likely ever.

Well, shit, Lacey thought. *That's a downer on an otherwise perfect morning.*

Perhaps it was the setting, or the few moments of extra downtime she had. But she allowed herself another indulgence. She and Nathan had taken a picture together, during his surprise visit the night before she left New Orleans.

She refused to keep it with the other photos on her phone. Too accessible. She had deleted it from her phone's album, but not before she had emailed it to herself and buried it in a folder. It took at least three clicks and much scrolling to reach it.

There was nothing salacious about it, the picture didn't reveal any portions of their anatomies normally hidden from view. But it did reveal much to Lacey—the expression on both their faces exposing hidden depths. It was an unusual selfie, Nathan had taken it. Neither one of them were looking at the camera. Nathan was looking at Lacey, and Lacey faced him, but her eyes were cast down, a shy smile on her face.

Out on the back patio of her cabin, thousands of miles away from where the photo was taken, she focused on Nathan's features. Sandy hair, a full head of it, with very little gray. He was eleven years older than Lacey—if the events of this past summer hadn't turned him gray, she wondered if anything could. He'd had several attempts made on his life. Lacey had come to his rescue twice.

She still marveled at it all. The first time she had used her power had been on Nathan. Her memory of the actual healing, especially that first one, was very hazy. It was like her memory switched off the first time her power switched on.

Nathan's shirt was on in the picture, but she could still make out his broad shoulders and muscular arms. She thought of the scar on his back, behind his shoulder. Proof of the bullet wound she'd healed on him, that first time. Even though she couldn't remember the details, she knew, with every fiber of her being, that she had healed the wound that produced that scar.

She wished she could separate that feeling from her feelings for Nathan. But it was impossible. They were too intertwined. She had first used her remarkable gift on him, and she was drawn to him, and she couldn't think of the potential of her gift and the potential of a relationship with him separately.

Dammit.

Lacey checked the time. She would allow herself ten more minutes to think about him.

That's way too much time, but what the hell.

Nathan was a big guy, and ridiculously fit. There was a sense of power in Nathan's form that she couldn't stop thinking of.

When she'd heard the knock on her door, the night before she was supposed to leave for California, she had thought it might be her neighbor, Mr. Max. Or possibly Tonti. Though Ambrose's low growl should have given it away.

Lacey wasn't sure what to do when she'd opened the door to find Nathan standing there, dressed like he'd just come from a job interview. (He had.) Part of her wanted to shut the door in his face, but a bigger part of her wanted him back inside her home, inside her life, and inside her again.

"I'm sorry," he said. "I know you must be getting ready to leave. I wasn't even sure you'd still be here. I just . . . "

"C'mon in. I leave tomorrow. Early."

"I won't keep you." He stepped over the threshold and stood awkwardly, by the side table where she kept her keys.

She took his hand, but he wouldn't move at first. He just stared.

"Have you done something different with your hair?"

She ran her free hand over the side of her head. "No. Other than wash it today, no."

"It looks good. You look good."

"Quit trying to flatter me."

He finally relented and followed her to the kitchen. He took off his suit coat and hung it on the back of a chair, then loosened his tie.

They spent an hour just talking in the kitchen, about unremarkable stuff. But it had made Lacey feel so comfortable, it lessened her anxiety about her upcoming departure. It felt like the way things were supposed to be, when you spend time with someone you care about. Who cares about you back.

She had sent Ambrose out into the yard, and walked over to where Nathan was seated at her kitchen table. His arms clasped behind her back. He rested his forehead against her ribs, below her breasts.

She laid a hand upon his cheek.

Looking up at her, he said, "I don't know that I've ever wanted someone so badly. It's a pain like I've never felt before."

She sighed. She was on fire for him. She found it hard to breathe.

"Me, too," she managed to say.

He stayed seated at first. Slowly, both hands slid underneath her t-shirt and up her sides. His hands caressed her breasts, ever so gently. He stood and unclasped her bra with a single, deft move.

Her hands at his waist now, she unbuckled his belt. She saw him swell. She got down on her knees and took him into her mouth. As she tasted him, felt him with her tongue and with her lips, he exhaled, forcefully and with a slight shudder.

"Oh, God, what you do to me," he said above a whisper.

His hand on Lacey's shoulder, he disengaged, and hooked a finger under her arm to pull her up to face him. He reached back to grip the kitchen table, and leaned back onto it with some force.

"Is this oak?"

Lacey caught his meaning. She was fairly certain the table would hold them, but didn't really care if it didn't.

"Yes," she leaned into him, kissing him hard on the lips. "Yes."

He pulled her down on top of him, sending her table centerpiece crashing toward the window. She knew they wouldn't stop for protection—she'd believed him, perhaps naively so, when he'd told her before that he'd been snipped, and had been in a monogamous relationship for over a decade. She straddled him and made herself ready to take him in. Her knees ached against the hard wood of the table, but not as much as she ached to feel him inside her.

She eased onto him, and pressed herself against him. She braced her hands on either side of his arms, her breasts just grazing his chest. They uttered a moan in unison, a sound that separated, then rose and fell as she worked herself against him. In a fluid move—it happened so quickly Lacey barely realized it—his arm encircled her and their positions were reversed.

He was atop her, thrusting with an amplified power that she longed to match.

She closed her eyes and let her longing cascade through every nerve of her body. When that exquisite feeling reached its peak, she cried out. The sound of her passion was answered by Nathan in the next instant.

He exhaled and rose up onto his forearms, sparing Lacey from being smothered by his full weight. He gently eased himself off the table, offering Lacey a hand and helping her down.

"Well, that's a first," she said.

"Really?" Nathan looked at the table. "It's almost as if it was built for that type of activity."

Lacey thought briefly of Fox, of similar comments he used to make. But before he died, the spark between them had withered to the point that they remained mere suggestions.

Lacey walked toward her bedroom.

"It does seem like that, doesn't it?" was all she said.

About a half hour later, they had both put most of their clothes back on and sat in her living room. Nathan pulled his phone out. "I need a picture of you."

"No, please. That's so awkward. I really don't photograph well," Lacey said.

"I find that hard to believe."

"It's the truth."

"Fine, then I'll get the both of us."

Before she could protest again, his long arm reached out in front of them and snapped several photos. He toyed with her when she asked to see the pictures.

"No, you won't want to see these. You were right, actually. You look like a goblin in these pictures."

She pushed at him and smiled. "I said I'm not photogenic. I didn't say I'm a monster."

He finally relented, and she'd asked him to send her the one she now held in her hand. On the back patio of a cabin nestled in the foothills of California's Central Coast. Ambrose rose up, his attention captured by some small critter out in the brush. He looked at Lacey.

"Sorry, Bro, you can't go chase that whatever-it-is. I've spent too much time this morning chasing after lost causes myself."

She willed herself to get back into the present.

18

The following day, Lacey wandered the grounds. There was an all-encompassing peacefulness about the place. Cabins were tucked away throughout the property, some nestled into the hillside. There were outdoor hot tubs filled with sulfurous natural spring water. A steep path up one slope led to the tubs, each surrounded by a privacy fence.

Even when the cabins were occupied, it had an air of seclusion. You could remain quiet and hidden if you wanted.

She was looking for Christine when she received a text from Eli telling her to put on a swimsuit and meet him at the hot tub farthest up the hill.

Yikes, she thought. *What is this about? Maybe, hopefully, finally, some practical healer training?*

She hurried back to the cabin, changed into a one-piece suit and threw a pair of shorts and a t-shirt on over it. It was the suit she brought with her everywhere in case she wanted to swim laps. Which never happened, because she never wanted to swim laps. But what if she hurt her ankle somehow? Then maybe she'd want to swim laps instead of run.

She let Ambrose out, he went out to his favorite sycamore and hurried back. It was too sunny out.

Walking up to the hot tub, she thought about how many miles she had run since college. Easily in the thousands. And she'd never had an injury. Nothing worse than sore muscles. She'd always thought she was blessed with good genes, which never made sense to her because her mother was always spraining something or tearing something else. Doing nothing more than a bi-annual game of tennis.

Pay attention, she could hear Eli saying.

Huh. So I've never been injured running because of my mutant powers?

But that didn't make sense, either. She'd only recently obtained her traiteur ability from Cecil. Maybe her healthy constitution just made her a good candidate.

There's still so much I don't understand.

She hiked up the trail to the top of the hill, wishing she didn't have flip-flops on. The very first hot tub was occupied, but all the rest appeared empty.

Eli would make me work harder to get to the very top, she thought.

A line of sky peeked out over the ridge of the hill, shot through with tree limbs and branches. She was about to go to the edge of the trail to see what she could see in the valley below.

"You're late," she heard Eli say. She looked down in the tub, and saw his head and bare shoulders. He looked like a bald bear.

"You didn't give me a time," she said.

He looked at her with his left eye. "You should have worn a two-piece," he said.

Lacey put her hands on her hips. It was involuntary. "Okay. Did you consider mentioning that in your text?"

"You're right. I'm sorry. That was my omission."

Well, that might be a first.

"I should have mentioned it, because I think you would be more comfortable in a two piece for the work we need to do."

He stood up and placed a leg on the step, revealing his entire form, unclothed. Lacey saw his big, muscular hairless-bear-of-a-man backside. She cast her eyes aside, but not before noticing significant scarring between his shoulders. She wondered what caused it, and thought of the brother he said he'd lost.

He turned to face her straight on, and she pivoted to face the opposite direction.

"Whoa, Eli! You might have mentioned you didn't have any clothes on. And wait, what kind of 'work' are you referring to?" She felt suddenly sick. She thought of sordid tales out of Hollywood. Men in power exposing themselves. Had all her faith in Eli been completely misplaced?

"Lacey, turn around please," he said.

"Really don't want to," she answered.

"Lacey," he said, his voice an octave lower and more soothing than she'd ever heard, "there is nothing predatory in my intention."

She turned her head to the side. A beam of light shot through the trees and landed just to the right of Eli's feet. "What are you trying to do, then?" she asked.

"Help you manage your ability," he said.

She slowly turned toward him. Her body faced the ridgeline, her head upward to look at the trees above Eli's head.

"There are things you can do to stop your clothes from catching on fire," he said.

She looked him in the eye. "You swear?"

He shook his head slightly. "I rarely swear. I can help you."

Still averting her eyes, she stalled by asking another question. She hadn't healed any "big" injuries during her time in California, so her question at least seemed relevant.

"I've been thinking about the two types of injuries you told me about at Kevin's funeral. How come I don't seem to burn up as badly with the second kind? The emotional, chronic types?"

"Your body acts as a conduit," he said matter-of-factly. "The power that courses through it for the trauma-induced, bodily injuries exacts a larger toll on *your* body."

"That doesn't sound good."

"No. That's why the sooner you learn to counteract that toll, the better."

"Okay. But, do you have to be naked for this lesson?" she asked.

Eli sighed. "No. But it's easier if I am."

She remained in her awkward twist, but relaxed enough to take a deep breath. While Eli struck her as odd in many ways, she never sensed that perverted was one of them. She also sensed that she might never get a handle on her power by remaining in her comfort zone.

She heard Eli sigh again. "This will be more efficient if you are unclothed, too. Clothing acts as an impediment in this type of work. Which is why a two piece would have been preferable," he said.

She cocked an eyebrow and looked him in his good eye.

"It would have allowed you to ease into it, I think," he said, in a voice so gentle Lacey felt like a child.

"It doesn't matter, Eli," she said, forcing herself to act

grown-up. "This is all so tremendously awkward, a matter of a few degrees is inconsequential."

The words surprised her as they came out of her mouth, but also emboldened her.

"Are you sure we have privacy up here, we're not going to offend anyone with our nakedness?" she asked.

"We are not likely to be disturbed," Eli said.

"Fine. What do I need to do?"

"First, relax," Eli said. He grabbed a towel and wrapped it around his waist.

That helps, Lacey thought.

"Take a deep breath," he said. "You need to be here."

Lacey relaxed her arms, inhaled deeply. "What do you mean?"

"Focus on the present. Release any thoughts of the immediate past, or the moments ahead."

She took another deep breath. She stopped herself from dwelling on the awkwardness just past.

"When you're ready, remove your clothes."

Lacey sighed. "Don't think I'll ever be ready, so I might as well just get it over with."

She took off her t-shirt and shorts. She glanced at Eli, a placid Buddha facing her.

"I know it's trivial, but could you turn around, please?"

Eli obliged, his words as he turned ringing serious and sincere. "It's not trivial."

Lacey tugged the straps of her suit and removed it, laying it down atop her other clothes. She remained hunkered down. "Can I get in the water?" she asked.

"Not yet," Eli said. "I'm going to turn around now."

He glanced down at her, crouched low to the ground,

guarding her pile of clothes like an alley cat.

"Stand up when you're ready," he said.

She'd compared Eli to Professor X and Buddha. In this moment, the look in his eyes rendered a modern-day Merlin, a complex magician with depths she couldn't fathom.

She stood up, her heart in her throat, her head feeling like it was in a vice from the pressure of embarrassment.

"Stand tall," he said. "Align your neck with your spine."

Eli's matter-of-fact tone relaxed Lacey a degree.

"Close your eyes," he said.

She looked at him straight on, and he gave her a nod of encouragement. She closed her eyes.

"Good. Focus on your head, your scalp. How does it feel?"

"How does it feel? How is it supposed to feel? It feels like my head," she said.

"Focus on the temperature."

Lacey took another deep breath. "It's warm. Almost hot. I can feel the blood rushing there because I'm nervous."

"Focus on the air surrounding you. How does it feel, compared to your head?"

"Cooler," Lacey answered. As if on cue, a breeze blew in from down the hill, rustling the leaves on the trees on the ridgeline above her head.

Goosebumps broke out on her arms and legs. She shifted where she stood. Eli didn't speak for what felt like an eternity. She willed her eyes to remain closed.

She noticed her body swaying. She planted her feet more firmly to try to stop it, but it only made it worse.

Because the ground is shaking, not me, Lacey thought. She opened her eyes and didn't see Eli.

Oh, crap. This is not good.

"Get dressed," she heard him say from somewhere beyond the trees. "We'll have to resume this later."

Lacey quickly put her clothes back on and Eli reappeared fully-clothed once she was dressed. He led her down the hill. Even though the shaking felt gentle, Lacey watched the tall trees around her carefully, expecting one to come crashing down upon her at any minute. All the awkwardness she just felt was replaced by fear.

The shaking stopped before they reached the clearing at the bottom of the hill.

"We need to stand by for any aftershocks," Eli said.

There was a parking lot beyond the clearing. They walked toward it, and Eli stopped at a bench set back about ten yards from the lot. He remained standing. Lacey's legs were still shaking, her heart beating wildly. She sat on the bench.

Eli scanned the horizon in all directions, as if he expected any aftershock to announce itself in the sky.

Satisfied, he folded his arms and planted himself across from Lacey, who gripped her knees on the bench. She looked up at him, and involuntarily looked to where his right eye was tracking. Seeing nothing, she returned her focus back to him.

"Well, that was exciting," she said.

"Unexpected," Eli said.

"Isn't that the nature of earthquakes?" Lacey asked.

Eli stared at her. She refused to follow his eye's gaze.

Can he predict earthquakes, too? Lacey thought.

"Yes," he finally answered. Lacey at first thought he was reading her mind.

"They are unexpected," he continued. "For most people. There was an earthquake the day I left home. The day my brother was killed."

Lacey held her breath and felt her fear subside. Was Eli about to open up to her? She released her knees and leaned toward him.

"This was in Kurdistan, where I was born. My mother could always feel it, the moments before an earthquake struck. She had the gift of prescience. My brother and I both happened to be in our mother's home that morning—we were young men, each of us living on our own by that time."

Lacey felt a growing warmth just below her heart. She stood. She had a growing need to reach out to Eli.

He stopped his story as abruptly as he began it.

"Lacey, no."

She stood silent against the bench. A rough patch in one of the slats scraped against the back of her knees.

"Why?" she finally said.

"Please, sit. There is another reason I am telling you this story. I'm not seeking relief. This is a pain I do not want healed."

She hesitated and reached back to grip the back of the bench. "I don't understand."

"Please, Lacey, sit." Eli took a step toward her, placing a hand on her shoulder. "I will be well. Earthquakes will always remind me of that day, and pain will always resurface, and I don't want that to ever change. The pain will subside in time."

Eli removed his hand from her shoulder.

Lacey nodded. *I almost understand that.* She sat on the bench.

"In that way, the earthquakes are related. The earthquake in Kurdistan many decades ago, and today's earthquake."

Back to not understanding.

Eli paused, turned to the side, and faced Lacey again.

"There is a term, it's used in quantum physics, called 'action at a distance.' Einstein came up with the concept, though he called it 'spooky action at a distance.'"

Lacey raised an eyebrow. *Quantum physics. The book Cecil gave me!* She didn't say anything, not wanting to interrupt him yet.

"The idea is that one object can affect another object, they can move each other or change each other, even though they may be far apart. In both distance and time. Even though there's no physical interaction. Are you following me?"

"Not really. But . . . " Lacey stood, ready to move her legs again. " . . . I was given a book on quantum physics. By the person who . . . "

She paused, realizing she'd never discussed Cecil with Eli. She knew so little about him, she hadn't been sure what to say.

Eli waited, patiently.

"By the person who passed along, or transferred all this. My ability, I mean."

Eli nodded, remaining silent for what felt like an eternity. "That's good. I have thoughts on that, which I will share momentarily. In the case of this earthquake, I am the one being affected, my thoughts and actions are being affected through space and time. You will need to discover what affects you, though. The modalities are always different."

Lacey's head started to hurt.

"Read about this concept, in the book, if you haven't yet," Eli said. "It is possible it was shared with you for that purpose. To help you understand the 'why' of your ability. I can help you with the 'how,' but I'm afraid I can offer no insight on the 'why.'"

The ground began to shake again as Eli said "how," and

they both stopped in their tracks when the shaking continued, unabated this time.

"Should we go inside somewhere, Eli?" Lacey tried to tamp down her rising panic.

He scanned the horizon again, as if confirming a prior assessment. "No. We're clear of any man-made structures in this spot. We should remain here."

With everything that had just passed between them, Lacey was inclined to trust Eli. And she was tremendously relieved that she was not alone.

19

Lacey couldn't comprehend the sight in front of her. There was road, and there were cars, but they were stopped. A little further ahead, the top of a building appeared where it shouldn't be. It looked like it was rising out of the road.

She looked at the time on her phone. Had it really only been less than forty minutes since she and Eli "sheltered in place" on the bench at the resort?

They had parted ways once they felt the worst was over. Eli had said there was no way to be sure, but she had Ambrose to look after, and Eli wanted to check in with the management, to see if they needed assistance.

Just a few minutes later, Eli called, asking for her help. He told her to change into long pants and closed-toe shoes and said he'd pick her up at her cabin in five minutes.

Ambrose seemed unfazed by all the shaking. She let him out, changed clothes, and righted a few items that had toppled on the kitchen counter. Everything else in her cabin seemed in order.

She walked outside the front door, and saw Eli approaching in a truck. When he stopped, Lacey hustled over to the passenger side and let herself in.

He began driving before she had fastened her seatbelt. "The earthquake took out a building," he said.

"Oh my god! Here at the resort? Is everyone okay?" Lacey felt her heart in her throat.

"No, not here. Everyone I encountered was okay. At least, no one was physically harmed. The building is a little further south from here. It was an older apartment building, I was told."

Eli had spent much of the drive talking about earthquake building codes. She wasn't very interested in it, and almost wished he'd revisit his more personal stories, but couldn't think of a good way to ask, "Could you please tell me more about your dead brother, instead?"

Also, his driving made her nervous, for reasons she couldn't quite explain. Eli, so sedate in most ways, was the same behind the wheel. Cool, measured, calculating. But Lacey couldn't help but think that he might just calculate that driving the car off a cliff would be the most appropriate course of action at any time.

As they approached the building, Eli pulled the truck off the highway. In the distance, there was what looked like it was once a three-story building, collapsed on one side. The roof was canted at a hard angle, crushing the collapsed side, and pointing up into the open air above the non-collapsed side.

There were other apartment buildings around it, and fast food restaurants and strip mall establishments across the street, but none of them seemed any worse for wear.

She let Eli lead the way. "All these other building we're seeing should be evacuated by now."

They made it to the perimeter of the scene, flanked with first responder vehicles and a van with a satellite atop. A handful of civilian types watched, phones at the ready.

Lacey paid close attention to the paramedics. She hadn't

told Eli about her idea. A full squad of people with SLOFD emblazoned in glowing letters on their backs were in full, orchestrated action.

A team of people navigated some rubble, carrying a person on a stretcher. There were shouts, and a police officer who had been standing directly ahead of Eli and Lacey rushed over to assist. Eli urged Lacey to quicken her pace, and they passed by the preoccupied stretcher team and crossed over the perimeter.

He directed her toward a less crowded area of the scene. They were shielded from view of any watching law enforcement. Huge chunks of wall lay about like they had landed from the sky. Lacey realized that might actually be the case.

"How many stories was this building, Eli?" she asked.

"Four."

Oh my God. It only looked like three from the road.

One chunk of wall still had a flat screen television attached to it. Wires and components dangled from it.

They entered the more intact side, through a door that flapped open. And Lacey felt it before she heard it. A popping in her ear drum, and then a noise beyond deafening. An intolerable pressure that forced her to stumble and nearly brought her to the ground. They were in a tight space, what was probably the entry hallway, and couldn't see what was happening. Everything sounded muffled after that, but she heard an official type shouting something about clearing all civilians from the scene.

She turned her head toward Eli and found him crouched, low to the ground. His eyes were closed, and she panicked. She didn't realize how much she relied on his guidance until that instant. She'd followed his unauthorized entry to a major disaster scene without a second thought.

His hand moved, palm flattening against a piece of flooring, and then fingers flexing upward. He opened his eyes and looked at Lacey.

She blew out a long breath. "What just happened?"

"An explosion," Eli said, rising. "Maybe a gas line. Hopefully nothing ignitable nearby."

Lacey got to her feet. "Hopefully," she said, resisting the temptation to roll her eyes.

"Eli, why are we here? Aren't we only making things worse for the first responders?"

He didn't respond.

"She should be somewhere near," was all he said.

Who, she? Lacey thought. *What the hell?*

Eli walked down the hallway. He passed one open doorway, peered inside, and said to Lacey, "This one's clear."

Lacey looked past him. She could only see four doors in this section of the building, and three of them were open. Everyone seemed to have gotten out of this side already. Except the woman Eli was looking for.

He stopped at the closed door. He tried the doorknob, and found it unlocked. But it would only open after he gave it a forceful shove. Lacey followed him inside.

Through a window with a skewed curtain rod, Lacey saw a thin tower of angry orange flame, billowing smoke flaring off the top. It was not too far in the distance, maybe fifty yards in the opposite direction of the way they came in.

"Ignitable," Lacey said under her breath.

"We'll need to make this quick," Eli said.

"I'll say." *Before we all burst into flames or tumble into the earth.*

The apartment was in shambles. Besides the maze of toppled

furniture and upturned items, there were stacks of paper and food containers strewn about. Like a hoarder lived there.

The air got very close. An acrid smell, a mixture of smoke and alkaline, filled Lacey's nostrils.

Eli said in a very low voice, "Rose? Rosie?"

So she *is Rosie*, Lacey thought. *I'd be intrigued if I wasn't so horrified.*

Lacey chimed in. "Rosie?" She meant it as an assist to Eli, but it came out as more of "Who is Rosie?"

"Rosie!" he said, louder.

A muffled voice answered, "Here." Lacey couldn't tell where it came from. Eli stopped.

Again, a little louder, "Here!"

"This way," Eli said.

Their path became nearly impassable. And impossibly dark. Eli pulled out a penlight and clipped it to his shirt pocket. Lacey made the mistake of looking at it straight on and wound up with a floater dead center in her vision.

"I'm over here!" the voice said, growing in clarity but becoming hoarse.

A human form finally appeared to match the voice. Lacey blinked and saw a woman half-standing, her back up against a bookcase, and half-sitting, one leg stretched forward in front atop a toppled chair. There was a doggie bed behind her.

"Rosie!" Eli said. "Did you get what you came here for?"

That's an odd question, Lacey thought. *But this is Eli, after all.*

Rosie shook her head, a tear escaping her eye. Lacey noticed an inked tear below the other eye.

"I can go find him while Lacey helps you," Eli said.

"No," Rosie said. "I found him. He didn't make it."

Eli nodded solemnly.

Lacey's heart dropped, and her face must have mirrored her panic.

"My mother's dog," Rosie said to Lacey.

"I'm so sorry," Lacey said. She was, indeed, sorry, but also relieved that the "he" wasn't human.

Lacey looked down at Rosie's outstretched leg, and suddenly understood why she wasn't moving. Her calf was turned in a way it shouldn't be.

Without thinking, Lacey asked, "Are you in pain?"

Rosie answered only with a look.

Nice job, stupid question, Lacey thought. *Why don't you just quit talking?*

After saying to Rosie, "Here, I think I can help," Lacey followed her own advice. She stopped talking, and reached her hands forward toward Rosie's leg. All words and all thoughts of self-consciousness slipped away. She wasn't sure where Eli was. Her only thought was a faint image of a tree, with one sagging branch.

Rosie raised her eyes to Eli, who had stepped beside her. Eli nodded reassuringly. Rosie closed her eyes.

Lacey felt an instinctive urge to remove her clothing. She felt like she was on fire. Disrobing, and the tree branch, were the only thoughts she had. In that instance, those two thoughts were her universe.

Something like a breeze came over her, she felt cooler, and the urge dissipated. No longer fixated on her clothing, she focused on the sagging branch.

A sound penetrated her thoughts. A plaintive note, a chord that resonated on a rising pitch until it became a wail. Lacey thought the breeze was howling through the tree. The sagging branch seemed to right itself. The howl faded.

The smell of smoke—separate and closer than the pervasive scent of the destroyed building—roused Lacey from her reverie. That, and several hard slaps on her back from Eli's hand.

"What, what, ow!" Lacey said.

There was a thin line of smoke coming from her t-shirt, just below her ribs. She grabbed her side and patted, a gentler touch than Eli's.

Rosie was panting, her face broken out in perspiration.

Lacey pieced together the events of the last few moments. Not sure what to say, she looked to Eli.

"We're getting there," he said.

What does that mean?

"Rosie," Eli said, turning away from Lacey, "are you ready?"

Rosie blew out a breath, and looked down at her leg. "I must have been in shock before. That doesn't look as bad as I thought it was."

Lacey gave Eli a sideways glance. He didn't react.

"Yeah, we better get going," Rosie continued. "This place is ready to come down around us."

"Should we grab the body?" Eli asked.

Lacey grimaced at Eli's bluntness.

"We can't. He's crushed, beneath the bed frame. There's no moving him," Rosie said, serious but not affected by Eli's manner.

Lacey wondered if Rosie might be Eli's cousin or something.

Eli nodded, and the precariousness of their situation crashed in on Lacey. The tree was a distant memory. Another BOOM. Her hearing still muffled from the first explosion, Lacey realized she had no idea how near or far this new one was.

"We'll help you," Lacey said, hurrying to Rosie's side.

There was no way they could fit three aside, so Lacey maneuvered in front of Rosie to provide some feeble support. Eli and Lacey hopped, shimmied, and scurried their way back into the living room, supporting the mostly dead weight of Rosie between them.

"Is your mom out of town?" Lacey asked.

"What?" Rosie struggled to answer.

Lacey realized the question seemed to come out of the blue, but it seemed a legitimate query, and she was struggling herself to keep her mind off their current danger.

"Your mom. She lives here, right, with her d . . . " Lacey stopped herself from saying dog.

"Oh. She . . . " It was an obvious labor for Rosie to answer.

Real good. There you go again, Lacey thought. *Heal someone, then practically kill them over again with stupid questions.*

"She's down in Los Angeles, isn't she, Rosie?" Eli responded.

"Yes. She's in L.A . . . for work," Rosie said. "I've been after her . . . to move out of this god-awful place. Now . . .

"Just my luck . . . I happen to be here to check on her dog when the place comes crashing down!" Rosie released a high-pitched laugh, struck through with pain.

Finally, they escaped the fatal maze of the ruined building. Lacey and Eli, flanking Rosie, brought her to a triage area.

Eli spoke to the paramedic. He brought his finger to his temple, and her tone changed from hostile to cooperative in a matter of seconds.

Eli must be working his mind tricks on overtime, Lacey thought. *Getting us in there, and smoothing things over now.*

They stood by while the paramedic checked Rosie over. Lacey tried to take mental notes on everything she was doing.

"You did the right thing," Eli said.

"What?"

"That was the right thing to do," he said. "Asking Rosie about her mom, trying to bring us all out of the situation."

"She could barely walk, much less answer me, Eli. I felt pretty stupid for asking."

"You'll do better when you get out of that frame of thinking," he said. "Your constant self-critique. It limits you more than you realize."

"Easy for you to say. You're like some supernatural Zen master."

"No," Eli said. "It's not easy."

The paramedic approached them. A few inches shorter than herself, Lacey noticed the way her uniform suited her. It seemed tailored to the woman's petite frame. Lacey wondered how she would look in uniform herself, then chastised herself for her vanity. And then criticized herself for being self-critical.

Thanks, Eli.

"We're going to bring Rosie to Bayside Hospital. But we'll need to wait a bit for a bus. An ambulance," the paramedic said, correcting herself. Her badge read "Nicholson." She had an East Coast clip to her speech that sounded very foreign on the Central Coast of California.

"Fortunately, the building had a lot of vacancies. I was told this side was cleared, but we'll need to do another walk through now."

She picked up her radio and spoke quickly to the person on the other end. Eli walked over to Rosie, who reclined on a makeshift cot.

Lacey stood, watching Nicholson the paramedic, and started to worry about other people nearby, people who might need her assistance. She thought of straying to find another triage area, but the police presence had tripled since they first entered the building.

Which strengthened her intention of getting properly trained.

Eli approached her. "Rosie's asleep."

"Oh. Did they give her something?"

"No. Her pain is manageable. Sleep is what she needed most."

"I don't understand."

Eli took a deep breath. "I helped her fall asleep, Lacey."

"Oh."

He can do that?

She wanted to ask more about it, and how he knew Rosie, but her concern for the other injured people still on site won out.

"You know, Eli, since we're here . . . "

"You want to see if there's anyone else you can help."

"Yes. Can you help me do that?"

Eli didn't answer for several moments. She couldn't anticipate how he'd answer.

"Yes," he finally said. "Let's go."

20

Galliano, Louisiana
One spring in the mid-twentieth century

It didn't feel like four years had passed since the tornados hit. Everyone who had been outside that day realized how fortunate they had been. No, not fortunate, *blessed.* Two houses, just on the other side of the bayou from the Becnels, took direct hits from the tornado. One was never rebuilt, and the other family had only just returned to their rebuilt home in the past year.

Camille was now getting ready to graduate high school. Birdie felt a pang of sadness when she heard Camille talk about college.

Both Camille and Brother treated Birdie, and each other, differently since that day four years ago. While they weren't disrespectful prior to that time, they each had a capacity to be dismissive in that unique, adolescent way. That way had been tempered with compassion, and a bit more reverence.

And there was another baby in the house. A toddler, now. For nine months, two years ago, Mrs. Becnel became a different person. Active, engaging. And pleasant. Collaborative in her dealings with Birdie. More present with her seven children. But after Esme was born, she withdrew even more than before that time. Birdie knew not to check on her unless it was specifically requested.

Even more than before, it was better that way. After countless episodes of hay fever, flu fever, and even one averted case of scarlet fever, Birdie knew these children better than she knew herself. They operated like a fine-tuned machine. The older children would return home from school, and knew better than to shirk their chores.

It was during Easter break, again, when Birdie found herself with a house full of children out of school and in need of occupation.

She had devised a game for Foxy. It was sort of an everyday-object Easter egg hunt. Sometimes it was a red bean, sometimes it was a rubber ball, sometimes it was a doll, once loved but now sitting on a shelf, abandoned for more big-kid pursuits.

On this April day, it was a baseball. Birdie had hidden it somewhere sure to get a rise out of Foxy.

Brother was in Mr. Becnel's study, messing with the radio. He knew to play it low, at a level not to disturb his mother. And he knew just how to leave it so that his father would never know he was there. Those were the conditions he and Birdie had worked out.

Camille was sneaking around, playing Candid Camera.

Evangeline was in the girls' room, reading. She had just reached that age where she learned that a good story was one of the best escapes from the relentless tug of teenage concerns.

Birdie took a deep breath. *Sometimes things get close to perfect,* she thought. Morris had been well enough to take on a few jobs for the past several weeks; the Becnel children were all happy, occupied, and harmonious; and the strawberries at the market had been the best she'd seen in four seasons. The Becnels who gathered when she entered the galley door with them howled with delight. "Birdie's gonna make strawberry shortcake!"

"Who says, children?" Birdie teased. "Maybe these are all for me."

Foxy looked at her as if he'd been betrayed. Birdie knew the thought of *not* having her strawberry shortcake was a fate he didn't want to contemplate.

She winked at him and said, "The game is set. It's something round. Now go!"

Foxy forgot about the strawberry shortcake. "What is it, Birdie?"

"Now, Foxy! You know the rules. Only hints can be given."

"Oh, man!" He knew the rules, but Birdie knew that didn't mean he couldn't push them. Wasn't that part of the game, anyway?

Last year, Birdie had found a magnifying glass, unused and practically discarded in a kitchen drawer. She had cleaned it up and offered it to Foxy as an aid in his searches. It was the only assistance that was permitted. And with Foxy's young eyes, it really served mostly as a prop, anyway. Birdie had always wanted to find a deerstalker cap, like Sherlock Holmes wore, to offer Foxy to complete the picture.

Birdie checked the pantry for sugar and flour to make the shortcake and got to work.

✳

Hours later, a little commotion ensued when Evangeline finally emerged from the girls' room and ran right up against the wrath of Amelie. She was nursing a broken heart. Jacque Songy, big man on campus (and quarterback) at O.L.P.S. High School, had just spurned her, after an intense three-week courtship, for Marie Lebreton. Amelie had no time for anyone or anything but her burnt feelings.

"Maybe if you spent a little more time finding out about the world around you, rather than chasing after Jacque No-Brains Songy and feeling sorry for yourself, you'd be a little more pleasant!" Evangeline chided her older sister.

"Maybe if you spent more time showing some *compassion*, you'd be a *lot* more pleasant," Amelie replied.

"What would you know about compassion?" Evangeline mumbled under her breath.

Birdie appeared on the landing in the middle of the upstairs hallway. She raised an eyebrow at Evangeline.

Amelie smirked, until Birdie turned that eyebrow to her.

Both girls stared at their feet, and muttered a nearly inaudible "Sorry" in unison.

"Supper will be ready in a half hour, children," Birdie called behind her as she descended the staircase and headed back into the kitchen.

Thirty minutes later, seven of the eight children had gathered in the kitchen. When Mr. Becnel was around for dinner, Mrs. Becnel would come out of her room, and the ten Becnels would eat in the fine dining room. But this evening, Mr. Becnel was in Houma, having dinner with business associates, he said. On evenings like this, which happened more often than not, Birdie and the eight children would dine together in the kitchen. Birdie rarely sat, she was always bustling around, so none of the children picked up on the difference—or the breech of service etiquette that Birdie knew she was committing.

Birdie did a head count of the gathered children.

"I think we're missing someone. You children think we're missing someone?" she said with a wink.

Brother piped up. "No, I don't think so. No one important, that is."

He then flinched and swatted his arm downward for no apparent reason.

The twins giggled and looked down at their feet.

Camille still had her camera around her neck; she usually laid it on the countertop before sitting down to eat. Recently, she'd started helping Birdie serve dinner. At least when they all ate in the kitchen.

Birdie turned her back to the table, knowing what was coming next and willing to play along with the game. The twins' giggles morphed into fits and squeals of laughter. Then, there was a tug on her skirt.

She whirled around, hands on her hips, careful to put a look of surprise on her face. "Foxy! How did you magically appear? And I see you used your deductive powers to find the prize." She nodded at the baseball in Foxy's hand.

In that instant, Brother groaned over the attention his younger brother received, the twins started clapping hands in unison, Amelie tried to shush them, Evangeline and Esme each watched, amused (Esme from her high chair), and Camille snapped a photo.

"All right, children, settle down. If I don't get you fed, the good Lord Himself will strike me down," Birdie said.

Camille put her camera down and went to Birdie's side to help dish up.

"Do you show your parents the pictures you take?" Birdie asked Camille in a low voice.

"Gosh, no. Mamere would just criticize," Camille answered. "And Papa's too busy."

Birdie nodded. "Make sure you keep it that way, you hear?"

Camille's eyes widened, then she nodded solemnly.

Birdie set dishes down in front of the twins, and she and Camille eventually got the whole table served. Birdie took her place next to Esme.

"Brother, it's your turn to say the blessing," she said.

He groaned.

"Oh, fine, you don't want to thank the Lord for the strawberry shortcake we're gonna have for dessert? I'm sure he won't mind if you don't have any."

Brother huffed, and begrudgingly recited the family grace.

Sometimes things get close to perfect, Birdie thought.

21

San Luis Obispo, California
Current day

Two days after the earthquake, Lacey was counting her blessings. Rosie was on her way to a rapid recovery, and Kandace had postponed the work she wanted Lacey for in town. Though she would still need to go to the studio later in the week, the day ahead of her was all hers.

What Lacey was most grateful for, however, was the turn her relationship with Eli had taken. In the span of less than twenty-four hours, it had become a friendship. A strange one, unlike any other she'd ever experienced, but a friendship nonetheless.

Their mission through the remainder of the earthquake scene was largely uneventful. Eli had helped her gain access to a victim who was stable, but had multiple lacerations. She fixed those up nicely. And there was an EMT who was struggling mightily but silently, the quake having triggered memories of a past trauma. He also seemed to enjoy some relief after Lacey's touch.

EMS had cleared the rest of the scene concurrent with Lacey and Eli's stealth maneuvers.

On the way back to Eli's truck, Lacey reflected on Rosie's healing.

"It was you, wasn't it?" she asked. "The 'breeze' that kept my clothes from bursting into flames?"

"It was a channeling of energy," he answered. "You will learn it. You're already beginning."

Lacey looked confused.

"The 'breeze' wasn't all me," he said.

"Oh. Really?" Lacey felt inexplicably proud of herself. Suddenly, her goal of becoming a first responder, who wouldn't have to strip down on every call, felt more attainable.

Back in the truck, Lacey felt less nervous than before with Eli in the driver's seat. They had picked up Christine—she was the connection to Rosie—and brought her to the hospital. Eli and Lacey sat together in the waiting room.

As the hours stretched on, they found themselves alone in a break room, drinking stale coffee. And Lacey felt emboldened enough to ask about Eli's power. He had been typically cagey when Lacey pressed for a full accounting of his abilities. And when she had asked if there was some sort of secret society, or marker, or maybe even just a directory of people who possess these unique abilities, he had actually laughed.

"It doesn't work like that," he had said.

"Well, how about if I start something? Maybe when I meet people who have a special kind of power, I can label them. Make them my 'Superfriend.'"

It had been an unusually light-hearted moment between them. Eli had warned her against assigning labels of any kind, to anyone. But he had agreed to be her Superfriend.

Lacey had spent most of the following day sleeping.

Now, wandering the grounds, Lacey saw Christine on the

path ahead of her, close to the dome. And it dawned on her in that instant that the wedding in the Healing Arts dome that Christine mentioned, the day Lacey first arrived, must have been Christine's and Rosie's. Lacey had learned, in the truck on the way to the hospital, that she and Rosie were recently married. She just hadn't realized *how* recent.

Christine was moving so tentatively, Lacey felt obliged to offer help.

"Christine," Lacey called, a few feet behind her.

Christine turned. "Oh, Lacey! There you are. Can you spare a few minutes?"

"Sure," Lacey said. She caught up with her at the door. Christine had the key and had opened it.

Filtered sunlight cast rainbow prisms all through the entry foyer of the dome. Lacey caught her breath. One word came to mind.

"Oh, I know, it's magical, isn't it?" Christine said.

"Huh, that's just what I thought," Lacey said, staring at Christine, wondering what Superfriend powers she possessed.

"Christine, how is Rosie feeling? Is she giving herself time to heal?"

The doctor at the hospital had said she was lucky to come away with no worse injury than a stress fracture. Lacey and Eli both knew it had been a lot worse than that just a few moments earlier. But Lacey was still paranoid that maybe her healing effect would wear off if Rosie didn't take it easy.

Christine laughed. "Getting Rosie to stay off her feet is no easy feat. But she's following her in-home exercises religiously. And says it doesn't even hurt to bear weight on that leg. It's rather miraculous, actually."

She tilted her head at Lacey. Lacey couldn't tell if Christine expected her to say something, and wasn't sure what she would say if she did.

Christine finally ended the impasse. "I'm glad you're here," she said. "I could use your help with that vase. The aftershocks."

Lacey looked to the corner and saw a large, ceramic vase lying on its side. It was her turn to tilt her head now, at Christine.

"I'm sorry, I'm just curious," Lacey said. "How did you know it had toppled?"

Christine looked for moment like she didn't understand Lacey, then laughed.

"Don't be sorry," she said. "I should apologize to you. Most folks around here are pretty used to my compensatory vision."

"Compensatory?" Lacey asked as she moved toward the vase.

"It's as good a name as any for it, I think," Christine said, following Lacey. "I can see shapes and contrasts, like what you might describe as being in a very dark room. And my other senses might be more finely attuned than those with normal vision."

They each took a side and righted the heavy vase.

"It's pretty impressive that you can tell who I am by the sound of my voice," Lacey said.

"Your accent is a dead giveaway. I don't need hyper-acute hearing for that."

"That's so funny," Lacey said. "My accent isn't really what you'd call a strong New Orleans accent."

"Maybe not to you." Christine returned to the reception desk and turned her head around the circular room.

Lacey stood by and tried to identify the fragrance in the air. Lemongrass. She was immediately transported back to

Angele's house, growing up. Angele's mom, Miss PJ, always had lemongrass incense burning.

An unadorned trellis lay against the wall, near the vase. Lacey imagined it festooned with flowers, and remembered the wedding. "Were you and Rosie married here?"

"Yes! That's right," she considered, "I first met you that afternoon.

"It was so wonderful, Lacey," she continued. "We had some chairs set up, and a little altar over there." She pointed toward the vase.

"The energy in the room couldn't have been more perfect."

Lacey let her imagination run for a bit. What a lovely, intimate space, with the scent and the dancing light. St. Daniel's was much more imposing, but was also the only place that could accommodate the more than 300 guests at hers and Fox's wedding.

"How long has it been since you lost your husband, Lacey?" Christine asked, turning toward her. "That is, if you don't mind me asking."

"No, it's okay. It's been about eighteen months. But I've seen so many changes this summer, it's beginning to feel like a lifetime ago."

Christine removed her glasses and placed them atop her head. Lacey tried not to stare at the glassy star shapes at the center of Christine's eyes, where a pupil would normally be. They were strangely beautiful, in an otherworldly sort of way.

"It's okay, Lacey," Christine said, laughing. "You can look. I can only imagine how my eyes appear, but they do seem to fascinate other people."

Lacey relaxed. "They're really beautiful, Christine. I hope it doesn't sound awful to say that."

"No, Lacey." She reached out for Lacey's arm and clasped her on the forearm, a warm reassurance. "It's wonderful that you see beauty there."

Christine's expression changed, and she turned her head toward Lacey's arm, then lifted her opaque gaze toward Lacey's face.

"Oh, my," she said. She nodded and slowly released her grasp on Lacey's arm. "Changes, indeed."

Lacey folded her arms across her chest. There was a burning sensation where Christine's hand had been. She was struck mute with surprise.

Christine is *a Superfriend!*

"Breathe, Lacey," Christine said.

"What just happened?" Lacey asked, finding her voice.

"I'm sorry, Lacey, I didn't mean to intrude," Christine said. She took a step back. "But as soon as I felt your arm, I could tell something was going on. Impossible to ignore."

Lacey took a deep breath. "What do you mean?"

"The compensatory vision," Christine said. "It gives me an inkling of when someone might need my assistance."

Lacey wondered just what Christine's Superfriend power might be. It made her lightheaded.

I need to sit down.

"Do you mind if I find a place to sit?" Lacey asked.

"Of course. There's a small room, just beyond that wall." Christine pointed right.

"Is it okay if I come with you?"

Lacey didn't answer. Christine followed anyway.

Lacey turned the corner and found the source of the lemongrass scent. A small room with no furniture except a small table and some large pillows arranged around the walls.

An extinguished incense burner rested the table. It reminded her of the worship space at the New Orleans Healing Center, except much smaller.

"I would have thought the incense would be lit, the scent is so strong," Lacey said.

"Leaving things burning is not the best idea in earthquake zones," Christine said.

"Oh, I suppose you're right." Lacey placed her hand against the wall and sunk down into one of the cushions.

"I'm sorry, Christine, I'm not sure what came over me. I'm just starting to get used to . . . to . . . what's going on with me."

Christine stood in the doorway. She didn't answer.

"Lacey, I'm a licensed masseuse," she finally said.

"Okay . . . " Lacey said.

Christine laughed again. "I'm sorry, I don't usually foist that set of skills upon people, they usually set appointments with me. But this is a slightly unusual circumstance. Would you be open to some impromptu massage therapy?"

Lacey didn't allow herself time to think before answering, "Yes."

"I will get my table," she answered.

Lacey tried not to dwell on the fact that she knew very little about Christine. There *was* something strangely magnetic about Christine, and Lacey's intuition told her she was utterly trustworthy.

She thought of Cecil. Lacey felt a sudden, intense pang of longing for home. For New Orleans.

There were similarities between Cecil and Christine. The instant affinity, the effortless persuasion. A sense of goodness and light. No rough edges like Eli.

"You seem better," Christine said when she returned.

"A little, yes. Thank you."

Christine cleared a spot on the floor and laid out her table.

"Are you sure I'm not keeping you from something else, Christine?"

"I think this is where I'm most needed, Lacey."

"Am I that fragile?" Lacey asked with a slight laugh.

"No, certainly not," Christine said. "Okay, I'm ready. You can leave your clothes on or take them off," she said. "Whatever you're comfortable with, but it might be more effective with your clothes off."

"More effective sounds good," Lacey said. "Give me a moment."

Lacey stripped, folding her clothes in a neat heap.

"Lie here, face down," Christine said. She covered Lacey with a sheet once she was on the table.

"Thoughts and feelings are likely to arise, Lacey. Make note of them, but try to keep yourself detached. Try to not let any one thought or feeling take hold of you."

"Okay," Lacey said, her voice muffled.

"If there's one thing that keeps coming up, it's usually important. Remember it enough so that you can reflect on it further."

The last bit sounded a bit ominous to Lacey. She gave a muffled, "Hmph."

Christine worked on Lacey's shoulder. She thought of Nathan. He had been shot through his shoulder. She had healed it.

Her lower back. Warmth flowed into her pelvis. She thought of Nathan first. Then Trevor.

Her quadriceps. Helga. Gunshot wound to the leg. She had healed that, too.

Her hands. She thought of Kevin. She felt a flicker of grief, a shadow of Fox. She thought of Kevin's sister, Holly.

When Christine began to work on her feet, Lacey lost sense of time. She could have been on the table for a minute, or an hour. She resisted the sense of panic that aroused.

Lacey found herself back near the top of the ridge, near the hot tub. It wasn't a daydream, or imagination. It was a near out-of-body experience. She wasn't sure if she felt Christine's touch anymore. Again, she resisted the panic.

Someone moved through the trees, just on the other side of the ridge. A shadowy presence. No face was visible, but Lacey sensed one. A flash image of red eyes, and menacing, bared teeth appeared to her. Because she was there, but not there, she didn't feel threatened. The presence seemed to be near a wrecked car, but she couldn't see it, she only sensed it. She could only see trees and a human form. And the human form was feeding. Devouring something, like a wild animal would.

She heard chatter at her feet. She looked down and saw a weasel. She yelped.

"Was that painful?" she heard a voice say.

Lacey looked for the weasel, but it was gone. All faded to darkness.

"Lacey, are you okay?" the voice said.

Lacey finally recognized it.

"I'm fine, Christine. I'm sorry."

Lacey tried to remember Christine's admonition to not let one thought take hold, to little avail. She was back on the table, and remembered where she was, but she was fixated on the shape through the trees. There was something so familiar about it.

Pay attention.

"Okay, Lacey, lay here for as long as you need. I'm going to step out of the room for a moment."

"You're all done?" Lacey asked in an absent voice.

"Yes. Take your time," Christine answered.

Lacey opened her eyes and blinked in the low light. She stared at a pillow. It had a Mayan pattern. It was set back against a solid pillow of a brilliant, deep burgundy. She was still on the hillside, confounded by the menacing presence and the car wreck.

What the hell was that supposed to mean? And why am I so compelled by it?

She rose and pulled her clothes back on.

Things can affect each other. Even through space and time.

The little weasel at her feet. The Weasel. Edmund Villere. She hadn't thought of him since before Kevin's funeral, yet there was the matter of his trial. Very much in her future. But the familiar presence in the trees was not him.

She folded the blanket Christine had used to cover her.

A ferret. Ferrets are domesticated weasels.

That was it. Gus Savin has a pet ferret. Gus Savin was the presence in the trees, she knew it, even though she didn't really know him at all. She knew it as much as she knew the sun would rise tomorrow.

Spooky action at a distance.

So, I have some vision of Gus Savin with a car wreck in the trees, Lacey thought. *Yes, I have an unnatural fear of car wrecks. And Gus Savin feeding on something like a savage is an image I could do without. So what the hell is it all supposed to mean?*

Christine came back in with a glass of water. Lacey folded herself down onto the Mayan pillow. Her eyes were leaking.

"Lacey. Can I help?" Christine asked.

Lacey shook her head and said in a quiet voice, "I'm not sure." She kept talking, because somehow, she thought it might help. "I saw some things, and I don't understand them. Some pretty creepy things. And I don't know how any of it relates . . . to what's going on with me."

Christine's glasses were back on her face, covering her eyes. "Whatever you saw, I think you'll need time to reflect on it. On what it means. But regarding your special gift . . . what's going on with you . . . I might be able to offer some insight."

Christine sat down cross-legged onto one of the cushions.

"I was quite young, nine years old, when *my* gift first manifested. I had lost my sight years earlier, when I was so young that I barely remember what it was like to see. I was staying with an aunt, Aunt Janie, one of my mother's sisters."

Christine paused and smiled. The peace that usually radiated from Christine was amplified.

"Aunt Janie would read to me, stories that my mother wouldn't. Stories that my mother thought would scare me. But Aunt Janie had such a flare for drama, she would make the stories come alive. And they always had a happy ending, so that even the scary parts were worth it. The ending just seemed that much happier for the trouble the heroes faced."

Lacey listened, silent, wondering what any of it had to do with Christine's gift.

"So, that one summer, for the time I stayed with her, Aunt Janie would bring me to an ice cream parlor. I was returning to my mother in a few days time, and it was likely to be our last trip for ice cream. Our routine was always the same—hand-in-hand we'd cross the street, me following Aunt Janie's lead.

"While crossing the street, a noise behind us startled me,

and I squeezed Aunt Janie's hand, tightly. I heard Aunt Janie catch her breath, and I thought I'd hurt her.

"'I'm so sorry! Are you okay?' I'd asked."

"What was the noise?" Lacey asked, wanting to let Christine know she was listening.

Christine's peaceful smile softened, touched by a hint of sadness, Lacey guessed.

"It was just a truck lowering its tailgate. I had asked Aunt Janie the same thing, but she didn't answer right away. We were across the street, I could tell, and near the door of the ice cream shop. Aunt Janie's silence began to frighten me."

Christine took a deep breath and pulled her shoulders back. "I remember that initial fear. That fear of not knowing what was going on. I believe that's the very worst thing, in the beginning."

"So . . . ," Lacey asked. "Was your aunt okay?"

"She was . . . then. We eventually went into the parlor, and ordered as we usually did. But Aunt Janie was strangely quiet."

"What I would find out later—later that same year—is that my touch has a special power. Some healing power, but no more than any typical masseuse. No, the single, extraordinary thing I would discover is that my touch has the ability to open peoples' eyes."

Her smile returned, and her hands spread out, palms open, on either side of the cushion.

Again, Lacey felt the need to speak, since Christine couldn't see her awed reactions.

"Like, you can give sight to other people?" Lacey thought what a terrible irony that would be, if Christine couldn't use it on herself.

Christine laughed. "In a manner of speaking. In some

instances, but not all, my touch can cause visions. Sometimes it's the future, sometimes it's the past, sometimes it's a potential future."

Lacey inhaled. "Really?"

It was an involuntary response. She felt foolish for how it sounded.

Christine laughed again. "Yes. I've always thought it fitting, that the first time it ever happened was with Aunt Janie, with her love for the fantastic."

"So, how . . . ," Lacey asked.

" . . . Did I discover this?" Christine responded. "Aunt Janie became ill later that same year. My mother and I visited her, around the holidays. My mother didn't say as much, but I knew we were going to say goodbye to her."

"Oh. I'm sorry," Lacey said.

"Remember, Aunt Janie always loved happy endings. She died happy, and at peace. But her final story, the last one she told me, was especially for me. It was about a young girl, who had something like Midas's touch. But instead of turning things to gold, she helped people see clearly. If it was dark, she'd provide light. If it was foggy, she'd provide a breeze to blow the mist away. And she said the young girl helped countless people through her life, and lived happily ever after."

Christine wiped her fingers underneath her glasses. "Oh my goodness, how I cried when she told that story."

"You were the girl?" Lacey asked in a soft voice. "How did Aunt Janie know?"

"When I clasped her hand in the street that summer, Aunt Janie had a vision of her own death. And of my ability to facilitate such things . . . in other people."

Lacey felt a panic rising. "But it's not always about death, you said . . . "

Christine's happy demeanor returned. "No. It's more like future or past events. That's just what it happened to be in my aunt's instance."

"Wow. Do you ever find it, like it's too much to handle?"

"I struggled a bit, early on. Going through puberty and coming to terms with a gift like that, all at the same time, was a trial I'm glad I'll never have to repeat."

"But now?"

"There's not a day goes by that I'm not grateful for this gift." She folded her hands in her lap, and her smile turned beatific.

Lacey felt a torrent of questions well up. Had Rosie ever received one of Christine's touch visions? Or was it best to keep it out of a relationship? Was Christine ever part of the other person's vision? Why hadn't Lacey received her ability earlier? Though she realized Christine couldn't answer that last one.

Christine eased herself up off the pillow. "I hope you'll find that place of gratitude, Lacey. I think you will. You seem to want to find it."

Lacey struggled to find the right words. "I . . . I do. I think I do. Thank you, Christine."

"It was my pleasure, Lacey."

22

When Trevor contacted her, out of the blue, later that evening, Lacey realized something. She was ready for a break from thinking about her "gift." Trevor had no clue about her ability. That made their conversations—all their interactions—much simpler than the ones she'd had over the last several days.

Maybe that's the reason everything between them had felt so easy thus far. She'd always had the lingering suspicion with Nathan, that part of his feelings for her were tied to the fact that she had saved his life. At least twice. Like a patient who falls in love with their doctor.

There was no such complication between Lacey and Trevor. The entire affair had been a whirlwind, and based solely on mutual attraction.

Was the attraction mutual? Or did Trevor just read Lacey as an easy hit?

Stop it. Overthinking this will kill it.

And she definitely didn't want to kill it.

His message had said something about fact checking. She had sent him a picture, taken from the top of the ridgeline, of the vast ocean below. And that he was going to be in the area and wanted to make sure she wasn't sending doctored photos.

The thread was fairly pragmatic, light on the usual innuendos and double entendres.

But still, her heart had leapt in her throat. The thought of sex with Trevor, out on her lovely, secluded veranda, with the sun setting in the background, got her engaged in a way she hadn't been since . . . no, not since Nathan. Really since the last time with Trevor.

And a respite from her "training," such as it was, felt like a good idea.

For just a little while, she didn't want to think about Superfriends, or the entire universe in need of healing, or feeling grateful for her power, or anything else remotely related to it. She just wanted to be. And being was easy with Trevor.

Wasn't Eli always telling her to live in the moment?

Wednesday afternoon, Christine told her in passing that she was needed up at the "Rendezvous" hot tub. Lacey expected Eli, even though it was a different location than the site of their training exercise the day of the earthquake. She wondered why he hadn't contacted her himself, but was prepared this time, nonetheless. She wore a two-piece under t-shirt and shorts.

She climbed the steps up to Rendezvous, and found the privacy gate bolted when she arrived. A little exasperated, she knocked gently, and nearly squealed when she heard Trevor's lilt attempt his best American, "Who is it?"

Lacey was speechless with excitement for a moment. "Who do you think it is?" she answered, trying to take her voice an octave lower.

"Oh, it's you," he said, the brogue returning.

The door opened inward to reveal Trevor standing completely nude and dripping. He must have already been in the hot tub.

Lacey looked behind her to see if anyone else could see him. He didn't make any effort toward modesty.

Lacey hustled into the cabana. She grabbed the door from Trevor and quickly shut and latched it.

"How did you get Christine in on this?" Lacey asked.

"Who?"

"The tall, elegant woman, visually-impaired . . . "

"Oh! The blind lass."

Lacey shook her head.

"Simple. She was in the gift shop when I reserved this tub. I asked the bloke behind the counter if he knew you, and he didn't seem to, and . . . " Trevor made a motion toward his eyes.

"Christine," Lacey interjected.

"Anyway, she heard me say your name, and she volunteered to play her part in this little game."

Trevor was still standing like a statue, in the same position.

"Eyes up, love," he said. "I'm sure my manhood is terribly distracting, but you're making me feel like an object."

Lacey laughed and looked him in the eye. "Well, maybe I'm just glad to see you."

"Likewise." He took her hand, an incongruously gentle gesture, and led her to a small table to the side of the door.

His clothes lay in a heap, next to a carton containing single-serve, plastic bottles of wine and two plastic glasses. Lacey noticed the unused clothes hooks on the wall and smiled to herself.

"For someone who seemed in a rush to get going, you practiced some patience in not opening the wine."

"I didn't want to drink alone. I'm in the buff alone most of the time."

That painted a picture in Lacey's mind. She lifted his jeans from the top of the heap and let them drop again.

"Ah, you're a neat freak, aren't you?" he said, grabbing one cap-topped bottle. "I suspected that all along. Sorry, love, I'm not."

He poured out the contents of one bottle into a plastic glass and handed it to her. "So, I've concluded your photo was indeed, not faked."

She lifted herself onto an open space on the table, sitting atop it, and played along.

"I don't have that skill, anyway. Why were you so interested?"

"I came up here to try to surf. Spent most of the morning out there." He poured another bottle into a glass for himself. He set it down next to Lacey and stood before her, leaning in.

"Sorry I didn't wait for you with the hot tub," he said. His voice was low, his face inches from hers. "It felt too good after that workout."

"That's okay. I can think of something else that might feel good." She moved in quick and kissed him hard. He responded without missing a beat. His hand moved to the side of her face, gentling stroking her cheek and tousled hair.

Lacey's senses went reeling.

Trevor turned his focus entirely to Lacey. She was pinned by his arms around her; his lips had moved to her neck. She braced herself with her hands on his hips, her hands fitting atop his hipbones like they were made for just that purpose.

Trevor's hands moved up and inside her t-shirt. The latex of her bikini top was too tight for his hand to slide inside, so he ran both hands over her breasts. Lacey longed to disrobe, to feel skin on skin, but didn't want to stop the momentum.

Lacey opened her legs to allow Trevor to move in closer. She could feel him hard against her. Hell, she could see it, too. But he made no motion to move inside her. She wondered how long he could stay tumescent like that.

She grabbed him and began to stroke. She longed to taste him.

Lacey hopped off the table and got on her knees before him. Trevor answered with a deep, harmonic moan. One hand on her shoulder, and the other twisted in her hair, he watched her tend to him.

"Sweet Mary, love," he said. His hand in her hair fell to her shoulder. His grip tightened and he pushed gently.

Before Lacey could react, he had her by her sides and lifted her back onto the table. Her nerves arced at the touch of his hands to her ribs. She breathed in sharply, and was bombarded by the sweet, clean scent of eucalyptus.

Trevor pulled her toward him, so she would have teetered on the lip of the table if he wasn't holding her so firmly. He pulled on the waistband of her shorts. She praised her luck for having chosen to pull on her looser swim shorts. He tugged them to just above her knees, lifted one leg out, and pulled her even closer.

"Grab a condom, love."

"Where?" Lacey hadn't seen any on the table.

Trevor held her fast with one arm, and rooted around underneath his pile of clothes with the other. Lacey reached for the packet as soon as she saw it.

"Take care of it quick," he said with a twinkle in his eye. Lacey slid the condom on as Trevor kept her steady on the table. Then he drove inside her, a swift, fluid movement that rose in intensity.

Lacey felt the edge of the table drive into her buttocks with each thrust. The pain heightened the experience. She gripped the table with one hand and cried out, certain that it could be heard along the hillside.

She didn't care.

Trevor's moans remained low, but increased in frequency, until they stopped. His movements slowed, until his thrusts became a gentle rocking. He pulled Lacey into an embrace and set her on the ground before him. She stepped back and out of her shorts, which still dangled from one leg.

Trevor winked, took a long pull from his wine glass, and with three quick steps, had submerged himself in the hot tub.

"That is a fabulous idea," she said with a big smile. She took her clothes off, making sure Trevor was watching. She made a show of it, grabbed her wine glass, and joined him in the hot tub.

✳

After her and Trevor's reservation time had elapsed up at Rendezvous, Lacey checked in with Eli with a quick phone call. He told her he didn't need her. Just like that. Not, "Enjoy the afternoon." Not, "Nothing's going on, I'll see you tomorrow." Just that: "I don't need you."

Even though she felt more connected to Eli now, his terseness still bugged her.

She shook it off and turned to Trevor. "Are you up for a hike?" she asked.

His eyes lit up. "A roll in the hay on the rolling hillside?"

She pushed at him with a smile. "Aren't you tired?" And wondered if he would try to take her off trail. The thought of the dry scrub at her back, ants, and possible reptilian visitors did not turn her on.

"Plus, I hear there are rattlesnakes," she said. She suddenly wondered how she would heal a snakebite.

"Ha! I can handle a rattlesnake. I could use the rattle as percussion. Would make a great story to tell onstage."

Lacey realized she probably didn't need to worry about curing Trevor of anything.

Though they hiked up the hillside together, they may as well have been miles apart. Trevor didn't say much, and took his time taking in the sycamores, the sage, giving way to pines the higher they rose. Lacey tried to draw him out with a few comments, but his answers were pat. It was clear he didn't want to engage. She tried to respect his space, but couldn't help but wondering what had caused his sudden mood swing.

Her mood notched down to match.

"The color's completely different," he finally said.

"What?" She had no idea what he was talking about. Nothing had preceded the comment.

"In Ireland. The sky can be this same color, certain times of year, but the earth it's covering is a completely different color."

"Isn't that why they call it the Emerald Isle?" Lacey answered.

"You think?"

So is that it, maybe? He's homesick? I can understand that.

Still trying to allow him his mood, she waited for his reaction when they reached the peak of the hill. They were almost there. She'd had her breath stolen from her the first time she saw it.

He stopped dead still when he crested the hill. "Well, this is terrible," he said without a hint of a smile. "Take me back this instant."

It wasn't until he winked that she realized he was joking. "We need to work on our comic timing," she said.

They stood where Lacey had when she'd taken the picture. The one that enticed him to make the three-hour drive from Los Angeles. They were two small dots on a hill, side by side, the great expanse of the Pacific Ocean stretched out before them, whitecaps appearing just as squiggly lines marring a massive blue mat.

"How's that for color?" she asked.

He nodded and gave her a one-sided smile.

The sun was still high, but beginning its descent toward the watery horizon.

"C'mon," Lacey said. "There's something really cool, over here to the left."

"Yeah, because this isn't cool at all." He smiled and pecked her on the cheek.

They walked a short distance along the crest of the trail, heading south. They passed through a few copses of trees, but nothing marred the view of the sprawling ocean beside them. The cars below, along California Highway One were so distant, they appeared as industrious ants in a path to a colony.

This is the California I've always wanted to see, Lacey thought. *So why do I feel a tinge of homesickness now, too?*

They reached a wooden swing, suspended from a sturdy tree branch. This was the first time she'd seen the swing unoccupied, though she'd only seen it twice before. Lovers' initials spotted the tree trunk. Lacey wondered if Trevor might add something to the woody manuscript. It seemed like something he might do. But with the sudden revelation of his moodiness, she wasn't sure she wanted him to.

"Whose idea was this?" Trevor said.

"Not mine," Lacey answered. "Doesn't seem like a bad one, though." She steadied herself on the swing and began to sway; low, easy strides. A breeze came up out of the north. She closed her eyes and let the wind have its way.

Trevor came behind her to offer swing assistance. His strength made her feel unsteady.

"Not too hard," Lacey said.

She expected a snarky response, but he responded only by easing up on his pushes.

It seemed the perfect lover's moment—a mountaintop, a swing, the ocean, the breeze. But Lacey felt lonelier than she had when she'd made the hike alone. She and Trevor had great chemistry, but it only seemed to apply when they were intimate. She tried to think of something to make light, but nothing came.

"I need to start thinking about getting back down to L.A.," Trevor said.

Lacey planted her feet and stopped swinging. "Sure. Of course." She hopped off the swing. "I'm sure I've taken up enough of your time already."

She meant it honestly, as a courtesy, but it came out tinged with bitterness. She looked toward Trevor, to gauge how he took her comment. He seemed not to hear it.

Well, this is turning out to be a drag, Lacey thought.

Trevor returned to his carefree form when they reached the resort. "We have a gig in Santa Barbara next week. That's close to here, isn't it?"

"Closer than L.A., sure."

"Think you can make it?" he asked.

"Sure," Lacey said, trying to sound bright. "I'll get the details from Jimmy. I'll plan to come."

They reached the parking lot, and Trevor stopped at a car with a Utah license plate.

"Do you need anything? Change of clothes or anything? I'm in a little cabin right across the way."

"No, love. I'm good. I'll see you soon?"

"Yep. I'll make it happen."

It sounded more convincing than Lacey felt.

She turned her back when he drove off, and found one of the benches at the edge of the parking lot. She made sure he was gone for good. She was stunned by the roller coaster moods she'd just experienced with Trevor. She felt profoundly lonely, and made herself feel worse by recognizing how alone she truly was.

Sure, she'd met a few Superfriends, but the only one who truly seemed to understand her potential—more than she did herself—was Eli. And he was not quite the balm for loneliness. And for as much as she enjoyed her time with Trevor, and wanted to be "in the moment" with him, he only seemed to remind her how she longed for something more permanent. Who knows, maybe he felt the same way. Maybe some corresponding part, in both of them, knew this wasn't going to be permanent.

This sucks, she thought.

23

Lacey awoke the next morning, feeling surprisingly refreshed. If she ignored her feelings for Trevor (or rather, her confused feelings and the longing they inspired for something else), she had to admit, the break toward a "normal" interlude seemed just what she needed. Plus, it was Thursday, almost at the end of a really weird week.

She didn't have to meet Kandace at the soundstage until Noon. And Eli had told her—again—that she wasn't needed today. Feeling the morning wide open before her, and determined to *not* think about her love life, or Eli's terseness, she started to imagine what her future career might be like. Dressed in a uniform, riding in an ambulance. Having to explain to her partner why she needed to strip in front of the injured person they were tending to . . .

That might be a minor issue.

Eli had said they could continue the lesson they'd started before the earthquake hit. But then he'd told her he hadn't been the only one helping her when they rescued Rosie. That she had helped herself. How?

She sent Ambrose out onto the patio and opened the window near the bed. It looked out onto a wooded area. She peered out, wanting to be sure no one could see her. She stripped completely naked, still not understanding why the lesson required her to remove her clothes, like Eli had said. She couldn't summon the healing feeling, the heat, because there wasn't anyone nearby in need of healing.

If she wasn't going to get so hot that she would ignite anything, why did she need to take her clothes off?

She heard it before she felt it. Announcing itself through a rustling in the trees, a breeze came through the window. The skin just below her throat tingled, then she felt a shiver radiate from that point all over her body.

Okay, I guess I wouldn't have felt that so intensely with my clothes on . . .

The wind died, and Lacey felt her temperature return to normal. She closed her eyes, for what felt like an eternity, then opened them again when nothing else happened. She stopped herself from tapping her foot.

What next?

Maybe there's some part of me that needs healing. Maybe that could increase my body temperature by a few degrees.

She thought about her messy emotions, her conflicted feelings, and concentrated on them. Nothing felt different in her body at all. So, maybe her emotional state wasn't "broken," or in need of healing.

You mean I'm supposed to feel like this??

Never mind, focus on the task on hand.

So, she really had no control over her ability. Eli had called her body a "conduit" for her power. But he had also hinted that she could control her body temperature—at least cool it down—so that she could counteract her power's ill effects. Ill effects like her clothes catching on fire.

Where's Eli when you need him?

She thought of ice, and snow. She looked out the window and tried to imagine the scene in winter. She tried to make her mind a blank.

It wasn't cooperating. She wondered if she was the only person in the world who had ever done this. Then immediately realized that she wasn't. She couldn't be. Birdie had some similar power, though she didn't know exactly what. She imagined Birdie trying to find some quiet place to be alone, with Fox's father and myriad aunts and uncles as children, knocking at the door, nagging to know what she was doing. She couldn't stop herself from smiling at the thought.

She thought again of "spooky action at a distance." Was that what Birdie was to her, and she to Birdie? Affecting each other through time and distance, even though they never knew each other? Only connected through the "conduit" of the Becnels?

She felt a shiver just below her throat, same place as before. It turned sharp and hard, an ice dagger. It began to spread. She opened her eyes, fear growing, half expecting to see a sudden summer snowstorm in the scene outside her window. Nothing had changed, the sun was still shining.

Her teeth began to chatter.

"Well, sh-sh-sh-it!" She could barely get the word out. *Okay, please, how do I stop this?*

She resisted the urge to wrap herself in the blanket from the unmade bed. She closed her eyes again and took a deep breath. Her teeth stopped chattering, but her limbs still shivered. She imagined standing outside in the sun, dressed in a comfy sweater. Then, she thought of coming back from a run, on a pleasant fall day in New Orleans. Still warmer than a fall day in most other parts of the country.

Her legs and arms stopped shivering. She opened her eyes and still saw goose bumps on her arms. But she was no longer uncomfortable.

She looked around the room and could hear Ambrose pacing outside on the porch. He was ready to come back in. She threw on some clothes and opened the door for him. She was lost in her thoughts.

Okay, so I definitely brought my body temperature down. But how?

"Was I thinking cold thoughts, Bro, was that it?"

The dog looked up at her as if to say, "How am I supposed to know?"

So, I was thinking of cold things, and then I thought of Birdie. About how we're connected.

I stopped thinking of my own issues for a fraction of a second.

"Is that it? I just have to detach a bit? And stop focusing on my problems?"

Could it be that easy?

She made an intention to ask Eli that very thing, and got ready to head to the soundstage.

The coffee mug, Diet Dr. Pepper, and wobbly straw was there, but no Kandace. Horatio was a sight for sore eyes at the gate, but he was the only thing that was familiar. The studio had been cleared. The table Lacey had used as a desk had been cleared. All that was left was cavernous, echoing space. Lacey peeked around the corner where Kandace's office had been. That, at least, looked the same.

It was eerie, and it was sad. Lacey had been frustrated and bored working here before, but it was still preferable to the profound sense of loss permeating the place now. Lacey felt Kevin's absence as acutely as at the funeral. She stepped inside the doorway to Kandace's office, found a folding chair, and sat.

Why did Kandace need her to come in? She had closed all the books when the production went on hiatus. Her throat felt tight and she wanted to get back to the Mineral Springs.

"When did you get here?" she heard a voice say.

Lacey whipped her head around. Kandace strolled into her office, more at ease than Lacey had ever seen her.

Lacey stood. "Just a few minutes ago. I couldn't find you, so I just came here."

Kandace plopped down behind her desk. "Go ahead, pull up the chair, we have time," she said.

Lacey looked at the chair again and pulled it closer. But not too close.

"What are we going to be doing today?" Lacey asked.

"Oh, I need your help with some files," Kandace answered. "But it can wait for a bit.

"Did you ever go to that restaurant?" Kandace asked. "The one you were looking up that one time?"

Lacey struggled to figure out what the hell Kandace was talking about. And her radical change in demeanor. She was so relaxed—and well, normal. It was not a bad thing.

"Um, you mean Taverna?"

"Yes, that's the one."

Lacey thought of her dinner with Trevor, her first night

with him. "Yes. It feels like a while ago now, with everything that's happened, but, yes."

"I wound up going back," Kandace said. "But not with Roger. It was a lot better."

"Oh," Lacey said. "That's . . . good."

"I met someone," Kandace said, her words falling on top of Lacey's. "Roger doesn't know yet."

"Oh, yeah? That sounds intriguing," Lacey said.

Kandace proceeded to offer details about someone who sounded surprisingly authentic. Black hair, green eyes, she wasn't really crazy about the way he dressed, he was a little too sloppy. They had gone together to Taverna, explaining her aforementioned reference. But they had also gone hiking, and Kandace named the trail. Turtle Rock, in Morro Bay. Either she was getting better at delusions, or this person was actually real.

"Wow," Lacey said. "You did all that in one weekend?"

"Oh, Lord, yes, it was a whirlwind. But he's been gone this week, traveling for work. He's supposed to be back next week."

"Oh," Lacey said. She had an insight, but didn't want to burst Kandace's bubble. Something about a whirlwind weekend, and then "disappearing" over the week. And the sloppy way the man dressed.

"He lives here, in San Luis Obispo?"

"Yes, that's how he knew the trail at Morro Bay, and what to order at Taverna."

Lacey thought of Fox, and wondered how many women like Kandace he had suckered. She shuddered, but for the first time ever, felt sympathy for the poor women who hadn't known he was married.

"So. Are you going to tell Roger?" Lacey asked. She

reasoned an imaginary boyfriend was better than a possibly married one.

"Not yet," Kandace said. "I'm not sure where this is going to go. And plus, I haven't really heard from new guy."

That confirmed Lacey's suspicion. "I think that's smart," she said. "You don't want to throw away a good, long-term thing just yet. I mean, you have a lot invested in your relationship with Roger, don't you?"

Lacey tried not to reflect on the absurdity of her statement.

"Yes, that's a good point," Kandace replied. "Thanks for listening."

That sounded sincere, Lacey realized with shock. Maybe there was more to Kandace beyond "work-boss mode."

"So, there is a bit of work to do," Kandace continued. "Would you mind helping out with some filing?"

I suppose it's all part of my ill-defined job, Lacey thought. "Sure."

Lacey and Kandace spent two hours together shuffling through boxes of paper, mostly Movie Marvel reports that never needed to be printed in the first place. Many were several years old, covering productions Lacey had never heard of. She kept encountering a report heading titled "Ripe Transgression," which made her giggle. But after the thousandth page with that heading, Lacey wept silently over all the sacrificed trees.

Lacey grabbed a cushion from storage and sat cross-legged on it while she sorted. Kandace brought in a chair and craned forward from the waist toward the boxes on the ground.

About an hour and a half in, Kandace switched gears completely. She leaned back in her chair, arched her back, and exhaled loudly. Following her lead, Lacey unfolded her legs, clasped her hands in front of her and stretched them over her head.

"You know, I heard something recently about Kevin, and I really don't know what to think about it," Kandace said.

Lacey tried to play off her surprise and Kandace's mention of the subject. "Who'd you hear it from?" Lacey asked.

"That doesn't really matter," Kandace said.

Lacey tilted her head to the side and waited for more, not surprised that Kandace wouldn't reveal her source.

"Someone was just saying, what if it wasn't just an accident? What if he had been run off the road?"

Kandace looked at Lacey as if she knew the answer. She had certainly thought of foul play, but she wasn't sure where Kandace was headed with this conversation.

Lacey shook her head, and pushed herself back on her cushion. "Wow," she said. "That would be awful."

Kandace seemed convinced this was the answer. "If he was run off the road, who would've been behind it? Or could it all have been just a freak accident?"

"Well, let's think about it," Lacey said. "Allison would be the one witness, if that was the case. Has she said anything publicly about the accident?"

Kandace stood up from her chair. She paced the small room littered with boxes. The setting, and Kandace's affected manner, made Lacey feel like she was in a bad television show. *The X-Files*, where the files were a bunch of lame accounting reports. Thinking of her setting, a soundstage for bad TV movies, she realized how ironic that seemed.

"Allison has said she doesn't remember anything about the accident," Kandace said, turning to Lacey with a dramatic pause.

"She was hurt pretty badly," Lacey said from the floor.

"Maybe she has some short-term amnesia about the accident." Lacey tried to give Allison the benefit of the doubt, but something bothered her. She remembered having a great first impression of Allison, but then feeling like she'd cast a spell upon her. There was too much that seemed hidden about her. Suspicion unfurled.

"Do you know if anyone is trying to jog her memory?" Lacey asked.

"I think so," Kandace said, her back to Lacey now. "I mean, someone has to be, right? That's a pretty big piece." Kandace turned back around, chewing on a straw. "Yeah, they would have to be. I heard a rumor—I don't know how true it is—that Allison might sue Kevin's estate. But if that's the case, they would want her version of events, right?"

Discussing the accident with Kandace, out in the open, triggered something right in the center of Lacey's brain, a little spark that she could make no sense of. A stronger, more patent distrust of Allison welled up, and Lacey felt immediately guilty for it. The poor woman had almost died, and also been witness to Kevin's last breath. But there was something about her that put Lacey on edge.

"Did you see or talk to Allison at all, at the funeral?" Lacey asked.

"No," Kandace answered. "I mean, I saw her to tell her how sorry I was, but that was it. She seemed like she was in a lot of pain."

"I saw her, but didn't have the chance to say anything," Lacey said. "Heck, I barely even saw you. There were a lot of people there."

"Did you see Wonder Woman there?" Kandace asked, eyes suddenly wide.

Lacey smiled. It was funny that Kandace used the character's name, and not the person who played her. Kandace actually looked star-struck, an open-mouthed smile and stars in her eyes. "Yes. She's hard to miss."

"I actually had the opportunity to say something to her, but I couldn't," Kandace said. "I couldn't think of anything that sounded appropriate for the setting."

Lacey wondered if that was the first time Kandace had ever successfully censored herself.

"Yeah, what do you say when you meet someone at a funeral? It's all supposed to be about the connection to the person who's now gone."

Lacey caught Kandace's reaction, then each cast their eyes away. Lacey felt guilty about their cavalier conversation. She endeavored to get back to the task at hand.

"So anyway," Lacey said. "I've gone through all these boxes."

Lacey swept her arm to the stack of ten boxes at her back. "They're all ready for the shredder."

They tied up the remaining loose ends, and Lacey left the studio just a few minutes later. She said goodbye to Horatio at the gate, thinking it would be the last time she'd see him. She thought about it, and realized he was the only person she'd interacted with at the facility who actually worked there full-time. Everyone else was itinerant, just like her. Moving with the production.

She wondered how Horatio felt about that.

24

Lacey was done with the Central Coast and all its wild beauty. Her skin was dry, her eyes were bloodshot, her limbs were tired. She thought of summoning some healing energy to use on herself, but felt too tired to attempt it. And, if she was honest with herself, some part of her *wanted* to feel done, dry and wrung-out.

How does that make any sense?

It had been three days since she'd seen Eli. And Christine had taken a few days off to help Rosie. Lacey had spent most of those days alone. During which, she'd figured out that Eli asking her to come up to the Mineral Spring must have been a pretense. The production status was still in limbo, and she'd done nothing to assist with scouting. So if the idea was that she'd come up here so that Eli could help her understand the "how" of her healing ability, how come he'd gone missing in action?

And the smell of the sulfur springs was beginning to feel less earthy, and more noxious. Just plain noxious.

Noxious was in her head on Monday morning, as she walked Ambrose around the grounds. The air was still, and the smell of sulfur permeated everything. Ambrose had already made friends with nearly every staff member, but even he seemed less sociable than usual. He passed them all up, giving each a slight nod of the head but no further greeting. Lacey couldn't tell if the staff wasn't in a friendly mood, either, or if it was her own foul humor that colored everything.

Ambrose seemed to be on a mission. With little pausing to sniff, he dragged Lacey up the hill. He was better with the steep inclines than her. Maybe it was because his breed was born in the Alps. For Lacey, having lived her whole life in the flat land (except for sinkholes and potholes) of southern Louisiana, the hillside retreat posed a challenge.

Out of breath and out of sorts, Lacey wasn't paying attention to where Ambrose was leading her. By the time he finally stopped, the sulfur smell was so strong, her stomach was in her throat. And they were back at the hot tub furthest up the hill, the one where Eli had attempted his "training." She didn't remember the smell being that strong before.

"Why here, Bro? What has you all amped up for this spot?"

Things got even weirder when he started barking. Not his usual, single acknowledgment kind of bark, but a prolonged, stream-of-consciousness bark. Like a clarion call.

"Ambrose! Hush! You might lose all the friends you've made here with all that ruckus."

He stopped and tilted his head toward her, as if to say, "I've got my reasons. Go figure them out, dummy."

Ambrose went down to his haunches, then all the way down to the ground. He stretched his massive chin out on the pine-needled ground before him.

"Well, I guess you're done then, huh?"

He let out a high-pitched yawn.

What the hell is going on, here? What is it about this place?

Lacey made a few steps in each direction, not sure what she should do. Suddenly, she was overwhelmed with déjà vu. She had reached the place she saw when she was on Christine's massage table. A wooded area at the top of the ridge, near the hot tub.

When she motioned as if she was headed to the crest of the hill, like in her vision, Ambrose perked his head up and let out a low, "Woof."

"So I should go, eh?" she replied sarcastically.

He tilted his head the other way this time, and returned his head to the ground.

She stopped when she thought she heard something nearby. Voices, or a low murmur that sounded like voices. A seed of fear lodged in her throat, just above where her stomach had seemed to take permanent residence. She took a few more steps forward, hoping that the rise in the ground before her would keep her hidden from view.

That's when she realized it wasn't voices. It was a buzz inside her head.

She took a few more steps forward, so she could see over the rise. She didn't see anything except a ray of sunlight spotlighting a patch of earth, about ten yards away and down the hill.

Curiosity fought with her fear. She looked back to Ambrose, whose head was still resting on the ground. He raised his eyes up to her but didn't move.

"Okay, I guess I'm going it alone."

The buzzing in her head grew stronger the closer she came to the patch of earth. It couldn't be called a meadow, just a small clearing in between a few trees. Suddenly, she felt a presence nearby. More than one presence. She turned her head sharply, scouring a 360-degree view, but didn't see anyone. Not even a shadow.

"Don't get spooked," she said quietly. She wasn't sure who she was saying it to. It had little effect on herself. While she wanted to turn around and hightail it back over the rise, a stronger compulsion drove her forward.

Her legs felt weighted with lead on the last few steps to the sunlit patch. When she reached it, and stepped inside the circle it created on the ground, she could hear the peaceful hum of cicadas in the distance. It did nothing to lift her unease. She took a deep breath, but her muscles remained tense. She looked all around her again. Nothing seemed out of the ordinary, nothing that would explain why she felt so frightened.

Except . . . except all around her, outside the circle, the trees seemed to move. A slow slide, all in unison. Was it another earthquake?

But they weren't sliding-falling, they were sliding . . . dancing?

A sharp pain struck Lacey's temples. Completely lateral, as if the two grip ends of a vice were ratcheting down onto her skull. Instant nausea welled up, and her hands flew to her head. She was surprised to find nothing there—nothing external causing the pain. It felt that real.

She doubled over, hands still clutching her head, unable to propel herself out of this cursed place. The dancing trees vanished, and a flood of images began to swirl around her. She squeezed her eyes shut, but that only made the images clearer.

What the fuck is happening? She wanted to scream the words, but she couldn't form them. The vice had moved to her throat.

The flood of everything around her slowed, and channeled

into one rectangle at the center of her vision. It was like watching a video on your phone in the dark, with inky blackness all around you.

She watched a woman driving a truck. Suddenly, the frame expanded, so it was as if Lacey was in the passenger seat. The dials on the radio, the song that was playing, the cracked leather on the dash, the clothes the woman was wearing. It had to be at least sixty years in the past. She looked at the woman. It was obvious she didn't know Lacey was there, she didn't acknowledge her. Lacey studied the woman's features. She knew her. She knew her, because she had seen her picture at the Becnel's house in Golden Meadow.

It was Birdie. Lacey looked out to the road. A one-lane highway; a dark, moonless night. The truck's headlights the only thing penetrating the darkness. The stars were veiled by a thick swath of hazy clouds. Lacey knew what was about to happen. She remembered what Tonti had told her about how Birdie died. The pain in her temples intensified.

She wanted to scream at Birdie, "Stop the truck! Pull over!" But the words wouldn't form, and she knew Birdie couldn't hear her anyway. Lacey tried to calm herself, to tell herself that it was a dream, it wasn't really happening to her. But nothing would quell her rising panic.

Then Birdie began to sing. A quiet, low melody escaped her. Lacey's panic subsided as she listened. *Pay attention*—the words resonated in her mind. She studied Birdie's profile as she tried to identify the melody. Lacey caught it after just a few notes. It was one of her favorites, a song that had seen her through many a dark nights. "Amazing Grace." Lacey felt tears well in her eyes.

Lacey realized she may never get another chance to see Birdie this way. She wasn't sure in which way she was seeing her, but there she was, plain as day—or dark, moonless night—before her. Lit by the glow of the dashboard lights, Birdie was beautiful. High cheekbones, perfect skin, luminous eyes. But her beauty was more than outward appearance. Something about the expression she wore, the sound of the notes she sang, Lacey thought of the kind of beauty they say is "inside and out." Lacey ached in a way she had never felt before. She wished she could learn about her power from Birdie. She sensed she would certainly have been kinder than Eli, at least.

Birdie finished the refrain from "Amazing Grace." She turned her head slightly, keeping her eyes on the road, and smiled. Lacey would swear she was smiling at her.

Then everything went bright. A tremendous flash, a bone-crushing impact. Lacey felt it all happening to her for an instant, and then all pain was gone. The vice grip on her temples was replaced by a sense of water flowing around her head, as if she was swimming.

The frame shrunk back to phone size, she was back in the clearing, but something was happening at the site of Birdie's crash. Lacey strained to see. Birdie was slumped over the steering wheel, there was blood pouring from her head. *She must still be alive,* Lacey thought. It was almost reflexive now, her instinct to heal—if it was actually happening now, and not in some distant past she wasn't sure why she was witnessing—Lacey might have been able to save her. When blood still flowed, there was hope.

The image continued to shrink. There was someone at the window. A person dressed in white. A linen suit, a man's suit. The vision was tiny, but the sense of foreboding encompassed all. A man's hand reached out, placing it on the driver's side window. Birdie let out an ungodly scream. A death rattle followed. Primal fear lodged in Lacey's gut—she knew she was *not* witnessing an angel, or Death, visiting Birdie in her final moments. She knew the person at the window was human. Maybe not a normal human being, but a living, corporeal, mortal being all the same. And she knew who it was, too. It was someone she knew, who she had just met in the flesh recently. She knew it because this all matched the vision she had with Christine.

The man who visited Birdie in her dying moment was Gus Savin. He had been feeding on something in Lacey's vision. Now she knew what—who—he'd consumed. It hadn't been Birdie's flesh, or blood. It was something more intangible. Her soul? Or her power?

A cloud overhead obscured the sunbeam, the circle in the clearing disappeared, and everything around Lacey was cast in a late afternoon pall.

She didn't let herself hesitate this time. She sprinted out of the clearing, out of the woods, and back over the ridge to Ambrose.

25

Lacey spent the evening watching movies on her laptop, and longing desperately for days without horrifying visions, and car crashes, and a hilltop rife with "spooky action at a distance." Ambrose laid his head in her lap for most of *Beethoven*, but opted for his doggie bed when she started *Legally Blonde*.

She'd tried to reach Eli for two hours, calling consistently every fifteen minutes. The only worry she had when she'd still received no response after the eighth time, was that he'd scold her for her insistence. Figuring he'd be in touch in "Eli time," she just gave up.

There was no one else here that she felt comfortable with, not comfortable enough to talk about what she saw. And what she sensed. She didn't know how to get in touch with Christine, and didn't want to bother her and Rosie, anyway.

And there was an owl outside her window who was driving her insane. Ambrose slept heavily, to the point of snoring. Apparently, the constant hooting didn't bother him at all. She cranked up the movie volume to her headphones, and wished she wasn't in the wilderness anymore.

She could go back to her rental in San Luis Obispo, but she

knew that would do nothing to quell her alienation. What she really wanted was to be home, and to have something to do, and have someplace familiar to feel alone and confused in.

Lacey fell asleep a few minutes before Elle Woods made her brilliant defense of Brooke Taylor Windham.

*

A loud hammering at the door to her cottage woke her. She checked the time—*what the hell?* It was 5:30 a.m. She made sure she still had clothes on—she did—and rushed to the door. Ambrose stood beside her.

It was Eli, looking more serene than his incessant knocking would indicate. The smooth profile of his skull was backlit by the sun, just beginning to peek above the horizon.

"Eli, what is it?" the words came out groggy, but she was terrified that something else horrible had happened.

"They've cast a new lead. Everybody's on their way here, we'll be filming here at the resort, call time in two hours."

"Wait, what? I haven't heard anything from Kandace. What am I supposed to do?"

"Kandace is off the picture. You're still the production accountant. I'll need your help today."

What the hell? "Okay. Give me a half hour?"

"Can't," he said. "May I come in?"

"Uh, sure?"

He stepped over the threshold and grabbed Ambrose's lead, which was hanging just inside the door. He called the dog over, hooked up his leash, and said, "I'll take care of him. Be ready to go when we get back. Wear long sleeves, long pants, and closed-toed shoes."

Lacey couldn't make sense of anything. Why had Eli just shown up with this news, instead of calling or texting? What had happened to Kandace? How long had the new lead been cast?

She scrambled to wash her face, brush her teeth, and find a long-sleeved shirt. She really wanted coffee. And she really wanted to know about Kandace. What does *off the picture* mean? Did she choose to leave? Or was she fired? That seemed the more likely scenario.

She found herself feeling something unexpected: sympathy for Kandace. Yes, she was a pain in the ass, but she was just beginning to figure out how to deal with her. And her intentions always seemed good. It was just her execution that left something to be desired.

And she was beyond angry with Eli. Why had he ignored all her calls? Why did he just show up without any warning? And why was he always so damn cryptic about *everything*?

Lacey was grateful for the immediacy of all these questions and feelings. It pushed the vision in the clearing further back in her head. And now, at least, she'd have something to do.

She was ready to go when Eli and Ambrose returned. She reached out for Eli's forearm, stopping him when he let Ambrose back in the cabin.

"Eli, did you not see any of my calls?"

"I'm sorry, Lacey. I was not in a place where I could have really listened to you."

"You could have texted, 'sorry, can't talk,' or something like that."

"I'm sorry, you're right, I should have done that."

How am I supposed to answer that?

He removed her hand from his forearm. "We'll be able to talk later. But now, we must go."

She followed Eli to the parking lot.

"I will need you to drive into town, to pick up a piece of equipment from the studio."

"How will I know what you need?" she asked, still frustrated. "Where is it? And why am I even agreeing to do this?"

Eli stopped. "Lacey. I will apologize again. I'm sorry I'm not able to help you right now. But I need your help, with a very simple task. That needs to be performed in a short window of time. Can you do this?"

Lacey huffed. He sounded sincere. Even a little sad. "Fine. Where is it?" she repeated.

"It's in the edit bay. It's marked. You'll know."

"Okay."

"Be back here by seven o'clock."

"Fine. But, Eli? I *really* need to speak with you later. I'm serious."

Eli looked at her a moment and gave her sharp nod of assent. "Later, after filming."

A short-lived trickle of satisfaction went through Lacey. She held it together until she was seated in the driver seat of her Accord, and Eli was out of sight. She banged her fists repeatedly on the steering wheel and let out an exasperated cry. She was still furious but she was also finally validated. He'd help her sort out all these things later.

Nine hours of running around is a good cure for frustration and restlessness. By the time Lacey had made it back to the resort (by 6:53 a.m.—she was very proud of herself for that), the parking lot was full with trucks and crewmembers running about. Some she recognized, but many were new faces.

I'm going to need to get these people's names eventually. Or else payroll's gonna be a bitch.

At the studio, she had taken a moment to peek into Kandace's office. It appeared untouched. Coffee mug with straw sat near the monitor, and a faint syrupy smell led Lacey to believe it must still contain some Diet Dr. Pepper.

They didn't even let her get her stuff?

Her sympathy for Kandace grew.

The equipment in the edit bay was indeed marked—with a tag looped through the handle of the canvas bag that read "Lacy." Lacey wondered if it was Eli who didn't know how to spell her name. The thought made her want to punch him.

But throughout the course of the day, she managed to talk herself off the ledge. It had to be someone at the soundstage who marked the bag. It was a very minor thing, but it still made her feel better. And Eli must not have responded last night because he was busy getting everything ready for today.

But how hard could it have been to just send a quick text?

She was curious about the new lead. She wondered if he'd have one-tenth the charisma of Kevin Horner. And then felt immediately guilty about thinking of his wattage and star power. He was a human being, with parents, and a sister, and other people who loved him, and he was gone.

Lacey caught her first glimpse of the new actor when she emerged from the brush, power cable in hand. Eli had told her to place some cable to run something—he had told her what it was, but she didn't retain it. She had been careful about placing it far enough out of the way, and marking it so that no one would trip on it. After twenty minutes of this effort, she received a text from Eli telling her that they'd chosen a different location on the other side of the road. And to pull up the cable.

I don't have the time to even be frustrated by this.

She brushed her hands on her jeans and saw Marco talking to someone she could only assume was the new lead. He was taller and leaner than Kevin Horner. Prettier, too—that was the word that first came to Lacey's head. Later, she'd learn his name was Jason Booker.

She wiped her hands against each other, looped one arm through the cable, and kept a respectful distance from Marco and Jason as she headed to the new site. She couldn't hear anything they said, but Jason's eyes were like a young buck's, caught in oncoming headlights.

Eli and a new guy—Lacey assumed he was the new A.D.—had everything ready to go across the road. Lacey wondered if Eli had known this all along, and had sent her on a fool's errand. She narrowed her eyes and pursed her lips as she approached Eli.

"Lacey, this is Hunter," he said. Hunter responded by nodding his head slightly in Lacey's direction and shouting "Wilson! Don't fuck this up!" to someone Lacey couldn't see.

She narrowed her eyes further at Eli. He something-like-a-smiled at her.

Soon, everyone was in place for the scene. It felt like only seconds had passed. Lacey stood silent and motionless, and watched Jason Booker. It wasn't until she heard him say, "I care about Sinead, and that's the heart of the matter," that she realized they were doing an exact re-shoot of the scene she'd witnessed on the soundstage just three weeks earlier.

It made Lacey snap out of the work-induced fog she'd

gotten herself into. She wondered why they weren't shooting it on the soundstage, like the first time. She guessed maybe they were hoping the gorgeous backdrop might distract the viewer from Jason Booker's terrible acting. There was no getting around it, and she didn't feel the tiniest bit of guilt for thinking it. His stage presence was stiff, his delivery was robotic. He was really terrible. Maybe the perception was worse because she had the memory of Kevin Horner to compare it to. There would be no breaking out into Don Henley singing. At least, she sure hoped not.

And her more pressing, personal concerns bubbled up. Standing silent, watching the awful scene unfold, she had an impulse to scream, shout out, feign fainting—anything to stop the travesty of a movie production she was watching unfold. Because what she really wanted to do was talk to Eli, and tell him about what she saw on the ridgeline, and find out what he thought of it.

Lacey was spared the trouble of causing a scene.

The first thing she noticed was Jason Booker freezing and going silent. The next thing she saw was Hunter throwing a script to the ground. Lacey figured Jason had forgotten his line. But when everyone turned around to face Lacey, she panicked. Until she realized they weren't looking at her. She turned slowly, and saw a man in a suit and a woman in a wheelchair.

Allison.

Arms crossed, neck brace, one leg in a cast. With sunglasses and perfectly-styled hair. Lacey felt like she was watching a scene in a movie. She went a little dizzy when she remembered she was actually *on* a movie set.

Someone who wasn't Hunter yelled, "Cut!"

Hunter and Eli marched over, and Eli leaned over and

whispered in Lacey's ear as he passed. "Come with me, but wait outside."

Huh?

Lacey stood at an awkward arm's length as Hunter started yelling obscenities at the man who accompanied Allison. He stood silent in his dark suit, yellow tie, and sunglasses. He made Lacey think of Secret Service detail. If he would have allowed himself any sort of expression at all, he might have been amused by Hunter's tirade.

When Hunter stopped to breathe, Eli said in a low but powerful voice, "Let's step out of this heat. We can talk in the trailer."

It's really not that hot, Lacey thought. Secret Service Man pushed Allison toward the Airstream, and Hunter huffed over in that direction. Eli's floating eye gave Lacey an indication that she should follow.

Lacey thought Allison might be staring at her, but it was hard to tell with the sunglasses. The permanent scowl on her face made Lacey step back a few paces, to get out of her line of sight.

There were three steps up to the Airstream trailer; Lacey assumed it was Marco's. A point validated when the door opened and he appeared. Lacey wondered how Allison would make it inside. Suit man wheeled her up to the steps and offered his arm. Allison swatted it away and griped, "No! I want *her* help." She aimed her index finger behind her. Lacey thought the bandage around Allison's head might hide an extra set of eyes, because her finger pointed squarely at her.

Eli nodded at Lacey.

Why me?

She reluctantly approached and offered an arm without

looking Allison in the face. Wiry fingers clamped onto Lacey's sleeve. She winced reflexively.

"I'm still very weak," Allison said. It was more of a command than an apology.

Lacey felt heat radiating from her arm where Allison held it. They were connected no more than a minute as they ascended the steps together, but Lacey was drenched by the time she handed Allison off to Marco. He had another wheelchair waiting, which struck Lacey as exceedingly odd.

This day just keeps getting weirder.

Eli offered her a towel he must have produced from one of his many pockets. As he walked up the steps to join the others, he whispered, "Wait out here. Allison and I will be out shortly. You will join us."

Lacey stared at him and wiped her brow with the towel.

And stupid me, thinking it wasn't hot.

She tried to remember how to cool herself off. She closed her eyes and thought of snow. But then heard muffled shouts from the trailer. She opened her eyes and felt the tiniest bit cooler.

Maybe I'm getting the hang of this.

She held the towel in her hand and shuffled from foot to foot, waiting outside the Airstream. She tried to find a spot where she wouldn't be seen. She felt weird about loitering around outside some meeting. A meeting about what? There was no telling. What on earth was Allison doing here? And was Secret Service her lawyer? Or her private security guard?

She felt weird, physically, too. She knew some of her power had been spent on Allison, she knew enough now to be able to tell the signature—breaking out into a sweat like that was a dead giveaway. But she felt very spent, more so than the short amount of time should indicate. And why did Allison *insist* upon her help?

I feel weird. And I want to go home.

She thought of her home on Florida Boulevard. Tonti might be on the porch right now, drinking a fleur-tini, antagonizing her neighbor, Mr. Max. She wanted to be there. For the first time in a very long time, she was excited about what the future could hold for her in New Orleans.

The city certainly has a need for emergency medical services. She was ready to get on with it.

She heard the door to the Airstream open. Eli beckoned her over. Lacey positioned the original wheelchair to receive Allison before going to fetch her.

I'm going to make a great paramedic.

Lacey felt close to faltering on the way back down with Allison. *Okay, this isn't good.* Eli held on to Allison's other side, and he took over and helped set Allison down.

Lacey took a deep breath. Eli looked over to her, his expression unusually solicitous. She nodded at him, *I'm fine.* He started wheeling Allison, and Lacey followed.

Weirder and weirder.

"I miss him," Eli said. Lacey wasn't sure whether he said it to her or Allison. She knew he was talking about Kevin. She waited for Allison to respond.

Allison tilted her head. Almost as if she recognized a cue, she lifted her sunglasses just enough to dab at her eyes. "I do, too."

Lacey didn't know what to think. Nothing about her gesture seemed sincere, but her words sounded true.

Lacey hurried to keep pace. Eli was rapidly wheeling Allison away. She had no idea where. They crossed a bridge that forded a shallow ravine. No water ran underneath.

Lacey saw soon enough that they were headed back to the main resort. Eli wheeled Allison up the steep incline to the doors of the Healing Institute with no apparent effort. Lacey thought of trying to wheel back down, how easy it would be to lose control.

She tried to stop thinking of that.

Eli left Allison dead center of the Healing Institute's studio space. Lacey followed and stood behind the chair, trying to mouth to Eli behind Allison's back. Her mouth formed the words *What do you need me to do?*, her eyes raised in a question mark.

"Lacey, come stand by me," he said out loud. "We both need to look Allison in the eyes."

Lacey was surprised at how quickly Allison removed her sunglasses. She glared at the two of them, but mostly at Eli. A defiant and haughty stare.

What the heck is this about?

"I know what caused Kevin's accident," Eli said.

Oh, shit. He does? Lacey strained to keep her face forward and emotionless.

"I know it wasn't alcohol or drug impairment, I know it was not swerving to avoid another driver, I know it was not an earthquake. I know it was you," he said pointedly to Allison.

Lacey felt her stomach quiver. So her sense of doubt *was* right.

"That's ridiculous," she said. She fidgeted in her wheelchair.

Lacey's distrust grew.

"You were under his skin from the moment he met you. You saw that, you exploited that. You injected another needle and twisted it at a most inopportune moment, and the consequences nearly claimed you, too."

Lacey tried to make sense of Eli's words. As usual, he only

confused her further. But even so, whatever he was saying seemed to confirm her nagging suspicion of Allison.

Allison's eyes narrowed, but her grimace softened. It was as if an invisible hand pulled a mask over her face. The defiance almost covered up by the engaging warmth Lacey remembered, from the first time she saw Allison in action.

"How could I have caused the accident?" Allison said, hurt apparent in her voice. "I didn't grab the wheel, I didn't even *touch* him! All I was doing was talking."

"You were manipulating him."

"How is talking manipulating?" she said, a genuine confusion registering in her voice.

"You know very well how talking is manipulating. You've had a gift for it your whole life. And you've used it to further your own lot, with no thought of the impact to others."

What was Eli talking about? What did he know about Allison's past? Dumb question. He's probably been in her head.

"What do you want, Eli? You can't prove I did anything wrong. *Can he, Lacey?*"

The question fell hard on Lacey. Allison's voice was putting her at war with herself. She had an impulsive desire to say anything, even if it was a lie, to prove Allison innocent. But to her core, Lacey knew that was wrong. She managed to whisper a strangled, "Stop it," and felt her doubt turn to certainty.

There *was* something in Allison's voice. Something powerful. And she'd used it to kill Kevin and get his money. Anger flared up hot and heavy. To use and abuse such a bright life that way—it was so deeply wrong.

"*Lacey, answer—*"

"No." Eli was silent for several moments. It had the intended effect on Allison. "Leave her be. No, I cannot prove it."

"Well, then, what?" Allison squirmed in the chair.

"You disappear," he finally answered. "You release your ridiculous appeal for Kevin's estate. You withdraw this fallacious suit against the production."

She's suing the production?

"Or what?" Allison replied. She folded her arms and the grimace returned.

Eli took a deep breath. It looked like he was preparing to say something, give her the full threat. *This is what'll happen, Allison,* her name said like a sneer, Lacey imagined.

But then he closed his eyes. It seemed it was only for an instant. But in that instant, Allison's expression utterly altered. The grimace morphed into an open-mouthed, silent scream. Her eyes, still without the sunglasses, registered something Lacey had never seen before. If she was forced to name it, it would be terror. But the word seemed inadequate.

Whatever it was, it was spreading. Just seeing Allison's face struck Lacey's heart, and an abject fear took root. She planted her feet and tried to calm herself. *Whatever this is, it's not aimed at me.*

In that moment, Lacey realized it was Eli doing something to Allison. That only made her fear grow.

Allison's face relaxed into a vacant stare. She looked unconscious with open eyes.

Lacey turned to Eli, too frightened to speak. *What did you do?*

Eli sighed. "Please bring her outside. The lawyer will meet you there."

Lacey finally found her voice. "Eli, I can't hand her off like this!"

"She'll recover quickly." He turned and walked toward the room she and Christine had occupied just last week.

The fear lodged in Lacey's heart started to grow warm. She wheeled Allison to the door, and made sure Eli was nowhere in sight.

Lacey thought about paramedics. Weren't they obliged to offer assistance to whoever needed it? Regardless of what crimes they may or may not have committed?

Regardless of her black heart, I can't, in good conscience, leave her like this. Dammit.

She placed herself between Allison and the door, crouched down, and gently grabbed Allison's forearms. She went immediately woozy, but remembered she had a very specific intent. *This is triage. Just get her past this shock. That's all.*

Lacey released her. Allison blinked. Lacey looked long enough to see a more normal expression, then scurried behind the chair. Through the glass, Lacey could see the lawyer ascending the hill.

She wheeled Allison through the door as the Secret Service lawyer guy opened it. Wordlessly, he grabbed the handles of the chair, and pivoted so that they both would descend the hill with their backs to the decline.

Allison aimed her gaze at Lacey. She couldn't see her eyes, but her lips thinned and one side of her perfect teeth showed. It was an evil smile that turned Lacey's blood to ice.

Oh God. What did I just do?

26

Lacey still hadn't talked to Eli about her ridgeline vision. She was too freaked out by what had happened with Allison at the Healing Institute. What had Eli done to her? And was Lacey in danger of it happening to herself?

As soon as she had handed off Allison to her lawyer, she went searching for Eli. She found him counting yoga mats.

"Eli . . . what just happened? And what did you *do* to her?"

"I didn't do anything to her," he said, his back to her.

Lacey walked so that she could see his profile. There was a look in his eyes she'd never seen before. His hand shook as he fingered through the mats, his lips moving in a silent vocalization. She couldn't believe Eli could be fretful. That Eli could be vulnerable.

"Eli, I've never seen anyone look that frightened. And I've seen people die."

He stopped counting. "Don't forget how new all this is to you. How do you know? Were you really looking?" He moved on from the mats to a basket full of foam blocks.

"Eli . . . " Lacey didn't feel like she was getting anywhere. "*I'm* frightened."

He set down the basket and turned his head to her. His floating eye went clear across the room. "Of what?"

Lacey threw her hands up. "I'm seeing things I don't understand, things that aren't happening, and then the stuff that *is* happening makes no sense! I can heal people, but only certain people, in a certain way, and my body heats up like a soldering iron when I do it. So, I don't know, pick something."

"No." He pivoted his body to face her. "Your ability is not what's frightening you. The visions, maybe. But you left something out. The thing that's frightening you most."

"Okay, fine. It's you! You're scaring the hell out of me!" At that very instant, he was. "You practically turned Allison into a vegetable with, what was it, some Jedi mind trick? How can you say you didn't do anything to her?"

And what's stopping you from doing the same thing to me?

Eli became still. "Do you feel I've betrayed a trust?" His voice was so quiet, Lacey strained to hear.

"I'm not sure, Eli." She'd lowered her voice, too. "I want to believe you would never do that to me. Or to anyone who didn't have evil intentions. But I don't know enough about how this all works. I'm too vulnerable."

Eli sighed. "Let me bring this back to the recent occurrence. To my interaction with Allison. I will try to explain it, and will let you judge for yourself."

He took a step toward Lacey, but maintained a respectful distance.

"Allison's mind space is a very dark place. There are many different places her thoughts, and actions, can lead her to. There was a suggestion of one of those conclusions."

"There was a suggestion?" Lacey tried to process his words. "You mean, you planted a vision in her head?"

"That's not entirely accurate, but if it helps you reach an understanding, then, yes."

Lacey stood silent. That kind of power was dangerous. And its effect was the opposite of what Lacey wanted to use her power for. Was Eli really her Superfriend, after all?

But then again, Allison had a dangerous power. That she did not use for good.

Did that make her a Superfoe? And does that justify what Eli did?

"I need to go," she said quietly.

She didn't know where. She just knew she needed to.

Allison's intrusion had shut down all activity for the day. Lacey received a text from Eli: *Work's over today. Tomorrow likely dark too. Wait until you hear from me.*

Great.

While not really great, it spared her the awkwardness of working so closely with Eli when her trust level had dipped so low. But about the last thing she needed, or wanted, was to be idle.

At least she had something to do. Her brother's gig—and Trevor's—was in Santa Barbara tonight. Two of the guys from the crew were planning to go, so she could ride down with them. She didn't want to be alone. And it would give her a good excuse to avoid going home with Trevor. She still felt conflicted over their moody hike at the Mineral Springs. Her previous infatuation with Trevor had been replaced with confusion. She wondered if that was a normal feeling at the end of an affair.

None of this is as much fun as I thought it was gonna be.

Scott and Hans talked about video games the whole car ride down to Santa Barbara. Lacey tried to interject some movie knowledge—she'd seen her share of movies based on video games—but neither of them bit.

How can they both work on movies and not know movies?

They arrived early enough that Lacey felt comfortable seeking out her brother. She knew better than to engage him too close to set time.

Scott and Hans treated Lacey with a little more deference when she told them she was going to pop backstage for a few minutes.

"You know the band?" Scott asked. If California had an accent, Scott had it.

"Yep."

"Dude, you should've mentioned it!" Scott chimed in. "Who do you know?"

"Um. All of them?" Once she'd had enough of playing coy, she answered, "Jimmy Campo is my brother."

They both tried an angle to get backstage. Lacey told them she'd need to check first.

She strode confidently away. She intended to disappear long enough so that she wouldn't have to hassle with getting them backstage.

She poked her head around a corridor and saw Dave Guidry talking to venue security. She was relieved. Her brother's best friend from childhood, she'd known Guidry for as long as she could remember.

"Lacey," he said with a slight tilt of his head. He nodded at the security guard, giving Lacey tacit approval.

Dave Guidry had never been an effusive type.

"Hey, Guidry. Is Jimmy back there?"

He nodded.

"Okay, then. See you later. Good luck."

Lacey prayed she would only find her brother, and she felt tremendously guilty for that.

You're an adult, for God's sake. People have flings all the time, and flings end. Handle yourself.

Her prayers were answered when she found her brother, bent over his guitar, looking like he was performing surgery. He pushed his reading glasses up to his forehead and said, "Budgie! You came to see me!"

She gave her brother a hug, laughing. There was just something funny about the reading glasses, his long hair, and his lanky 6'2" frame.

"Is Monica here? I'd rather hang out with her than the Jabronies I came with."

"Who talks like that?" he said. "And I knew this would happen. As soon as I introduced you to Monica, it would be all about her, and you'd have no more love for your brother."

"Exactly. I've been looking to ditch you like a bad penny."

Jimmy returned his glasses to his face and resumed work on his guitar. "Nah, she has a work thing tonight, she couldn't make it."

"Pity."

Lacey couldn't help herself. She tried to disguise it, but her head kept pivoting, looking around for signs of Trevor.

"Watch you don't get whiplash there, Budge." He looked up at her and smiled.

Lacey huffed. "This is your fault, you know. If you and Monica hadn't left me with him."

"Last I checked, you were a grown ass adult. With

supernatural powers, even. How could I suggest She-Hulk do anything she didn't want to do?"

"Stop. And I can't even talk to you about him, because he's your bandmate and I don't want to screw up your mojo."

Jimmy laughed. "This is squarely your fault, anyway. How long have I been telling you to lighten up and just have fun? You probably quit having fun as soon as you started thinking too seriously about it."

"Ugh. I don't want to talk about this with you. There's other, bigger shit going on."

"Did you have another gamma ray exposure?"

Lacey laughed. *Thank God my brother can make me laugh about this stuff. He's probably the only person who can.*

"No. Maybe. Sorta. Eli—Professor X—has been trying to show me some stuff, and it's got me freaked out. And some other stuff, stuff back home, has me freaked out, too."

Jimmy stopped messing with his guitar and gave his full attention to Lacey.

"Geesh, I'm sorry, you're about to go on and I'm dumping on you."

"I have a few minutes. Is there stuff back home I need to worry about?"

"No, no, nothing like that." Lacey began to pace. "There's stuff that happened in the past—well, may or may not have happened in the past—and it might have something to do with . . . my gamma exposure."

Jimmy leaned back in his chair and laid his guitar across his lap. "You're not making any sense, Budge."

"I'm sorry." She stopped pacing. "I guess I'm not really ready to talk about any of it. Like you said, I'm a grown ass adult. I'll figure it out."

Jimmy bent over his guitar again. "Do I need to come bust up on Professor X?"

"God, no. That's about the last thing I need, for you to go up against Eli. He's just . . . he's just a really weird guy. And I'm learning it would be a terrible thing to be on his bad side."

"Sounds like treacherous waters. Can you do long-distance-learning with him?"

"Yeah. Maybe. I'll figure it out."

"You keep saying that."

As if on cue, she heard Trevor's voice, emerging from a back room. He was laughing and talking to someone.

Lacey couldn't help herself from going rigid when she saw him. The someone he was talking to was tiny, doll-like, with overdone makeup. The look on her face was vacant like a doll's, too. Her hand was on his arm, and she was leaning so far into him, she looked like she might topple over if he wasn't there.

Get a grip, Lacey. People flirt all the time.

She looked his way and gave him what she thought was a coy smile. And then turned back to her brother.

"What was I saying?"

"That you'll figure it out." Jimmy couldn't stop himself from laughing.

Trevor and Doll-Woman had gone their separate ways. He approached Jimmy and Lacey. She tried to relax her posture, to little avail.

"Figure what out, love?"

"Oh, just work stuff."

"Hmmm." He moved right past her comment. He bounced on his heels, like Tigger. "Are you ready to hear *our* work? We're debuting a new one tonight. It's nothing short of inspired. Right, James?"

This is a different Trevor. A getting-psyched-to-perform Trevor. I'm not so sure I like this Trevor. Too hyper.

"This isn't work, Seamus. This is a calling. You might like the name of our new song, Lace," Jimmy said.

Lacey smirked. She loved most of the music her brother made. But the song titles, album titles, even his band names were questionable, at best. "Please, do tell."

"'Starving Hysterical Naked,'" he answered.

"Inspired by someone you know?" *Is he writing about my 'gamma ray exposure'?*

"Relax, Budge, it's from a poem."

"By Allen Ginsberg," a voice said from the direction of the stage. Dave Guidry.

"It's time," he called out. "Get your asses up here."

Jimmy picked up Lacey in a bear hug. "Stick around, Budge. You can invite the Jabronies to hang out after."

"Careful, Chump! Don't pull something before I get a chance to hear 'Hysterical Useless Naked.'"

He set Lacey down. "That's Radiohead. We're LeViticum."

Trevor gave her a quick peck on the cheek, like a child might offer his grandmother.

"Later, love."

Try as she might, the best she could offer was a forced smile.

Lacey, Scott, and Hans didn't stay long after the show. There was a quick meet-and-greet. Scott and Hans were starstruck—quiet, respectful, but not a whole lot of fun. That was likely one of the reasons everyone dispersed after less than half an hour.

She was peeved at Jimmy for disappearing, but it wasn't so unusual for him. She wasn't sure what she felt about Trevor. After all, he had asked her to come. Hadn't he? So why did she feel like the jilted fool?

On the drive back, she received a text from Jimmy.

Sorry about the Houdini, Budge.

Yeah Chump, what gives?

Story for another time.

Lacey sighed. *Whatever*, she thought to herself, opting to not respond to her brother's text.

In her head, Trevor was hooking up with Doll-Woman. And Jimmy was sparing her having to be witness to any of it. Or maybe they just wanted to get high and watch movies. Or play video games. (She suspected that's what Scott and Hans had on their agenda as soon as they arrived back in SLO).

Even if it was something legitimately mundane, she was pissed at Trevor. Or more precisely, pissed at herself for having expectations. And she usually loved getting to see her brother perform, and now Trevor had ruined that, too.

Thinking back on their new song, she hadn't been that impressed. She wasn't sure whether she should blame the song or her state of mind for that, though.

27

Lacey was back in the rental in SLO. After a few intensely busy days up at Sycamore Mineral Springs, Eli told her to pack up her stuff (and Ambrose) and get ready to work out of the studio again. She was immensely grateful for the flurry of activity on the production, because it had kept her mind occupied.

And Eli had been a different person these past few days. Almost warm, even. Lacey hadn't worked up the nerve to ask him about anything of a supernatural nature. Or on whether his banishment was enough of a price for Allison. What would stop her from using her Superfoe powers again?

On the one hand, there hadn't been time to ask about any of the supernatural things. On the other hand, Lacey had "compartmentalized" them. She still felt a chill down her spine when she remembered the Birdie vision, but it had taken on a dream-like quality. After learning what Allison did, and what Eli did to her, Lacey wasn't sure how to talk to him about what now felt like a bad dream. And she hadn't had the opportunity, with Eli acting like any other boss working on a deadline. Maybe just a little less harried than normal people might be.

And Kandace had returned! Lacey couldn't believe she was actually excited about that, but she was. Hunter, who was prone to belittling outbursts, was about one thousand times worse than Kandace had ever been. Though Lacey wasn't sure what Kandace was supposed to be doing. She was still on the payroll as A.D.; Hunter, who was still around, was listed as a producer. Kandace seemed to dislike Hunter as much as Lacey (and the rest of the crew) did. Somehow, having someone to unite against made her feel closer to Kandace.

All the turmoil on the set—for the entire production—made Lacey long for it to all end. And the end would come soon, if the production schedule was to be believed. Lacey was glad to return to San Luis Obispo and the rental. And the soundstage. As beautiful as Sycamore Mineral Springs was, too much had happened there. Too much stuff that wasn't good. Between herself and Trevor. Between herself and Eli. And between herself and . . . herself. The Birdie vision on the ridgeline was a silent constant, just below her surface. It didn't help that every time she turned her head in that particular direction, it was there, defining the western horizon.

She was ready for a pause. Where the only things that would happen would be mundane stuff.

And she did get a mundane pause that lasted precisely thirty-six hours.

She was at her desk at the soundstage, reassembled to an almost exact replica to what it had been at the start of the production. Looking over the schedule, there were only two more shoots. She had been calculating when was the soonest she and Ambrose might be home.

She had been online, looking into admissions into Delgado's EMT training program. The community college was only blocks from her house on Florida Boulevard. She would be able to walk to classes.

She was wondering how much class work there would be, before she could get out to practical training, when her phone lit up. It was Angele calling, not texting—that was unusual.

She picked it up, a little worried about what Kandace or Hunter might say about her taking a personal call.

"Hey. What's up?" Lacey answered.

"Yeah. I wanted to let you know that my dad's funeral is scheduled for this Friday. You don't have to come if you can't make it. But I figured you'd want to know."

"Jesus, what? Did you say your dad's *funeral*?" Lacey inhaled sharply. "Where are you right now?"

How long has it been since we last talked?

"I'm in New Orleans," Angele answered.

Lacey realized she hadn't talked to Angele since Kevin's funeral. There had been a few sporadic, "check-in" texts between them. The last she'd heard from Angele, her Dad was doing okay, and she had expected to return to California in a few days' time. How long ago had that been?

"What happened? Are you okay? How's your mom?"

"I don't have time to give you all the details. I'm okay; Mom's really sad. I've been having to take the lead on all the arrangements."

"Okay. Is there anything I can do?" Lacey wanted to ask why the hell she waited to call until the funeral was already arranged. But now wasn't the time for that question.

"No. But let me know if you're able to make it into town."

"Yes. I can." Lacey quickly realized she would have to ask

several people first. "I will try. I will let you know. Are you sure I can't do anything for you?"

"No. Thanks. I have to go."

Angele ended the call before Lacey had a chance to say anything else.

Lacey stared at her computer screen, stunned. She knew Angele's dad had surgery. Complications can happen after surgery. She felt a tremendous burden of guilt for not knowing about whatever had happened. Maybe it had all happened so quickly that Angele didn't have a chance to reach out.

Yet, Lacey hadn't even thought to reach out to Angele about any of the stuff that had transpired at Sycamore Mineral Springs.

Why was that?

On the surface, Lacey had told herself that she didn't want to bother Angele while she was dealing with family matters.

But Angele had been the first person she went to after Fox died. She was the first person she told about her newfound "mutant power" just a few short months ago. But that was the thing, if she was honest, that had opened a rift between them it seemed they were unable to breach.

Lacey had been prepared to quit the production in order to return home. She had said she wanted to be there for the funeral, but she knew she had other reasons, too. She kept those to herself.

She didn't have to quit. She would only miss two days, and she had two days to prepare for them. She would fly home to New Orleans late Thursday, and return late Sunday. Sunday was a scheduled non-work day.

Eli would look after Ambrose while she was gone. She'd had to ask him via text, because he'd been off site. On Wednesday, he was supposed to be at the studio, and Lacey steeled herself to talk to him. About more than just watching her dog. But finding a quiet moment was a challenge. He spent most of his time in the edit bays, always surrounded by a bevy of crewmembers. Around lunchtime, when a line began to form at the craft table, she thought she might be able to find him alone

She never got the chance.

When she turned in the direction of the edit bays, she saw Kandace making a beeline toward her, mug in hand.

"I need to replenish," she said, holding up the apparently empty mug. "Come with me?"

So now we're best friends?

"Sure," Lacey said, trying to hide her disappointment. She might need Kandace to cover for her while she was out, so it was not only out of the goodness of her heart that she accompanied her to the vending machines.

They were tucked away in one of the back corridors of the cavernous studio. Lacey never liked going there alone. It was too secluded. She suspected Kandace felt the same way.

"How's your friend Angele doing?"

Lacey had a well-rehearsed lie for the people on the set. While she was certain she would never see any of these people again, the nature of Angele's business meant she could be working with any of them for weeks, possibly months at a time.

"Oh, she's managing. I think she's relieved her father isn't suffering anymore."

The truth of the matter is that Lacey still hadn't talked to Angele, so she hadn't the slightest notion how she was doing.

"I'm not ready to lose a parent," Kandace said. "I don't

know what I'd do. I nearly lost it when Roger wound up in the hospital with appendicitis."

That's interesting. "Oh . . . ?" Lacey said.

"That's why I was out," she continued. "I freaked out, thought he was dying, and tried to take some time off, but that's just when they got Jason Booker to finish the shoot. So that's why Hunter came on."

So Roger is real. With a real appendix. Huh.

"So, you and Roger are good?" Lacey asked. "Did anything happen with . . . ?"

Kandace flushed red at the reference to "the other guy." "No, that was nothing. I found out he was . . . he wasn't available. And I don't even want to think about not being there for Roger when he needed me."

Yep, the other guy was married. In this instance, I hate knowing I was right.

"You know, Hunter wanted to fire you," Kandace said, and looked pointedly at Lacey.

It was Lacey's turn to flush red. But her reaction was from anger, not embarrassment. *I'm remembering why I don't like you, Kandy.*

"He wanted to fire me? Did I do something wrong?"

"No, no. Not that." She turned all her attention to the vending machine. Lacey swore she was doing it for the effect.

Lacey pursed her lips. *I wish he had fired me.*

"No, just for taking the two days off. Since we're so near the end, he wanted to try to trim the payroll.

"It was Eli who talked him out of it."

"Oh. I guess I should thank Eli," Lacey said. *Yeah, thanks a lot.*

"Yeah, probably. I'm still trying to think of an appropriate way to thank Mr. Savin. That's why I pulled you over here, I wanted to run a few ideas by you."

Lacey's heart went into her throat of the mention of Gus Savin. It was swiftly accompanied by a chill down her spine.

"I'm sorry, Kandace, I must have missed something. What does Gu . . . Mr. Savin have to do with this?"

"Uh, he's the executive producer of this whole shebang, right?"

"Yes, I know, but you need to thank him for that?"

"No, he's the one who got me back on this production. Like Eli did for you."

There were too many things swirling in Lacey's head to form a response.

"So I was thinking I should get a Southern-themed gift, just a little something to let him know I appreciate what he did for me. I figured you would have some ideas."

Lacey shuddered to think what Kandace might consider a "Southern-themed" gift to be. But she really didn't want to spend anymore thought or energy on thinking up a token of gratitude for Gus Savin. She needed to extract herself.

"I don't know, Kandace. He's an antiques dealer, I can't imagine there's anything he needs, or hasn't seen before. I think a nice, heartfelt note from you would be appreciated. I think that would speak to him the most."

Please don't ask for my help writing it.

"Really? Just a note?"

"Make sure it's on nice stationery," Lacey added. "Or a card."

"Okay. Well, that should be easy."

Kandace took a long swig from the Diet Dr. Pepper bottle, and poured the remainder into her coffee mug. She looked around.

"They've moved the recycling," she said.

"It's in the kitchen," Lacey answered.

Walking out of the corridor, Lacey broke off to head toward the edit bay. She poked her head in to find Eli seated, with three guys flanking him, captivated by whatever he was doing on the screen before him.

She sighed. "I'm ready to go home," she said under her breath. She went back to her desk.

Near the end of the day, Lacey was at her workstation, calculating when she'd be able to cut the payroll, when Hans appeared. His eyebrows were raised, which Lacey read as . . . concern?

We'll go with concerned.

"Are you busy?"

Hans had never sought Lacey out at the studio, not since he spotted her when he was up in the scaffolding.

"Uh, no. Not really. What's up?"

"Something's happened with Hunter. Says he's not feeling well. Figured since you helped me out that one time, maybe you could do something."

Lacey really didn't want to spend her energy on Hunter. Maybe Angele was right, that she should be choosier about who she helps.

And she tried not to think about why Hans might be asking her. Maybe he was just really impressed by the quality of her bandaging when she took care of his cut.

"Uh, not sure what I'll be able to do, but if you want me to come . . . maybe he just needs to go home and rest?"

"You can tell him that if you want."

Lacey didn't want to tell Hunter anything at all, for fear of being on the receiving end of one of his tirades.

What the hell, this job's almost over. And I'll have to get used to angry people, if I ever want to work as an EMT.

She followed Hans to the edit bay. Three editors sat in front of three different screens. None of them played any sound. Hunter sat in a chair against the wall, hand over his eyes, the back of his head resting against the wall.

"He's all yours," Hans said in a low voice. He turned sharply on his heel and left the room.

What the hell?

"Moondoggie says you know about migraines," Hunter said to her, one eye peeking through his hand.

Lacey assumed he meant Hans. "Uh, you have a migraine?" was all she could think to answer.

"I'm sitting in the closest dark, quiet place I could find, and I'm afraid if I move I'll throw up. What do you think?"

His voice showed the obvious traces of pain, but he still sounded like a jerk.

"Do you want a cold compress?"

"That's your brilliant cure?"

Lacey drew a deep breath. "It usually helps me. I'll be back shortly."

She was tempted to just leave him to his suffering and go home. Home, home—to New Orleans. Let Hunter and Kandace figure out whatever reporting they needed and altogether forget about their stupid *Magical Choices*.

But she knew exactly where to find a cold compress—she'd seen one in the first aid cabinet. And if the ice machine was working, she'd know where to get ice, too. She reminded herself that it would be best to not have feelings (or an ego) if she wanted to do this for a living.

Hunter peeked through his hand again when Lacey

returned. He made no motion to take the compress.

"Lean forward," Lacey said.

"Why?"

"It works better at the back of the neck."

"Ehhhh-uhhhhh," was all Hunter could manage as he moved his head forward about three inches and put his hands on his knees.

Lacey placed the compress on his neck. Hunter, usually so perfectly put together and coiffed, needed his neck shaved.

He must really not be feeling well.

As awkward as it was, tending to Hunter, staring at the backs of three silent editors, Lacey felt a sense of calm come over her. The fingers of one hand touched his neck, lightly, while the other hand held the compress. And that hand was warm, despite being pressed against the ice-chilled fabric.

Hunter continued to moan. They became less frequent after about a minute. He finally let out a deep sigh and reached one hand behind his head to grab the compress. Lacey felt a shock when their fingers briefly touched. She stepped back.

"Maybe you do know something about migraines," Hunter said.

Not really. But I know something about pain.

"Any better?"

"A little. You can go now. I'll get back to work in a bit. Did you get me that report?"

"I emailed it to you."

Lacey flexed her hand and smiled, ever so subtly, as she returned to her workstation. *Bet you're glad you didn't fire me now.*

28

Lacey sat with her parents at the back of St. Mary's church. They had arrived late, coming in from New Roads. Her mother had hinted that they might not be able to make the nearly two-hour trip in for the funeral, but Lacey successfully laid on the guilt and here they were. She'd simply reminded her that the Lees were their neighbors and friends for more than twenty years. That might have done the trick. But what probably sealed their fate was telling them that would be their only chance to see Lacey for another month.

Father John celebrated a full Mass. Lacey knew that had to be at Ms. PJ's urging. Angele's father, Mr. Bob, or Mr. Bah—his own riff on Ms. PJ's accent—only attended church at Christmas. He couldn't even be convinced for Easter. Angele had quit going to Mass before she graduated high school. But Ms. PJ had been a fixture at St. Mary's 7:00 a.m. daily mass while Lacey had been in grammar school there. She was certain she'd never stopped.

It was the first time Lacey had been to Mass in more than six weeks. She felt a tinge of guilt over it, but it was not as if she'd had any free time in California. Well, maybe when the production went on hiatus. She resolved to be less preoccupied with her worldly concerns when she returned home for good, and return to her semi-regular Mass schedule.

Attendance at Mr. Bob's service felt sparse. In addition to it being her first Mass in nearly two months, Lacey realized this was her second funeral in as many months. Though Mr. Bob's was about as opposite a Hollywood funeral as one was likely to get.

There would be no gathering at Ms. PJ's house after the funeral. But Angele asked Lacey if she would stop by later, anyway.

She had a few hours before Angele expected her, and her parents weren't ready to get back on the road. With time to kill, Lacey and her folks went to lunch in Metairie. The hibachi restaurant had been a favorite of both her mom and her the whole time they'd lived in St. Mary's parish. Her dad would just have to suffer through it.

Lacey was anxious all through lunch. She wanted to talk to Angele, she wanted to talk to Tonti, she wanted to get down to the Bywater before she left Sunday night. She was particularly anxious about the person she arranged to meet in the Bywater.

✳

Angele's mom, Ms. PJ, still lived in the same house where Angele had grown up. Lacey grew up across the street and two doors down. But her parents had sold that house and moved to New Roads about ten years ago. Lacey felt transported into the past the moment Ms. PJ opened the door and let her into the foyer. It still smelled of lemongrass, same as it had every time Lacey sought to escape her well-intentioned but annoying mother and hang out with Angele.

Lacey wondered if Ms. PJ still bought the incense out at the Vietnamese market. She'd complain how everyone would speak to her in Vietnamese, and she'd answer back in her native Thai, until finally they'd complete the transaction in broken English.

Ms. PJ asked Lacey to sit down, and proceeded into the kitchen. She knew she was putting a kettle on. She heard two voices speaking Thai. Lacey recognized Angele's voice, and wondered why she hadn't met her at the door. She got up from the dining room table and tentatively poked her head into the kitchen.

"May I come in?" she asked.

"No, no, Lacey, you sit down. You relax," Ms. PJ said.

"Mother, let her come in," Angele scolded. "Maybe Lacey doesn't want to be alone."

"Fine. But don't look, Lacey. I don't want to give away any of my secrets." Ms. PJ winked at her. It was an old parlay from when Lacey was a kid and would pester Ms. PJ for cooking lessons.

Funny how her desire to cook had completely dissipated by the time she married Fox.

Lacey smiled. Ms. PJ looked tired, but not especially sad. "Are you doing okay, Ms. PJ?"

"Oh, fine. But I miss Bah. I never knew how different it would be around here."

"I'm so sorry, Ms. PJ. I don't know if I got the chance to tell you at the church."

"It's okay. He's been sick. Sick for a while."

Lacey looked to Angele.

"Mother, we'll be in the living room."

Lacey followed Angele to the small and tidy living room. The furniture was all the same, arranged the same way as it had been since Angele and Lacey were teenagers. Mr. Bob's well-worn recliner looked like a shrine.

"Lee," Lacey started.

Angele held up her hand. "Look. There's nothing you could have done for him. His health had been declining for a long time."

Lacey had a million things she wanted to say, but held her tongue.

Angele brought her voice down to a whisper. "And doing your thing would have freaked Mom out in a big way. I wouldn't know how to explain it to her."

"You could have still mentioned to me how sick he was. Normal friends share things. Why did you assume I'd feel like I'd have to try . . . my thing?"

Lacey still had a hard time naming her ability. And she wouldn't let on to Angele that her assumption was correct—she would have felt compelled to help Mr. Bob.

"Because I know you. And look, it all happened really quickly. He was stable but not great for a few days after the surgery, and then, last week, it all went downhill pretty quick."

Lacey nodded. Looking at Mr. Bob's recliner, she said, "All this time, I never knew his name was Robert E. Lee." She still had the funeral program in her purse, with a photo that had to be from twenty years ago emblazoned on the front. The name above it read "Robert Eugene Lee."

"Yeah. He hated it. That's why he always insisted on Bob or Bobby."

Angele adjusted herself on the loveseat. Sounds of Ms. PJ bustling in the kitchen carried into the living room.

Lacey lowered her voice. "How's your mom doing, really? Do you think she's going to stay here?"

"God, I hope so. Because if I wind up moving back, and then she goes somewhere else, I'm going to be pissed."

Lacey cocked her head. "You're really thinking about moving back?"

"Yeah. Or at least making here home base. I'll still be traveling for locations, as long as I can pick up work."

Lacey was instantly glad her foray into movie production would be so short-lived. She always thought she wouldn't like the lack of job security, but was surprised to learn that what she really hated was being away from home for so long.

"I'll sure appreciate having you around a little more." Lacey looked at Angele sideways.

"The way things have been between us lately, I'm not sure I believe you." Angele sat stiffly on the loveseat as she said it. She was never one to dance around things. That was Lacey's job.

"But, you're thinking you're done with production accounting?" Angele continued.

Lacey caught herself fidgeting in her chair. She stopped and said, "Yeah. I've been thinking of a new career. But I'm not ready to drop what you just said."

She realized she didn't feel like dancing around Angele's attitude anymore.

"What's more to say?" Angele said. "People grow up, people change, friendships change. Hell, you've had multiple massive changes in just the past year and a half. You can't expect us to be the same as we were when the biggest things we had to worry about were our faces breaking out before prom. Which yours never did, by the way."

Lacey leaned forward. "I always thought friends would be

the ones to stand by you through the changes," she said quietly.

Angele pulled back, flattening her spine against the loveseat. "I have been standing by you. Pointing out the things you're too naïve to see. But you still don't listen."

Lacey's naiveté was suddenly glaringly apparent to her. She'd been naïve to try to hang onto a friendship with someone who had such a low opinion of her. Angele's no-quarter-given demeanor had been a good balance to Lacey when they were growing up. But Angele's edges were significantly sharper now. And Lacey was smarter than she used to be.

"I guess you're right," was all Lacey said. "Friendships do change."

"So what's the new career you're thinking of?" Angele said, relaxing, apparently ready to drop the subject.

Lacey was also ready to move on, but not so sure she wanted to share her new vocation with Angele. "It's something I could do anywhere, and especially in New Orleans."

"Exotic dancer?" Angele deadpanned.

Lacey shook her head. Remembering that Angele's father had just died, she was trying to be sensitive to her feelings. But she wasn't sure she had any.

"Well, what? It won't be so bad having you around here when I'm in town."

"A ringing endorsement of our friendship," Lacey said. "I'm thinking of becoming an EMT."

Lacey did not expect Angele's reaction. Her best friend began to howl with laughter. Which quickly turned into her obnoxious, staccato laugh.

The sounds of bustling in the kitchen stopped.

"Glad you find my life's calling so amusing."

"No, I think it's perfect! But you've heard about all the

drugs they do, haven't you? To keep them going through those long hours? I can just see you getting paired with some beefed-up junkie."

"Oh, God. Please?" Lacey was trying to watch her language with Ms. PJ within earshot. "Why is it me always making bad choices with you? Why can't it be about the work? Don't you think this kind of *work* is something . . . somewhere I could really make a difference?"

"Sure, healing gunshot victims. Giving them a temporary reprieve. And you pining after your partner, Biff Responder."

Lacey cringed and held her forehead with her hand. She didn't want to tackle either of Angele's insults. They belied what she thought of Lacey, and of humanity in general.

"Well, long story short, I really appreciate all you did to get me on the movie out in Cali," Lacey said. "It's been fun, but it's also helped me figure out what I do—and don't—want to do for the rest of my life."

And just like that, Lacey realized she wanted less of Angele in the rest of her life. Maybe she'd been conditioned to lean upon Angele's friendship in the past, and maybe that just didn't make sense anymore.

Ms. PJ entered the living room with a teapot and three cups on a tray. "What's so funny, Gelee?" she asked her daughter.

"Nothing, just Lacey, Mother." Her back had stiffened again. "You know she's always been able to get my funny bone."

"I know, always so serious. That's why I was always glad when you come around, Lacey." She poured three cups of tea and sat across from Lacey and Angele. "Get her to loosen up. I don't know how she got so serious. Me and Bah not like that."

Lacey asked Ms. PJ if she still made it to daily Mass.

Angele rolled her eyes, excused herself, and said she'd return momentarily. Both Ms. PJ and Lacey let out a sigh when Angele was out of sight.

29

Lacey was instantly charmed by the cypress wood storefront, painted a cheery red with big white letters welcoming passersby to the Bywater Bakery. It had opened while she had been in California, and she had wistfully read the reviews during her daily perusal of the news back home.

She thought it perfect that Nathan had suggested it for a meeting place. It was near to the other stop she needed to make in the Bywater, and this gave her the perfect excuse to try it out.

Something about the place made her less nervous. Because the thought of seeing Nathan again threatened to throw off any shred of equilibrium she possessed.

Her heart was in her throat as she walked through the front door. A bright young face behind the counter smiled at her. The aroma of freshly baked bread made her instantly hungry. Lacey looked around the assorted tables and counters, set against big picture windows. An older couple ate in comfortable silence, a group of five likely students debated over cups of coffee in a sheltered corner on the back wall. No sign of Nathan.

She couldn't decide if she was disappointed or relieved. She approached the counter and asked the bright young face for a cup of coffee.

"Nothing to eat, ma'am?"

It had been several hours since lunch at the hibachi restaurant with her parents, and the menu options looked amazing. But Lacey didn't want to be caught stuffing her face when Nathan came in. It was not the look she was going for.

"No, thank you."

"Sit wherever you like, ma'am, we'll bring the coffee out to you."

Lacey picked a corner diagonally opposite to the student debate team. She could see people come through the door, but was partially hidden by the pastry case.

Bright Young Face brought her coffee over.

"I just realized I didn't pay you," Lacey said.

"We'll bring you a bill before you leave." The young face grew brighter with a smile, and returned to the counter.

Lacey sipped the coffee and pulled out her phone. No messages from Nathan. No messages from anyone.

She felt foolish and lonely. She regretted reaching out to Nathan in the first place. And with the court date for The Weasel looming for sometime in the next few months, all the circumstances of their fraught relationship seemed just so damn messy.

But she couldn't stop thinking of him. There was too much unfinished between them. And her dalliance with Trevor had only made her realize that she longed for something more permanent. And she thought, there was the potential, the seed, of something more permanent with Nathan. She knew it made no logical sense. He was still married. But, try as she might, she couldn't get her heart to follow her brain.

She was wallowing in self-pity, vacillating between reaching out to Nathan to find out if he was still coming, or just getting up and walking out. She would leave a few bucks on the table for the coffee.

She was staring at her phone and didn't realize someone was standing in front of her table. No one had entered from outside, she was sure of it. Lacey looked up and saw a woman, blonde hair cut in a bob, with a yellow chef's coat. With the warm smile on her face, Lacey couldn't help but think of sunshine.

Sunshine Chef held a pastry on plate. "It's *pain au chocolat,* a new recipe for me," she said to Lacey. "I was wondering if you wouldn't mind being a taste tester."

Lacey looked to her side, wondering why this stranger was approaching her, but remembered her manners. When someone who appears to be the owner of restaurant offers you food, you don't decline. Especially when that food is a pastry.

"Of course, thank you so much."

Sunshine Chef sat in the chair opposite Lacey. "Do you mind?"

"Of course not. Please." She stared at the pastry. It glistened with butter, and a rivulet of chocolate escaped from one end, along with a bit of steam.

"We're still working on it, the chocolate shouldn't run like that. But I think everything else has come together nicely."

She seemed like she was waiting for Lacey to taste it, so she obliged. It saved her from having to find something to say. She burnt the tip of her tongue, but the pain was quickly overcome by the delicate mixture of flavors. It was a pretty amazing pastry.

Her mouth was full when Sunshine Chef slid a piece of paper, folded over with "Lacey" written in cursive at the center. "I have something else for you. Nathan asked that I give this to you."

Lacey covered her mouth and hurried to swallow. Her stomach had leapt into her throat at the mention of Nathan's name. It made swallowing a challenge.

"Oh," she said, mouth still partially full. "Are you, um, friends with Nathan?"

And if so, could you tell me why in hell he left a letter instead of meeting in person?

The sunshine smile returned. "Not good friends, no. I've known him for a little while, since he helped me close this deal. When I bought this place." She gestured her hand around the bright bakery.

Lacey was relieved that she wasn't a paramour of Nathan's. Though she still could be, but Lacey didn't get that vibe. Friendly business associate rang true. She kicked herself for thinking so much about it. And she remembered her manners again.

"Your place is really lovely, I'm so glad I made it down here. And this *pain au chocolat* . . . wow."

"Glad you like it." She rose from her chair. "I need to get back to the kitchen. Take your time, sweetie."

Lacey smiled up at her and thanked her again. Then turned her attention to the piece of paper on the table. Everything else faded around it. It almost glowed. Nathan's script was very pretty, almost feminine. At least he had remembered the "e" in Lacey.

She contemplated crumpling it up and stashing it in her purse. No, throwing it away with a flourish, right here in the Bywater Bakery. No, even better, leaving it right where it was on the table, so that Sunshine Chef could tell Nathan how she walked right out of this bakery without even so much as a look back at his lame note.

But the need for instant gratification got the best of her. She slid it from the table, surreptitiously, casually. She hoped no one could see how much her hand was shaking.

She pressed herself against the back of her chair, trying to become small and invisible. She opened it and blurred her eyes, so she couldn't make out words at first. All she saw was a page full of pretty cursive, smaller than her name on the front.

Finally, she took a deep breath and focused her vision.

Lacey,

I know this is a chicken shit thing to do. With all you've done for me, and I can't even work up the nerve to see you face-to-face. Though that is the one thing I really long for most in this world. To see you again.

But that's why I have to settle for this note. I'm afraid of what would happen if I saw you. Because I've decided to try to work it out with Lisa. We've spent a little time together with the kids. We've both realized how much better we are as a family, maybe more than as a couple. I don't know if that makes sense. But when I think of being someone worthy, someone worthy of saving, I think I need to be a better father.

You deserve to be with someone who isn't as mixed up as I am. I know that sounds chicken shit, and I think I know how you'll react when I say this: not seeing you hurts me more than you'll ever know. It's a pain worse than what lingers from those injuries you healed. I know you won't believe me when I say that. But what you believe doesn't matter. Because it's the truth.

I don't know how to end this, so I'll just repeat more words that I know you don't believe: I love you. But what you believe doesn't matter. Because it's the truth.

Nathan

Lacey wanted to crumple the note and toss it across the lovely, bright bakery. No, she wished she smoked, because she'd take her lighter and set it aflame. Instead, she refolded the note, ever so tenderly, and tucked it into her purse. She stared, stunned. Her eyes felt full, but the tears wouldn't fall.

She felt sick, and the air in her quiet corner felt too close. She looked at her coffee mug and pushed up out of her seat, remembering she needed to pay. Sunshine Chef had replaced Bright Young Face behind the counter.

"Don't worry about it, sweetie. It's on the house." Her look was sympathetic, and saved Lacey the effort of trying to fake sounding upbeat.

For an instant, Lacey wondered if Sunshine Chef's understanding look meant she had read the letter. But the suspicion disappeared just as quickly as it came. She got the vibe that Sunshine Chef implicitly understood the effects of hand-written notes, fraught encounters, and dashed expectations.

"Thank you," Lacey said. "And the chocolate croissant was amazing, too."

"Even with the runny chocolate?" Sunshine Chef winked.

Lacey nodded. She whispered, "Thanks again," and scurried out the front door. The sound of the words "runny chocolate" struck some unseen chord and busted the dam that had been holding back her tears. Rivulets streamed down her face as she rushed to her rental car.

30

The New Orleans Healing Center would have to wait. She
needed a good cry, and she wanted to be home. Lacey just
prayed Tonti wouldn't be there.

She had been when Lacey arrived in the wee hours of Friday
morning. It was surreal, returning home for the first time in
more than a month, and hearing the television blaring loud
from two rooms away. The other strange thing—Ambrose
wasn't there. It didn't feel right to walk through the side door
and not hear Ambrose running to greet her.

Lacey had prayed that it was Tonti who had turned on the
television. And not a poltergeist who had taken up residence
while she was away. She didn't know what to expect in this new
world of supernatural abilities.

She'd set her bag down in the laundry room and tip-toed
into the living room. Sure enough, Tonti was sprawled out on
the sectional sofa, mouth agape, snoring loudly. A bottle of
Blanton's was open on the bar, and a half-full tumbler, clearish-
brown from all the melted ice, sat on a coaster on the side table.

Lacey had never seen Tonti drink bourbon.

Nor had she ever seen her sleeping. Even in repose she was

formidable. She took up the entire longer section of the sofa, and one arm, splayed across the "L", took up half of it.

Lacey couldn't help but smile, despite being so travel weary. While it had taken some cajoling to get her parents to agree to meet her for Mr. Bob's funeral, here was Tonti, waiting to greet her after her long journey. At least, she'd assumed that was Tonti's intention.

It had taken several attempts to rouse her. When she'd awakened, it was the first time Lacey had seen Tonti appear vulnerable. She'd blinked and rubbed her eyes and said, "I need to call Hines." Her on-call and long-suffering driver.

"I can call you a cab or an Uber," Lacey had offered.

"No! Hines hates it when I talk about that. I guess I must pay him better."

Lacey had been too tired to make any sense of Tonti's words. "Okay, where's your phone?"

"Oh, I wanted to visit with you. There's so much to tell you. Greg got engaged, they've rerouted the trains, the vacant lot next door sold." Tonti pushed herself up to seated.

Lacey could only laugh. "That's a lot of information, Tonti. And big news about Greg . . . wow . . . we definitely need to catch up."

Lacey had recalled Tonti telling her about her youngest son's new girlfriend on a phone call. She thought Tonti liked her. Maybe Greg wanted to act before his mother's tides changed.

Tonti had sat, dazed, still half asleep.

"Can you meet on Saturday?" Lacey asked. "Maybe lunch or dinner?"

"Yes, yes, splendid idea. Brunch on Saturday. I'll come pick you up. Could you hand me my phone, child? I think I left it on the bar."

They hadn't said much else, or at least, Lacey didn't remember if they did. She was pretty brain dead after her travel. She was sure she would get the complete rundown, and then some, when she met Tonti tomorrow.

But for now, she was relieved to find her home empty. Late afternoon sun slanted through the front windows, highlighting lines of dust and dander. Even with Ambrose absent, you couldn't keep telltale signs of him from settling into the farthest corners. A faint musty smell pervaded the entire house. It made Lacey sad to think of her house vacant. Even with Tonti to bring occasional bouts of activity in her absence, it wasn't enough to breach the emptiness.

She intended to grab the bottle of Blanton's she had replaced on the shelf after Tonti left last night, but she never made it that far. Fixated on the emptiness, she tossed her purse to the couch and hurled herself after it. She collapsed face forward, producing great gulping sobs into her folded arms.

Some small voice kept telling her she shouldn't be so upset about Nathan's note, but that only made her cry harder. In all her reveries about returning to New Orleans and beginning an auspicious career as a supernatural first responder, Nathan had existed as a great potential possibility. Not a foregone conclusion by any means. There were too many questions about his family, the state of his unraveling marriage, the nature of his relationship with Lacey. But she realized she had wanted to tackle all those issues, and—if his marriage was going to dissolve—to find out just what she and Nathan could be. His stupid note removed all those issues. There was nothing left to negotiate.

She cried until there was nothing left.

✳

Saturday morning, Lacey's head still hurt from crying. She went for a run, choosing a direction to purposefully avoid her nosy neighbor. She knew he knew she was home, but wasn't ready to deal with him. She wanted to find out what Tonti knew about the sale of the vacant lot before she faced Mr. Max. AKA Kravitz.

She tried to focus on what she *would* have to look forward to when she returned for good. There was Kravitz. Not so much to look forward to, but at least a constant. There would be classes at Delgado. Fond memories of LSU, all interlaced with memories of Fox, came into her mind. She was older now. But *was* she wiser? Was she any more discerning, or would she go into her classes at Delgado with the same wide-eyed naivety that marked her time at LSU?

And there was Trevor. Would she see him anymore once she was back in New Orleans permanently? Maybe his musician's schedule made him more available to travel. But had their time together run out? Thinking of what she didn't have with Trevor made her think of what she wanted to have with Nathan, so she tried to stop thinking of them at all.

Focus on your future. And quit focusing on feeling so empty. Maybe that's a good thing.

Eli. Eli would probably tell her to embrace the emptiness.

Trying to focus on the benefits of being empty, thoughts of her vision at Sycamore Mineral Springs began creeping in. She passed a neighbor she didn't know as he got into his car. He wore a navy blue blazer with a crest. She would swear he glared at her before he drove off.

Stepping off the curb, about to cross Marconi Drive to get

to the park, a speeding truck appeared under the overpass. She jumped back before it clipped her. The driver shouted something unintelligible from his open window.

She suddenly didn't feel like running anymore.

She turned around and tried not to chastise herself. Up until now, the news about Angele's dad, and her ulterior motives during her visit home, had crowded out creepy thoughts about Gus Savin. But some part of her knew getting to its meaning was more important than her broken heart.

Good thing she would see Tonti in a few hours.

Lacey felt a slight flash of deja vu when Hines dropped her and Tonti off at Katie's. Had it really been just two months since they were there together last? It felt like a lifetime.

A crowd of people milled about outside in the sweltering heat. Lacey wondered how long they'd have to wait.

Tonti breezed up to the host stand, said a few low words to the host, and she grabbed Lacey's arm as the host led them through the restaurant to a set of stairs. Lacey followed Tonti as she labored up the steps.

"When is Scot going to fix that elevator, dear?" she said to the host.

"But Miss Evangeline, it works, you just said . . . "

"Oh, I know dear, I said I wanted to get my exercise. Won't be the first thing I've said that I regret."

Lacey made a mental note to use the elevator on their way out.

They were led to a secluded table in a corner. The host pulled out the chair for Tonti and she made a mini production of sitting down. Lacey sat herself and peered out the bright second-story window. It offered a view of shotgun rooftops and converted law offices. Lacey sneezed and it echoed throughout the empty, spacious room.

"I'll be back with your drinks," the host said.

Lacey wondered what Tonti had conjured up for them. "Tonti," she asked, "why are we the only ones up here? There's a crowd of people waiting downstairs."

"This room's only open for dinner, child."

Lacey shook her head. "You never cease to amaze me."

The host didn't return, but a tall blonde woman entered with a bottle and an ice bucket for chilling.

"Oh, Elizabeth! Look at you, how splendid. And it is the California sparkling, right? My dearest niece here has spent the last month on the Central Coast of California. We need to commemorate that."

Lacey tried to smile. *It's a nice thought, at least.*

Tonti spent the next forty-five minutes debriefing Lacey on Greg's engagement, the wedding date (it wouldn't be for another year and a half), and the places his fiancée Kelly should shop for the dress. Tonti spent at least twelve of those minutes discussing how the wedding would *not* be during Lent, how she was concerned when they chose a February date, but her research indicated that Mardi Gras would be late that year. And the next twelve minutes complaining that they didn't think it through, because they'll be competing for venues and caterers with all the Mardi Gras balls.

She only spent half that time delivering the neighborhood scoop. How she thought the house that would go up on the vacant lot between Lacey's house and Kravitz's would be a two-story, and how the couple building it were retired or near to it with no kids. Tonti speculated that Lacey's privacy would be much enhanced by the addition to the neighborhood, but that the unsuspecting new couple had no idea what they were in for with Kravitz.

They had finished their meals and Tonti had requested another bottle of sparkling wine when she said, "Well, tell me all about California, child! You haven't said boo about it, and you mentioned you've been seeing someone, and I want to hear all about your fella."

Lacey chuckled. Hearing Tonti go on about the world as she saw it for the last hour plus had strangely settled her nerves. And while she would never call Trevor her "fella," she did find it easy to describe him and all his charms. And she found, when she'd given Tonti the PG-rated version of her relationship with Trevor, she'd actually forgotten about Nathan for a brief moment.

She almost didn't want to bring up Gus Savin, because she finally felt more relaxed than she had in weeks. But the combination of the sparkling wine and the momentary bout of self-confidence fueled her.

"Tonti, have you ever met the antiques guy down in the Quarter—Gus Savin?"

"Why, of course, child. What brings him up?"

"Nothing, I met him for the first time out in California. He's a financier on the project I've been working on. I just thought it was kinda funny. I'd dealt with people who work for him for years, when I worked for Trip. But I'd never met him until now."

"He's one of those types who makes himself known on his own terms. Not quite a recluse, but he definitely doesn't seek out the spotlight. I'd be the same way if I had his kind of money."

Lacey stopped herself from laughing. She couldn't picture Tonti shying away from any kind of light.

"Is he really that rich?"

"That family's money goes back as far as the Louisiana Purchase, and probably even further. I remember speaking to him once at the Odyssey Ball, it had to be at least ten years ago now. He knew a lot about Galliano. He said he grew up there but spent his school years back east at some Eton-like boarding school. Which explains a lot."

The quizzical look on Lacey's face made Tonti go further.

"For one, it explains why I didn't know him growing up, child. We have to be close to the same age."

Lacey nodded. "Other than him growing up in Galliano and having a lot of family money, do you know anything else?"

"Like, what? Is he gay or straight?" Tonti rolled her eyes. "Oh, for heaven's sake, please don't tell me you're interested. I know I said I'd support you whoever you chose, but please, I can think of only one reason to get involved with that man. And I *know* you're not a gold digger."

Lacey's stomach went sour at the thought. "No, no, no, Tonti! That's not it at all. His whole involvement in the movie production just seems fishy to me, that's all."

"So you're playing detective. Okay. *That* I can support. Anyway, I think he's gay. Or certainly bi. Or maybe asexual. I've never known him to be connected with anyone, male or female.

"And I wouldn't worry too much about him backing the movie. He probably has money in many a Hollywood ventures. It's a good way to be close to the limelight, but not in it."

"You're probably right. That makes sense." Nothing about Gus Savin made sense to her, but she was ready to stop discussing him. The information about Galliano was definitely something to research further, on her own.

"And I've told you about Trevor, but I haven't said anything about how beautiful the resort is, the place where I stayed for a few weeks."

If she left out the earthquakes and the creepy Gus Savin visions, the place and her time there would seem downright picturesque.

31

Galliano, Louisiana

One summer in the mid-twentieth century

Birdie knew change was brewing. Momma had called it the Sense. She'd said Daddy had it the whole time she knew him. And it made sense that Birdie had the Sense, too. She took after her father. She'd received so many of her gifts from him.

She'd felt it before Morris had gotten the sickness in his legs. She'd felt it before Momma died. She'd felt it before that twister tore through Galliano. She couldn't remember if she'd felt it before Daddy died. If so, it would had to have been the first time.

Momma had told her about it when Léon got sick. It was maybe two years after Birdie had helped him after his fight with the coyote. Momma had told her dogs don't live as long as people, and Léon's time was almost at hand. Ronnie had told her she had given Léon an extra life, like how they say cats have nine lives. Dogs only get one, but Birdie had given Léon two.

This time, she knew it wasn't about anyone close to her. No, it was closer than that.

It was why she asked Ronnie, during a recent phone call, to look after Morris. To move him up to Ohio if he had to. It indicated the kind of man Ronnie was, the kind of man Birdie always knew him to be, that he accepted her words with no protest.

"Ronnie, don't ask why I'm asking."

"I know better than that."

"I know you and Morris have differences, but he respects you. More than most men he knows. He may put up a fight at first, but he'll listen to what you have to say. He'll follow you. You just need to show patience."

"Just don't put me in this situation for a while, you hear?"

Birdie just smiled when Ronnie said that.

It was why, during their last visit, Birdie took Cecil out with her on a day off. They each acted about ten years younger than they were, and had a great time doing it. They made stories about all the birds they saw on the river batture, they made stories about all the raccoons, possum, coyote and alligators they couldn't see, but knew were hiding, waiting for the light to go down so they could do their nightly dance.

It's why she took him near the cemetery, the same one where she had found Léon so long ago, and told Cecil about his grandfather, her father. How you wouldn't find his grave there how he said he "didn't want his spirit bound up in this place." His spirit was out in the batture, and off in the woods to the north, and in the nightly dance of all the creatures of this land. And how his spirit was also in Birdie, and in Cecil, in a very particular way. She explained to Cecil how his grandfather had passed along a very special gift, a way to help other people. She told Cecil she was sad they lived so far away from each other, and that she wished she could show him more. But that his father knew about his special gift. And that if he asked his father about it, and listened, really listened, he would know what to do.

That day, the day she had stayed late, waiting for Mr. Becnel, she had felt the Sense more strongly than she ever had before. Everything about that day had been normal, but just amplified by the Sense. She was in the Becnel's kitchen. This was as it was most days. Evangeline had a book before her at the kitchen table, and Foxy was at Birdie's heels. This was also as per usual. Mrs. Becnel was having a good day, and the three younger children were with her. This was a little unusual.

Foxy was talking up a storm about Madeleine Picoult, a girl from school. Evangeline was pretending to read. Birdie set a bowl down in front of her, filled halfway to the top with sugar and butter.

"As long as you're sitting there not reading, why don't you work on mixing that for me?" Birdie winked at her and returned to the stove.

Evangeline huffed and set her book aside. But the mixing bowl gave her a better vantage point for watching her brother and Birdie.

"Madeleine Picoult went to *the city* with her big sister. Just the two of them! Their parents let them go alone!"

"So, everything you've told me about Madeleine Picoult, Foxy: she hits other children . . . "

"She hits boys!"

" . . . And girls, too, you said. She goes into town with her teenaged sister . . . "

"She's seventeen," Evangeline interjected.

"You read that in that book, Sister?" Birdie asked.

Evangeline returned to her stirring.

"Any who, everything I hear about this Madeleine Picoult, she is not the girl for you, Foxy."

Foxy stopped his chattering and looked stunned.

"She's too much like you. You'll want a gentle girl."

"No I won't!"

Birdie laughed. "Maybe not right now this instant, but eventually. Someone who can help you raise your children. Because if they're anything like you, you're going to need that kind of help."

Something about the children, or child, Foxy would have. Birdie felt the Sense there. There was no way to explain it.

"I'm not bad!" Foxy took up his own defense.

Birdie wiped her hands on her apron and turned around to face Foxy. "No, child, you are not bad. You are a beautiful child of God who's full of spit and spirit. You would be blessed to have ten of you to raise. But you won't want to do it alone."

"When are we gonna eat?" he asked.

"Is that any way to speak?"

"I'm sorry, Ms. Birdie. I'm just kinda hungry now."

She crouched down and embraced him. "So ask, 'May I enquire when dinner will be ready?'"

He broke free and said, "May I require when dinner will be ready?"

"Not for another hour. Go play, child. Work out some of that spirit."

Foxy ran out to the living room. "How's that mixing coming, Evangeline?"

"Fine, Ms. Birdie. Do you think I'll be a good mama?"

"Oh, Sister, if you pay half as much attention to your children as you do to all the business going on around you, you will be a super mama.

"But you don't need to be thinking about that just yet." Birdie had noted how all the blossoming signs were there for Evangeline. Lord help her if she developed in the same way her older sisters had.

"Just you look out for yourself. You're probably the best suited for that. To look out for yourself and your family."

Birdie walked over to inspect the mixing. She grabbed the bowl from Evangeline.

"Fine job, Evangeline. Fine job."

It was after dark by the time Birdie got into her truck to head home to Morris in Larose. Mrs. Becnel had asked her to stay after dinner. She had said she wanted Birdie to stay until Mr. Becnel made it home from his business trip, better to have two adults in the house. But there was another reason, one she wouldn't say out loud. Birdie knew Mrs. Becnel also wanted her to stay to help Foxy with his homework. He had a math test tomorrow, and everyone in the house knew that Birdie was the best with math.

There was no moon that night, and the air was thick through the fields laying alongside Louisiana Highway One.

She imagined the lights from her truck's headlights were the only lights for miles around.

32

Lacey thought about "spooky action at a distance." She had tried to read more about it in the book Cecil gave her, but she still didn't understand. So instead, she thought about two places, separated by distance, and elevation. Here was the New Orleans Healing Center, roughly two feet below sea level. And there was the Healing Institute back in San Luis Obispo, with its hillside location. If one were truly in need of healing, it was a lot easier to walk through the doors of the New Orleans Healing Center than to traverse that steep incline to the spacious domed interior of the Healing Institute.

The exterior to the Healing Institute was certainly more sylvan than the surrounding St. Claude neighborhood of the Healing Center. But thinking of those woods just spooked Lacey all over again.

She took her time getting to the bookshop. She was hoping against hope that she would find Cecil there, just like the last time. Or rather, that he would find her there, as that's how it all appeared to go down.

What had she learned since that last time?

Cecil passed this along to me. I know that for certain. But I haven't seen him since I've known this.

The displays along the bookshelves had changed. The section with all the books about healing or healers wasn't where it was before. That's where she'd last met Cecil. She ambled down the aisles, attempting to casually peruse.

I've learned that I've truly moved on from Fox.

It hadn't even been two years. Was it possible to really move on that quickly? Oddly enough, the fresh heartbreak with Nathan helped. At least in that capacity. And she would always be connected with Fox's family. Through Tonti—she had made her undying devotion abundantly clear. And her name. She came to this gift through the Becnels (even though she still didn't understand how or why). She wanted to keep the name. She'd never really thought of *not* keeping it.

So Fox gave me a name, another family, and a thicker skin. I can live with that.

She felt a fleeting glimpse of something like nostalgia. For the innocence of first love, for the trust she was so willing to give. Truth was, that hadn't changed. She was still willing to give away her trust. The change was: she was stronger now. She could handle the pain when that trust was betrayed. And she knew to be more selective.

Trevor. I know he's not Mr. Right. No reason he can't be Mr. Right Now.

There was a different person behind the sales counter of the bookstore. Another young man, as disinterested as the other one who had been there when she met Cecil. She began to get the vibe that she wasn't going to find Cecil today.

She thought a little bit more about Trevor. With her romantic life a wide-open horizon, why not continue with him?

Any "bumps in the road" they'd experienced felt like her own doing, her own expectations getting in the way. And with the distance between them soon to grow longer, she'd have to let go of any expectations.

She sauntered into the "books of local interest" section. A photo collage graced the cover of a book on Mardi Gras, with the subtitle *Carnival Royalty*. Ordinarily, she wouldn't have given it a second glance. She had no problem with the celebration aspect of Mardi Gras, or its reputation for debauchery. There needed to be a place for those aspects of life, and she always liked how Mardi Gras gave sanction to them. It was the part of Mardi Gras that was hijacked by the social elite that always bugged her. She'd heard her old boss, Trip Carriere, talk about his membership in the Rex Organization enough. She'd learned long ago to tune it out or ignore it.

The book contained profiles of the kings and queens of Mardi Gras for the past fifty years. She knew Gus Savin had been Rex relatively recently. She knew it all too well, because Trip would take every possible opportunity to regale her with the tragic tale of when Gus Savin had robbed him of the crown. He had been convinced that the enviable title of "Rex— King of Carnival" would be his. Not just that, he would be the youngest man to ever receive the honor. Gus Savin received both those "honors" instead.

Lacey picked up the book. Slight nausea tickled at her esophagus. She flipped to the page featuring Gus Savin. Even though the picture was more than ten years old, he looked the same as he had when she met him just a few weeks ago. He was wearing a navy blazer, this one with some type of crest embroidered on the right side. Same floppy hair both he and

Trip Carriere sported. And there was the pinky ring, noticeable through a slight glint in he picture.

The profile didn't contain anything she didn't already know. Tonti's intel about Galliano had been the most intriguing thing she'd heard about him, anyway.

The man behind the sales counter began to take an interest in Lacey's loitering. Had she been there too long?

She looked around. She had no sense of Cecil. She didn't know why she thought he might magically appear, anyway. The whole idea seemed silly, now.

She didn't want the book, but it was the one she had in her hand, and she wanted to prove to the suddenly-interested store clerk that she was a paying customer.

Lacey hustled to the counter and paid cash for the stupid Mardi Gras book.

The clerk offered an insincere "thank you" as he handed Lacey her change, and promptly went back to being disinterested.

Whatever, Lacey thought.

Careful, young Lacey. That sounds rude. She heard a voice in her head.

Cecil?

Was she really hearing Cecil? She'd "heard" Eli a few times, but this was different. Eli never sounded like his actual voice, she just knew it was him. This voice sounded like Cecil's.

Look me up when you return to New Orleans permanently.

Again. It was Cecil's baritone, his inflection, everything.

Lacey hustled out of the store and moved to a corner of the atrium where she wouldn't draw attention to herself. Because she figured talking to the voice in her head might look a little weird.

Cecil? How? And what do you know about Gus Savin? And why did you give me this power? And where are you?

She thought she heard his laugh, but it was starting to fade.

I'll be here when you come back. We can talk about those questions then.

Those last words sounded like they came from the end of a long corridor.

"Dammit!" she said out loud. *Some Superfriend you are, Cecil.*

The voice in her head had gone silent. She was just starting to get used to the idea of Eli's ability. Was she really ready for another "silent conversationalist?"

Lacey looked around to see if anyone had heard her. She sank down to a nearby step and put her head in her hands.

About five minutes later, she was in her car headed home. It felt like five hours later. She wanted to hurry up and head back to California, so she could hurry up and finish her work out there, to hurry up and get back here *permanently*. Permanently, like Cecil had said.

She beat her hand against the steering wheel of her rental car. It wasn't as sturdy as her Accord.

She didn't want to spend too much time in her house. It felt too weird without Ambrose. So on her arrival there, she left the Mardi Gras book on a shelf, grabbed her bag, and left an hour earlier for the airport than she intended. She had hoped to return to California with some answers, and instead was returning with more questions.

33

Sitting at work, Lacey tried to focus on the positive aspects of her New Orleans trip. She could only find two. One, she knew a little more about Gus Savin, though that felt more like "beneficial" than truly "positive." The second thing felt really positive: it put the end date of this seemingly interminable production that much closer. The reshoots with Jason Booker were complete. She didn't think it was because he was such a competent actor. She figured it was because she wasn't the only one who was ready for it all to end.

Neither Marco nor Eli were on set when Lacey returned on Monday morning. Kandace and Hunter were orbiting around the soundstage, in circles that never intersected. Each would ask Lacey for the same report, sometimes only minutes apart. Lacey would email it to each of them, separately. At this point, it was easier to just oblige than to point out the inherent inefficiencies caused by the overall breakdown in communication.

Kandace had asked Lacey to come in on Saturday. With less than eight days to go, Lacey slept in that morning, took a leisurely walk with Ambrose, and decided she'd get to the soundstage when she got there.

I could get used to short-timing like this.

Her sense of calm left her when she saw Eli's car in the parking lot. He had told her he'd be back on Tuesday, and that they could finish up any loose business then. Lacey had been steeling herself, working on the phrasing of her questions, determined to finally ask him about her vision on the ridgeline. She had been working on tamping down the fear the vision inspired, but still wasn't sure what she felt about Eli's abilities. His powers of persuasion, she had deemed it.

But she had thought she still had three days to prepare. She wasn't ready.

And she definitely wasn't ready for what she saw next.

As she entered the building and crossed over to her workstation, she saw Eli talking to someone in the hallway that led to the offices. An oxford blue button-down with French cuffs, navy blazer hooked over his shoulder. Floppy hair cut in a style meant for someone younger. Gus Savin.

Lacey cut a hard right, hoping not to be seen. She made it to her workstation, a knot in her throat, heart beating fast. She stared at the blank screen of her monitor for about a minute, until she worked up the nerve to turn it on and pull up a reporting page. So it would at least appear that she was working.

Another two minutes after that, she found the nerve to turn her head toward the hallway. They were gone. She could see the light on in Kandace's office, but she wasn't about to head over there. Right there at her workstation was where she was expected to be. Kandace could come to her if she wanted something.

Waiting for Kandace to come to her was a bit of a problem, because she had no idea why she had asked her to come in. She sent Kandace an instant message—something innocuous so that she would at least know Lacey was in the building.

No response.

Lacey was getting ready to go see Horatio at the front gate, just to get her mind off whatever the heck was happening, when Hunter, of all people, came to her rescue.

He strolled in, looking like a completely new man. Head held high, he walked straight over to Lacey's desk. He'd gotten a haircut, and some telltale redness and leftover cleanser made it appear that he might have even had a facial.

"Since you're here, can you pull a payroll preliminary? Email it over as soon as you can."

He turned around before Lacey could answer. "Sure," she said to his back. His neck had been shaved, too.

It was the same report she had sent yesterday, but she was happy to have something to do.

Not long after that, Kandace eventually surfaced and sent a few requests over the course of an hour and half, but they only marginally helped pass the dragging time.

Lacey was actually paying attention to something on screen, making sure she'd clicked all the right boxes, when she jumped at the sound of Eli's voice.

"Lacey."

She whipped her head around. Eli was directly behind her, placid as ever. And alone, thankfully.

"Eli. You scared me."

"Seems I'm pretty good at that."

You don't know the half of it. Or, I guess you probably do.

Of the one thousand, seven hundred and thirteen questions

running through her head, all she could think to say was, "What's up?"

"You have time to take a ride?"

"Sure." Despite her best attempts, her voice cracked on the word.

Eli's driving no longer scared her. It was his other traits—and seeing him meet with Gus Savin—that put her on alert.

"Let me just finish the report I'm doing here, and tell Kandace."

"I already told her."

"Of course you did."

Lacey saved her work, grabbed her purse, and followed Eli out of the studio.

She did not get the chance to ask Eli where they were headed. As soon as he pulled his truck out onto the road, Eli began pouring his heart out, and it sent Lacey's mind reeling. All of his sharing was done in a very Eli-like way: measured words, calm tones, absolutely no hand gestures. Which was preferable, since he was driving.

He told her how he'd been recruited as a fighter as a young boy in Kurdistan. How he had followed his father and older brother into the only life they'd ever known. How his mother had shown him how to read people, how it was the only way he would survive. Her gift of prescience had told her Eli would have a life outside of that land. A life that would go on long after her life, and her husband's, and her older son's had all been snuffed out.

"My father died when I was twelve. Fragment from a mortar round caught him in the neck. My brother and I watched him bleed out."

Lacey had a hard time comprehending the words coming

from Eli's mouth. It was a reality that only existed for her in the movies, or on the news. It couldn't be the reality of an enigmatic man she'd been following around on a movie set for the past two months. Could it? And why was he being so open about it now?

"I left Kurdistan when I was seventeen. That was the day I told you about, the day of the earthquake. We were eating a midday meal at our mother's when it struck. She had asked us to come. She knew it would be the last day she would see either of us.

"Later that same day, I saw my brother shot in the head at point-blank range."

He fell silent after uttering those words. His voice never faltered as he delivered all of this information.

"I had no other option but to run, and leave my home. I knew it was time. My mother and I had already said our goodbyes."

Lacey rubbed her palm beneath her eyes. She longed for a tissue. Once she was sure he was done, she asked, "Eli, why . . . ?"

"Why am I telling you this?"

Lacey nodded her head vigorously. She was too choked up to speak.

"Because I know my past is something you've wondered about. And because there's now reason for you to know about it. No one can ever know the whole truth about another person, but it was time for you to have a wider lens on me."

Eli pulled into the parking lot of the resort. "Are you up for a short hike?"

She nodded, less vigorously.

They walked in silence, Lacey a pace behind Eli. After a minute, she realized where they were heading.

"I'm not wearing a bathing suit, Eli."

"I'm not going to ask you to disrobe," he answered. "And you've almost mastered that lesson."

I have?

"Yes, you have. Your 'homework' exercise helped you figure it out. Just remember to put some distance between your focus and your particular worries. Detach from yourself, and you'll have it down shortly."

"How did you know about that?"

Eli stopped and turned to look at her.

Lacey shrugged. "Stupid question, I guess."

I might finally be past the worry about him being in my head. Huh.

They stopped at the hot tub where Eli's lesson had been interrupted. And just a stone's throw from where Lacey had her vision. The wind rustled through the trees.

A faint whiff of sulfur, mixed with a stronger touch of eucalyptus, was oddly calming.

"I asked Gus Savin to meet me at the soundstage today," Eli said.

A gust of clarity finally helped Lacey find the words she'd wanted to ask Eli all along.

"Eli, what do you know about him?"

"Enough to know he needed some misdirection. That's what I attempted today. I believe I was successful, but I don't know how long it will last."

"You mean misdirection, like that thing you did with Allison?"

"Similar.

"You think you have no enemies, Lacey. That you've done nothing in your life that would facilitate the production of enemies. But by the nature of your gift, you've acquired enemies. Something like natural enemies."

"Superfoes?" Lacey said out loud.

"I don't recommend making light of this, Lacey."

"I'm not. I don't think I am. I'm just trying to process this. Did Gus Savin kill Birdie?"

"I don't know that, because I don't know Birdie. I just know that Savin has his . . . Superfoe . . . powers through acquisition. I suspect this has given him unnaturally long life. I know that he takes from others, and will continue to do so as long as he finds those with . . . abilities."

"Eli. Do you remember what you said about spooky . . . about action at a distance?"

"Of course."

"I think Birdie is my action at a distance. I feel some sort of effect from her, even though she was gone long before I was even born. And I think Gus Savin killed Birdie. I think he took her power from her."

Eli considered. "Then it is good I attempted to get him off your scent."

Lacey went pale at the thought of being hunted. "I don't want Superfoe enemies. I want to be a paramedic."

Eli let out a sound she'd never heard before. He laughed. A warm, mirthful laugh.

"That was funny, Lacey."

"Really?" *What about it was funny?*

"It was the way you said it. It struck my funny bone."

Okay . . .

"For as much as my endorsement means, I think you pursuing emergency medical training is a great idea. The perfect outlet for your abilities."

"But what about enemies? What if Gus Savin . . . picks up my scent? How can I go about my life with him out to get me?"

"You must not let the existence of enemies alter your choices. My father was killed by an enemy outside our ranks. My brother was killed by an enemy within our ranks. But I did not leave my land because that enemy had me in his sights next. I left because I believed I was meant to have an effect elsewhere. To help people—other Superfriends, let's say—receive the guidance they need. This is something that would not come to fruition if I stayed. I honored my mother, and my family, by the choice I made."

There was something impassioned in his tone, almost like he was trying to convince himself. Lacey tried to put everything Eli was telling her into the right context.

"So, you're saying I should go forth and EMT? And just because I'm naturally paranoid, it doesn't mean people *aren't* out to get me?"

He laughed again, a little less forcefully. "Some paranoia is healthy. I recommend you hang onto it."

Lacey sank to the ground and rubbed her temples. "I still don't know why *I* am the one who received this power. You wouldn't happen to know the answer to that, would you?"

"No. I think you'd need to ask the one who bestowed the power. If there is any reason at all. Action at a distance does not require a reason."

"I was afraid you'd say something like that."

"Lacey, you are a good person, with a purer heart than most. Who will do good works with the gift you've been given. Might that not be reason enough?"

Lacey blushed at the entirely unexpected praise. "Those might be the nicest words I've ever heard come from your mouth."

"I wouldn't have said them to you if they were not the truth."

"Thanks for all this, Eli. Here I was thinking maybe you were raised on another planet, only to find out you spent your childhood witnessing atrocities I can't even fathom. And that the King of Carnival, who might just happen to have vampire-like long life, wants to kill me, because I have something he needs."

"He doesn't know you have this power yet. He senses it, like a pig rooting for truffles, but he hasn't connected the dots yet. My efforts may have bought you some time. But I don't know how much."

"What if I don't return to New Orleans? What if I do my EMT training somewhere else?" Lacey wasn't sure she wanted to hear the answer. Because everything Eli had laid on her made her more homesick than ever.

"It may offer a little time, perhaps. But there are no guarantees. And I stand by my words: you can't let enemies alter your choices."

Lacey thought of a quote from the *Terminator* movies: "No fate but what we make." She was bolstered by the sentiment. But then she remembered that the cyborgs did eventually get the upper hand in those movies, and went right back to square one.

"Are you up for one final lesson?"

"That depends. Is it about Superfriends, or Superfoes?"

"Neither. But I think you'll like this one. Look up."

Lacey lifted her head. The sun was rapidly descending behind the tree line. Golden light filtered toward them, horizontally. The sky behind them turned pink.

"Watch the sun rise and set, whenever you can," Eli said.

"That's the lesson?"

"Yes."

She settled into her spot, folding her arms across her chest. Long, bright lines grew around them, the light the trees let through. She and Eli stood shoulder-to-shoulder, the light reflecting off Eli's smooth head. She imagined Eli was a modern-day Buddha. She snuck a look at his face, and realized she didn't need to imagine it.

"I can live with that one. You're my favorite Superfriend right now, Eli."

They waited until the sun sunk beneath the ocean. She felt her trust in Eli grow as darkness fell. Walking back in silence to Eli's truck, Lacey realized how much she would miss him when she returned to New Orleans. Permanently.

EPILOGUE

Two days later, Lacey watched the sun set with Trevor. He had shown up, unannounced, at the soundstage. Once Horatio had cleared him, Trevor garnered sideways glances from Kandace and Hunter. Lacey hadn't cared, and left early, as soon as he'd arrived.

They returned to Taverna, the same seaside restaurant where they'd had their first "date." The thrill of the unknown was gone, but their time together was back to being easy. And "Mr. Right Now" was just what she needed. Right now. She'd decided to let go of the rest and have some fun for her few remaining days in California. She needed to heal herself from her heartbreak.

She needed someone who knew nothing about her abilities. Someone who didn't care about what she was going to do with her life. Someone who might have been concerned if she told him someone was out to get her, but there was no reason to do such a thing. Not when the wine was flowing, the sun was setting the ocean ablaze, and her troubles felt like they were beyond that golden-blue horizon. And the promise of a harmonica serenade was in her future.

This time, they never made it back to the room. In the thick sand behind a dune, they fell into each other, laughing from the wine and the effort. His teeth brushed her ear, and she repositioned herself underneath him.

Trevor looked her in the eyes and smiled. "Ready for some sex on the beach, love?"

Maybe California hasn't been so bad, after all. Some positives, certainly.

Lacey smiled, then her eyes lit up at something she saw in the distance.

"What is it?" Trevor turned his head.

A shower of shooting stars was lighting up the sky.

✳

ABOUT THE AUTHOR

 **ANNE McCLANE** writes sci-fi and paranormal fiction. She is a New Orleans native who spent sixteen years out west before returning home to embrace the mysteries of the Mississippi River Delta. She has many years experience in publicity, public relations, and marketing, which has provided a fine primer for writing about the speculative, abnormal, and outrageous.

You can find her science fiction stories on Amazon, in the anthology *Just a Minor Malfunction . . . .* Learn more at her website: **AnneMcClane.com**

OTHER BOOKS IN THE TRAITEUR TRILOGY:

Book One: The Incident Under the Overpass—Lacey Becnel discovers she's obtained supernatural powers, under extraordinary circumstances

Book Three: The Conclusion on the Causeway—Back home in New Orleans, Lacey finds her calling

www.ingramcontent.com/pod-product-compliance
Lightning Source LLC
Chambersburg PA
CBHW070430120726
47910CB00003B/721